The characters and events portrayed in this book are fictitious. Any similarity to real persons, living or dead, is coincidental and not intended by the author.

ISBN: 9798656272780

Cover design by: Kate Rosewood

Like everything else in my life, this book is for my girls, Shelby and Saoirse.

Chapter One

She was born in 1760 and given the name Katherine Whyte. From the time she was a young girl she would hear the servants talking about her mother. Some would say Fiona suffered from madness. Some would say she suffered from an arranged marriage. Some would say the arranged marriage caused the madness, though most wondered why a marriage to such a kind man wouldn't instead have the opposite effect. Most steered clear of Fiona Whyte, and all hated to be summoned by her. She could quickly grow from temperamental to violent, especially when she drank wine.

As the children grew, Katherine's father William released their nanny, and Fiona threw a horrible fit, having not been consulted by her husband on the matter. When their oldest maid and cook died, Fiona beat another maid until she bled for not being able to cook fast enough. When that maid quit her duties abruptly thereafter, Fiona laid her hands on one of their male servants, Rupert, backhanding him across his face simply for being the one to tell Fiona of the young maid's departure.

Upon witnessing this spectacle of violence, and at the dinner table of all places, her husband William stood and crossed the room to pull the crazed woman off of poor Rupert, slapping her across the face three times until she fell to the floor. Fiona all but crawled out of the room, and William apologized to Rupert, telling him to take the rest of the evening to recover.

William had always been good to his staff, giving them the holidays to be with their own families, and giving them gifts on special occasions, though Fiona would always protest. Far and wide people knew of William Whyte, and were keen to be hired by him, though they also knew the rumours about his crazed wife and would weigh their options when considering employment at the Whyte home. Once word got round of Fiona's violent outbursts, people became less and less willing to work there.

William was much the opposite of his wife. He was loud, but gentle, only ever raising voice in anger to Fiona when her outbursts grew out of control. He taught his children to be mindful of the help— to treat them as though they were family, and they would in turn be treated the same, with respect and love.

A young Katherine was somewhat confused by this, knowing her mother was family, but there was little to no love or respect between her parents. And Fiona didn't show much affection toward her children either, though Katherine was alright with that. She was always on edge when alone with her mother. But never with her father. William was kind to her, and her brother Edward, and Katherine looked forward to the times they spent alone, when William would teach them new games or run around outside with them. However, William was the man of the house, a busy, noble fellow with friends in the highest places in England, and alone time with him was fleeting.

Eventually, all but two servants were either relieved of their duties or quit them, and as the children grew, William saw no need to replace them until Fiona could control her anger. Anyone in their right mind would either quit immediately or not take a position here at all. The only two left by the time Katherine was ten years old was Rupert, and his wife Eleanor. They had their own room in the house, and as long as their duties were complete, the house was clean and the meals were prepared and the children and animals cared for, William had no problem with them coming and going as they otherwise pleased when they weren't needed.

Katherine grew fond of Eleanor, often wishing she were her real mother. Eleanor's voice was soft and low, and her attitude was kind. Eleanor took care of Katherine when she was sick, and would sing or hum songs, which she eventually taught to Katherine. Katherine saw the affection between Rupert and Eleanor as a young child. She would mistake them for brother and sister and became confused when they would correct her to say they were married like her parents, because her parents' marriage was not sweet or loving as theirs was. It was filled with rage and violence and resentment.

It was due to her mother's awful attitude toward William and marriage and family that Katherine herself dreaded the whole idea. As she grew, she worried that she would become an awful, angry woman like her mother if it ever came to pass that she marry. She was not an ignorant child—she knew that she and Edward would each have to marry someday, most likely to people they didn't know, and the thought terrified her.

One day when she was ten, in time spent with her family walking around the streets of London, William doted on his son, proclaiming that Edward would grow to be a good, strong, wealthy man and make a wonderful husband for Miss Lucy Parker, to whom he was betrothed. It prompted Edward to ask about Katherine's future.

"Well, my boy," William said, "Katherine shall be a lovely lady and a noble, loyal wife to a young man named Henry."

"No!" Katherine cried out, suddenly emotional and slightly exhausted from their day. "I will never marry! I do not want a husband!" She began to sob.

William crouched to take Katherine by the shoulders. "Now, now, my girl. What's all this about? You *will* marry one day. Every woman marries. And Henry is a kind boy from a good family. Don't you believe your daddy would choose a wonderful boy for my wonderful girl?" he cooed.

Katherine sniffed and nodded.

William patted her shoulder and stood up. "Of course I would."

Fiona, who was never one for comfort or affection, muttered under her breath. "My father never had the decency to do so for me."

Katherine, who loved her father dearly and was already in a scrappy mood, snapped at her mother. "Daddy *is* a good man!"

The sting of her mother's hand came fast and furious against Katherine's left cheek. Not quite as fast but twice as furious was William's response. He brought his own open hand against Fiona's face; what began as a slap turned into more of a cupping of her face, just as hard, but continuing as it pushed Fiona down onto the sidewalk.

"Woman!" he shouted as he towered over her, appearing as tall as the buildings around him from Fiona's position on the ground. "You will never again raise your haggard hand to my children or so help me I'll have you hung!" He whirled around, grabbing Katherine's hand and leaving the moaning pile of petticoats behind.

"I do not know anyone called Henry," Katherine said a few moments later, her voice quiet, but still firm with defiance. She was determined to not recreate her mother's fate, and desperate to bring everyone's attention away from what had just happened.

"Well, perhaps you are correct!" William squeezed her hand, still something of a growl lingering in his voice. "We shall come to an agreement then, you and I. I would like you to meet young Henry. You will grow to like him, I'm quite certain."

Katherine shook her head. "I won't!"

William stopped and turned to give her a stern look and point his finger in her face. "You are a lady," he reminded her. "You will meet him and be on your absolute best behaviour. And if I am right about Henry, you will marry him. But if I am wrong, and he is some sort of awful scoundrel, then you will never marry and become a miserable old spinster of a woman. Do we have an agreement?" He held out his hand for her to shake.

She shook his hand and nodded, enjoying how once in a while her father treated her as an equal, and with that her first meeting with Henry Bullock was scheduled for the next week.

Henry was almost four years her senior. He was a lanky, tall boy with hair that would have been blonde long ago. The first thing Katherine noticed about him from across the parlour of her home was his piercing blue eyes. Fiona pushed Katherine forward from behind, more forcefully than she needed to. Katherine folded her hands in front of her and stepped to the middle of the room. She gave a small curtsy, as Fiona had told her to, and smiled.

Henry took a step forward and gave a nod in response. They both knew who the other was, and why they were there.

Katherine was unsure of what to say but feared her mother's wrath. Her blank mind raced as her eyes fluttered around the room looking for words and landing on the table in the corner. "Do you play chess, Henry?" she asked.

Henry opened his mouth to speak, but immediately snapped it shut, choosing to nod instead.

Katherine gestured to the table across the room, and Henry stepped aside, gracefully allowing the young lady to go ahead of him. Their parents seated themselves on the sofas across the room to enjoy each other's company and monitor the children from a safe distance.

It was a brief meeting; one game of chess was played. Henry didn't say much, but Katherine, who could feel her mother's eyes burning into her, felt the need to make conversation. She wanted to learn as much as she could about Henry, to show her parents that she was in fact making an effort, but he was a quiet boy, who blinked across the table at her for short periods of time, mostly shrugging in response.

"Do you have any brothers or sisters?"

He shook his head.

"Do you like the school you attend?"

He nodded.

"What is you favourite time of year?"

He shrugged.

Only when he made a play she hadn't anticipated, and she commented positively on it, did he show any sign of emotion— the tiniest pressed smile that disappeared as quickly as it had arrived.

Henry won the game.

One month later, Henry was brought to the Whyte home again. They played another game of chess, which was also very quiet, and again Henry won. Then the adults invited them for a walk around the property. Henry walked dutifully beside Katherine with his hands folded behind his back, and Katherine walked dutifully beside Henry with her hands folded in front of her skirt.

This time Henry's mother Anne tried to spark up a conversation. "Katherine, your father says you like to read. What's your favourite thing to read about dear?"

Katherine gave a polite smile in the woman's direction, without actually making eye contact. "Animals," she said curtly.

Anne continued. "Do you have a favourite animal?"

"I like cats. And butterflies."

"Butterflies aren't animals," Fiona corrected her daughter.

"Yes. They are insects," Katherine said, hoping to convey that she was aware of that but also not wanting to disrespect her mother. "But I just finished reading a book about butterflies."

Anne raised her eyebrows and nodded with interest. "Henry, have you done any reading lately?"

Henry, who had been gazing up at the sky as he strolled along the path blinked in surprise to be called upon.

"Henry?" Anne repeated.

Henry's father George, a portly fellow whom Katherine noticed seemed to always have shiny, damp skin, slapped him on the back. "Pay attention boy!" he bellowed and let out a loud nervous laugh.

"The last book I read was about Columbus and his travels," Henry finally added.

After a few moments waiting for him to elaborate, his parents' faces showed disappointment and they continued to walk with Katherine's parents ahead of the youngsters.

Katherine felt sorry for him. She understood entirely

what he was going through. She wanted to engage him, knowing it would also help her look like she was trying. "Do you like to travel?" she asked.

Henry shook his head. "I've never travelled."

"But did you enjoy the book?" Katherine asked after a pause, content with her recovery, but casting a glance to her mother.

He nodded. "Parts of it."

Perhaps she was getting somewhere. "What parts?"

"The boats, I suppose. I like boats."

Her eyebrows rose with interest, much like Anne's had a few moments ago. "Oh? What do you like about them?"

"I liked the drawings, actually," he told her. "I like to draw. My favourite thing to draw is ships. The ones in the book were exquisite."

"Perhaps you could show me your drawings—, " she began.

"Katherine!" William called from up ahead. "Keep up!"

She did not speak any more, but picked up her pace to catch up, Henry at her side.

And so it began that a few times a month the two families would meet. Eventually, however, the parents got lost in each other's company, allowing the children to roam the house and the vast property freely. And while Katherine did her best to keep up, Edward was home from school, and being the same gender and close to the same age as Henry, they had more in common; running about, digging holes, and leaving Katherine alone.

Not that she minded entirely. If their parents thought they were together, no one asked questions or barked orders. Therefor the boys would run and hide and play, and she would chase butterflies and dig for worms. One bright afternoon she happened across a two-toned ladybird just inside the treeline. The right side of its elytra was damaged and had faded to a brown colour, while the dark wing hung out from underneath it, loose and immobile. She picked the creature up, let it crawl up her arm, set it on a dandelion and followed it as it made its way across a pile of dirt and pebbles at the bottom of a tree. When the time came to go home, she bid her tiny new friend farewell, and had forgotten about it by the next time the Bullocks came to visit.

It was a week later. The children were made to stay for tea, and then were free to roam. Once again, Katherine kept up for as long as she could for fear of her mother, but as the boys hopped over rocks and climbed trees, Katherine's cumbersome dress and lack of upper-body strength slowed her down. She wandered back to the place she had found the ladybird and was both surprised and elated to see it again, the same insect with the same broken wing, in the same shallow ridge of gravel and clover she'd left it. She greeted it and played with it again. She followed it as it moved and spoke to it for hours, until it was time to go into the house.

The next day Katherine made a point to visit the same spot, and after some patient searching, the ladybird was there. She figured it must have made this area its home, since it could not fly away. She did not know what ladybirds ate and her book did not tell her much more than other tiny bugs, but she had brought it a piece of biscuit and a few berries and set them throughout the pebbles on the ground. Katherine ran to the stream on the other side of the trees and brought a cupped hand of water back. She set a leaf on the ground and poured a few drops into the leaf. Then she set her new friend on the leaf and was quite pleased to see it stand in the tiny pool, making subtle movements under its head where she believed its mouth to be, until finally it wandered away.

It rained for two days before Katherine was able to stow away to the trees again in the cool, damp sunlight. It had been ten days since she first came across this ladybird, and yet it was still here in this spot. Katherine had never had a pet, or even a friend, and now she felt as though she had both. She named it Dot, referred to it as a female since it was a *lady*-bird, and tried to visit every day. Some days Dot was very well hidden and Katherine couldn't find her. And she wasn't sure whether Dot was eating the food she was bringing or whether the insect was finding food of her own, but she was still alive weeks later, although the wing that had been dangling out had disappeared.

As the summer came to an end, Katherine began to wonder what she could do to keep Dot alive, whether it was possible to bring her into the house and hide the insect in her room somewhere. She would need to bring a plant, perhaps, and some stones. Maybe place all these things in a box of some kind so Dot felt at home. She began planning in the days that followed, even drawing out what she wanted her little ecosystem to look like.

Another Sunday afternoon brought another visit from the Bullocks. Katherine had stopped trying to keep up altogether the last few times, instead choosing to go find Dot immediately. She was successful, and after letting her crawl on her hands for a bit, set her on the fallen tree she usually used as a seat.

And then she gave a small shriek as the boys jumped out from behind two different trees. They had been quiet and stealthy, and she had been preoccupied with Dot. Katherine was startled to her feet.

"What have you got there, girl?" Edward asked, taking a step toward her. Katherine recognized the change in his voice, his tone, his accent. He was pretending to be a tough, cockney street kid. It was something she had seen him do before with other boys, around whom he felt he had something to prove, but only once or twice around tall, timid Henry.

"Just a ladybird," she told him, innocent and unassuming, her voice soft and her eyebrows raised slightly. "I call her Dot."

In a quick movement that neither she or Henry expected, Edward swung his hand and brought it down swift and hard, killing the bug.

Katherine gasped and cried out. "Edward!" She looked down at the flattened mess, then up, her eyes moving back and forth between the boys before her. Heartbroken tears spilled over, and with one loud sob she lifted her skirts and dashed toward the house. She could tell no one about her poor deceased friend or the ruined plans for Dot's future, as no one would understand or care, and she avoided the trees behind the house for days after that, worried she might stumble across the tree that poor, squashed Dot was likely still on.

As the colder seasons came, these meetings between the two families slowed down. Katherine was quiet around the boys after that, choosing to no longer follow them when they ran amuck. Eventually they came to a halt altogether when Henry began attending school with Edward. Katherine was being taught at home the ways of women; how to cook and sew. She took up painting and needlepoint and would often ask to help prepare meals with Eleanor. Edward would come home on holidays, and she all but forgot about Henry, save for one of Edward's return trips where he informed everyone over dinner that George was moving the entire Bullock family to Boston.

Katherine didn't think much of it, having not seen him in nearly a year, and her sentiment seemed shared by William. Fiona, however, shook her head in frustration, over and over again after hearing this news. She muttered something about loyalty and planning that Katherine couldn't quite hear, and William shushed her, telling her to no longer speak of the matter.

Fiona downed the contents of her wine while William spoke, then slammed her hand down onto the table. “We planned! We agreed— !”

“Woman!” William cried from across the table, slamming his own hand down, harder than she had done, causing everything on the table to bounce and shake. “There is nothing can be done about it now!”

Fiona ignored him, turning her anger to Katherine. “What have you done, girl?! Did you say something to offend them? Did you disrespect the boy somehow? I bet it was all your ramblings about insects!”

“Fiona!” William stood, his chair sliding back with such force it fell over. “I will hear no more of this! Bullock’s decision had nothing to do with Katherine!”

“You do not know that!” Fiona charged, standing to meet his energy on her own side of the table.

“I do! Bullock sent word months ago of his intention to take up a position in Boston. Why do you think they ceased to return here?”

Fiona’s nostrils flared and the whites of her eyes became clearly visible, but she said nothing and continued to stand out of spite.

William continued. “He spoke of how he believed arranged marriages were no longer relevant and asked to be graciously relieved of our contract. I agreed and wished him well and that is the end of it.”

“William what have you done?” Fiona howled.

William grumbled back at her. “It was at His Majesty’s request that Bullock take the position. We have no place to argue with the king, now do we?”

It silenced her. Both Katherine and Edward looked down into their laps, terrified to lift their heads for fear of losing them.

A growl came from deep within Fiona as she threw her cup against the wall, causing everyone in the room to jump. William shouted at her but was forced to duck as a bowl was thrown at his head, crashing behind him. Next, she slammed her plate to the floor at her feet with both hands before sweeping out of the room, shouting at everything and nothing as they listened to her make her way up to her chamber. They heard her slam her door, then open it and slam it again and again, screaming inaudibly.

William took his seat again after picking it up off the floor. He drank his ail but seemed to have lost his appetite, as had the children; Edward pushing his food around his plate nervously, and Katherine refusing to move at all, keeping her hands in her lap. The slamming stopped, but the screaming continued, waxing and waning. At times Fiona would open her door and scream down at William; for having known for months and not told her, for refusing them the life they had worked so hard for; for ruining their chances of marrying off their only daughter; for ever having married her at all. Then she would slam the door again. After nearly an hour of listening, without exchanging any words themselves, William ordered the children to bed and ascended the stairs to his own room, hoping to find some peace.

Chapter Two

Katherine lived a sheltered life for many years. Save for having to accompany her parents to church on Sundays and the occasional trip to the dressmakers, her life was confined to the grounds of the estate. She made friends with birds and snails and worms and of course her favourite, the butterflies. She asked her father for more books on insects and animals and spent most of her adolescence reading and exploring the grounds trying to find the creatures within them. Her mother insisted she stop reading books on lower life forms and instead choose literature that would potentially help her later in life. Katherine was given books on poetry, sonnets by Shakespeare, historical documents, all in an attempt to make her more agreeable in the eyes of outsiders. Now and then Fiona would present her with stories of love in hopes Katherine would learn what it meant to be a lady and what men expected from women.

Katherine helped groom and feed and care for the horses. She fed the chickens and collected the eggs. Several hours of a day were devoted to working with the staff, pulling up vegetables, which Katherine enjoyed because she often came across snails and worms and grubs and would challenge herself to identify them. One day, at the age of fourteen, she followed a beetle as it crawled and flew and crawled and flew past the treeline to the clearing behind the garden. Beyond the clearing was the wide stream; she knew that meant the edge of their property. It was nice here, quiet, though most things around her were quiet. This place felt special though. She remembered her brother talking about it, when he and other young boys would wander in and out of the trees, having their adventures, but Katherine knew the only people who went this far now were the servants when they came for water, and she had only been out this far herself a handful of times. She started coming back again and again, spending more time here, bringing a book, bringing food, bringing her painting tools. She dreaded the winters, knowing the stream would freeze over and the bugs would all die and she would once again be confined to the house.

Once in a while her father would entertain people; he would throw a party and many guests would stay for days. Katherine found these events both exhilarating and terrifying. She would get so excited to be around other people, and yet when she was, she felt nervous and awkward. She would never know what to say or how to act—until after the fact, when she would receive swift discipline from her mother on everything she said and did wrong. Luckily for Katherine, these events were few and far between, and she would have months to correct the behaviour her mother found offensive or unattractive before the next time she would see another outsider.

What Fiona did not find unattractive, however, was her appearance. The only praise Katherine received from her hard, cold mother was based on Katherine's looks. Her long, dark brown hair was usually pinned up and curled. Her mother would comment on her eyebrows being symmetrical, her waist being slim, her eyelashes being long and dark before her green eyes, though Fiona would often comment that she had no idea from where Katherine had gotten green eyes. And Fiona would take great pride in the comments made by friends and acquaintances on the rare occasion Katherine was allowed to be seen. They would call Katherine lovely, or even stunning. They would speak of how Katherine was blossoming like a beautiful rose. Fiona would beam at this, as though it had been said about herself. And the more people took notice of Katherine, the more Katherine was let out and allowed to be noticed.

With Katherine's age and beauty came new potential suitors. Katherine more and more would accompany her parents to the city, to the market, to church, to functions of every kind. The people Katherine met would introduce her to their sons, who were close to her age. Some of these young men and their parents would come to the house for lunch or dinner.

But after a time, something changed in Fiona. She became aware of the fact that people were coming to spend time with Katherine, not with William or herself. It wasn't that it bothered her— she wasn't much for company— but she made the decision to once again shut Katherine into the solitude of their house. Katherine didn't understand why she wasn't invited to town anymore, or why these people were no longer joining them for meals. And since no one would explain why, she figured she was being punished for having done or said something wrong.

Until one day when Katherine was sixteen Edward came to visit. He had long since completed school but was now living in a house of his own in London. It was a brisk morning at the end of autumn, and they could see their breath as they walked through the frosty garden, enjoying what could possibly be the last sunny day before winter arrived. Snow had not yet fallen that year, but a thick frost had come the night before, and the blanket of glittering silver and white crunched and sparkled under their feet with every step. As usual, Edward asked her how things at the house had been in an effort to make small talk.

"I hear they have been keeping you locked away again, sister," he said as he took a seat on the bench near the entrance to the garden.

"Yes," she sighed as she sat next to him. "I fear I may have said or done something to offend Samuel Milton. His family does not come to visit anymore, and mother instructs me to no longer speak to him at church. If ever I'm allowed back to church, that is."

"Oh? Have you offended God as well?" Edward asked with a grin as he nudged her with his elbow. He managed to get a smile from her and hoped she understood how silly her situation was. "What about that Wallace fellow?" he asked, though he seemed to already know the answer.

"James. Yes, him as well..." she trailed off, feeling her confidence fall. "I was dressed properly. I only spoke when spoken too. And I made certain to speak only of the things *they* did. I haven't any idea what I have done..." She shook her head.

It was rare that her brother showed tenderness. Normally his demeanor toward her seemed to be businesslike, but at this moment Edward took in a sharp breath and looked into her eyes. His face was caring, but his words were frank.

"Katherine. It is nothing you have done, save for simply growing into a lovely lady. There have been many young men who have asked about you. To me or our father or mother. We are all aware of it. We all want you to marry well, of course. Father would prefer it be a kind man who will take great care of you and your children, but also someone who will grow to love you as you are in your heart as well. Do you understand this?"

Katherine nodded, and he continued.

"Now while I would like to believe Fiona wants the same things for you, I'm sure she would not much care to marry you off for love as much as for stature. Father thought a match with Wallace or more so with Milton would indeed be fitting, as they are well-adjusted and gentle young men, who could also give you a comfortable life. However it seems Fiona has gotten her way again and convinced our father that someone better could be found. Fiona has seen the interest you have gained and now claims you could someday have your pick of any man in England. And unfortunately, dear sister, this could be both a blessing and a curse."

Katherine nodded in understanding and looked away. She knew that, even though she could have any man in England, if polite and charming young men like James and Samuel weren't good enough for her mother, then the choice really wasn't Katherine's to make. Katherine didn't want *any* man in England, she just wanted one. She wanted him to be a nice man, maybe someone funny, smart. Someone who would let her be herself and not grow angry or irritated with her if she made the smallest mistake. Katherine had yet to meet this man, and if Fiona had anything to do with it, Katherine never would.

She felt her brother let out a chuckle and turned to see a smirk on his face as he looked down to the ground. "Yes?" she asked.

He inhaled as though to speak, then shook his head and stood. "Come," he said, holding out his hand to her, "breakfast should be ready soon."

Katherine still wanted to know what he had found amusing, but she was also used to most information being kept from her, so she let it be as they returned to the house. Her family made conversation throughout the meal, mainly the two men, of business and government and the upcoming Christmas season, and then Edward spoke words Katherine hadn't heard in a very long time.

"Henry Bullock sends his best wishes." His eyes were set on her while he said the words before he turned his head to look in his parents' direction.

"Henry Bullock?" William called out from across the table, a grin spreading across his face and then he slapped his hand down on the surface. "I don't believe it!"

Edward smirked, likely after catching his mother rolling her eyes. "Yes. He wrote to me after they settled across the sea and we have remained in contact since."

"How wonderful! How have we not heard this before?" William continued, looking around at the rest of the faces at the table, not at all trying to hide his astonished delight. "Go on boy. Tell us! How have the Bullocks fared in America?"

"Quite well, I believe. They remained along the coast, and Henry has mentioned the increasing tensions with the Americans and the crown." William nodded in understanding, though Katherine had no idea what they were talking about. "He has written that people get angry with his father for his... conflicting loyalties and have broken windows in their home."

Katherine gasped at this. "How dreadful!" she said, making her contribution to the conversation. In her mind she remembered Henry and his lovely parents and couldn't imagine how scared the young boy must have been when this happened. And then she came to the realization that the boy she remembered would now be a grown man, a year older than her brother. She wondered momentarily what he would look like now, but it occurred to her that she barely remembered what he looked like when they were younger. All she could remember was that he was tall and had the most remarkable blue eyes.

She listened to her brother and father continue to talk but faded in and out like she usually did. This was the first she had heard of these "tensions" Edward was referring to. She had no idea there was any such conflict going on. Then again, she didn't speak with many people who would inform her of worldly news, and unless asked, her father would not bring it up on his own with the women.

"When next you write him, please let him know we are glad to hear he is doing well," William said to Edward. "And we send our best to him and his family."

"Oh yes, mine too," Katherine insisted cheerfully. "He was always such a shy lad when he was here, but also incredibly polite."

"Perhaps you should write him as well, Katherine," Edward suggested, reaching for his glass of water and bringing it to his lips, in an effort to hide yet another smirk. "You yourself spent a great deal of time with him."

"An absurd idea, after all they put us through…" Fiona scoffed, more to herself but loud enough for all to hear.

Katherine shook her head, choosing to ignore her mother and maintain eye contact with her brother. "Oh, no. I couldn't. It's been so many years. I only vaguely remember those days. I wouldn't know what to—.“

"Think on it, sister. No matter how short, even just a Christmas greeting. I'm sure it would be a great surprise for Henry to receive word from another old friend."

She gave a pursed smile. "Think on it I shall," she said with a nod. She pondered the notion for days. Would it be strange? Would it even be appropriate for a young woman to send a letter to a young man? She knew in her heart that it would be innocent. Her father gave no mention that it would be wrong. Fiona of course would, but she didn't care for most things. And besides, Henry likely had a lady already, perhaps even a wife, though Edward had not mentioned it. She saw no harm in it and the next day presented her brother with a simple note to go along with the next letter he would send to Henry, which he told her would be in a few days. She had wished Henry a merry Christmas, knowing it would likely arrive around then, and told him she was glad to hear that he was alive and well after all this time.

With that she went back to her life of solitude, which was always far more bleak in the winter months, as she did not care for the cold, and even a walk around the garden had no appeal. She painted warmer days and read of warmer climates and passed the time with her needlepoint, but most days she felt as though the walls were closing in on her and when she was ready to scream in the afternoons, would wander into the kitchen to help prepare the evening meal to take her mind off of... her mind.

The monotony was broken when, in early February, she received a letter. She never received post, and was quite confounded, staring at the envelope long after Rupert had handed it to her. She quietly found her way into the study and opened it.

Miss Katherine Whyte,

I pray this finds you in good health. Thank you so much for your lovely greeting. I was quite pleasantly surprised to receive word from you, as you can imagine. Your brother speaks fondly of you and your accomplishments. I would very much like to continue corresponding this way, if you think it appropriate, to hear in your own words how you are faring and how, if at all, life in England has changed since my departure. My father and mother send their best and warmest regards to you and yours.

Yours,

Henry Bullock.

She read it twice to be sure she had read it right the first time. She wasn't sure what to think. It was quite pleasant and sincere, as Henry had always been, yet she felt as though she needed to hide this from her mother. The thoughtful words were one thing, but continuing on as he had requested, no matter how innocent it was, would be an entirely different issue with Fiona. However, as Katherine thought more about it, she felt it would be rude of her not to respond, and truthfully it was rare that anyone asked to speak with her. She found herself torn with the idea, and it kept her up thinking and contemplating most of the night. The next day she felt tired as she hadn't slept much, and it had her in a sluggish, foul mood. The boredom that she was somewhat used to was absolutely unbearable this day, and it pushed her over the edge. She marched into the study and began to hastily write a response, but she immediately tore it up and started over.

Henry,

How lovely of you to respond, and in so timely a manner! I would also be pleased to continue in this way, if you would be so kind as to tell me about America, as not much has changed in London from what I can see. I am curious to know if you still reside in Boston or if your travels have taken you elsewhere in all these years.

She ended it kindly but she didn't send it out. The more she thought about it the more her mind allowed her to worry about the consequences. If she gave it to her father to send, he would have questions. And what if Fiona found out? Or what if Henry sent another one? She hadn't actually anticipated receiving anything from him in the first place. She'd simply done it on a whim at her brother's request. And so she hid Henry's letter and the one she'd just written him in her room and tried to forget about them.

Until a few days later when her parents returned from church and brought Edward with them for Sunday supper. She'd nearly accomplished her goal of forgetting all about it as she was cutting potatoes, and Edward found her in the kitchen. He watched her quietly for a bit, and she kept on with her task, aware of his presence but with little to say.

He inhaled sharply. "I received word from Henry Bullock again recently."

Katherine politely smiled though she didn't look up at

him. “As did I,” she said and continued to work.

“Hmmm,” Edward nodded, raising his eyebrows. “I was certain you would. He would ask about you from time to time throughout the years.”

She stopped and furrowed her brow in curiosity as she brought her face up to look at him. “Oh?”

“Yes, he always spoke fondly of you, remembering all of your efforts to be especially kind to him while he was here. Whether it just to appease our parents or genuine caring on your part, he found it quite endearing.”

As she usually did when she didn’t know what to do or say, Katherine made brief eye contact and smiled before looking away quickly.

“And I must say,” Edward continued, a small smile on his lips as he watched her avoid his eyes, “In all the time we’ve been writing one another, I can’t remember ever having received such a rapid response. Likely cost him a pretty penny to have them sent out so quickly aboard such a fast ship.”

She met his eyes again then nervously dropped them to continue chopping her potatoes. “How can you tell?”

“The post marking on it tells a tale.” He was silent again as he stared at her. “It’s been four days now sister. Have you perhaps sent anything back to him?”

She wiped her hands on her apron and shook her head, turning to put handful after handful of potatoes into a pot. “No. I… I wrote something, but I wouldn’t know whom I could trust to ensure its safe departure.”

The smile remained on his face and he cocked his head to the side. “You don’t trust me?”

She looked up at him from under her brow. “Of course I do—.“

"Good news then," he said cheerfully, loudly, not allowing for her to protest. "I'll wait here while you fetch it, and I shall send it at first light tomorrow."

She knew her face showed her confusion and she opened her mouth to speak, but again he wouldn't allow her to.

"Run along!" he told her, grabbing her by the shoulders and leading her out of the kitchen toward the stairs.

She did as she was told, hastily climbing the stairs and entering her room. She pulled the letters out from under the nightstand where she had hidden them and looked over each once more. She quickly thought of the things she would change but was also worried that if she started a new letter Edward would lose patience, so she tucked them into her pocket and went back down the stairs.

Throughout the rest of the evening she sat with bated breath, wondering if perhaps her brother was playing some awful trick on her and was going to reveal to their parents that she, a young single girl whose mother had high aspirations for her future, had written a letter to a young, presumably single man to whom she was once promised and who likely wouldn't meet her mother's standards. And that she would receive some form of dreadful punishment for it. But as the hours passed and nothing came of it, her thoughts changed instead to curiosity and she wondered why this seemed to mean so much to Edward. She had never seen him so insistent about... anything.

After she had readied herself for bed, she pulled out Henry's letter and read it again, taking note that he had dated it December 26th. She inspected it and it had indeed been postmarked when it was taken in by the ship— the very next day.

Thirty-eight days, she thought, doing the math and remembering back to the day it had actually arrived at the house. It would have been a fast ship indeed, making the trip in only over a month's time. She didn't know the exact day Edward had sent hers away, but it was sometime in early October.

She didn't know whether Edward was also willing to find a ship ready to depart immediately or how fast the ship itself would go. She didn't know whether Henry would make haste with his next response, or if he would even bother to reply to her innocent ramblings. She didn't know whether it was wrong of her to spend this much time thinking about it. But she expected that she would not receive another letter for months.

So three weeks later, when Edward came to the house and handed her another envelope, the shock on her face was palpable.

"He could not have replied to me already!"

Edward shrugged. "No, Katherine, I very much doubt your letter has even made its own journey across the ocean yet. To have arrived already, this would have had to have been written and sent at least a month ago. Perhaps a few days more."

Katherine looked down at her hand then back up to her brother. She didn't understand what was happening. Why would he write again so soon? The only way to understand would be to read whatever was in her hand.

"Excuse me," she said lowering her head, not willing to risk looking Edward in the eye as she ducked out of the room and walked quickly up the stairs. She closed her bedroom door and sat on her bed.

Miss Whyte,

Forgive my haste, and I sincerely apologize if this seems bold, or if you have made such a decision as not to return my sentiments. I have thought about you often throughout the years and was certainly most excited to have received your brief note. After I sent my response my mind became overrun with all the questions that have flown in and out of my head as I wondered what had become of my former betrothed. However at this juncture since I have yet to receive any word from you as to whether you wish to continue our friendship in this way, I would instead like to take this opportunity to thank you so very much for all you did in our youth to please your parents and mine. As I think back to our meetings, I remember all the trouble you went through to keep me entertained as a boy. Those efforts may have gone without acknowledgement by our families, and perhaps by myself at the time, but I can look back now as the man that I am and truly appreciate them. No matter the outcome of our current situation in life, I have always wanted to say this to you. I am eternally grateful to have once called you mine.

Most sincerely,

Henry.

Katherine set her hands on her lap with the letter still in them. Something stirred within her, and it made her want to weep. She could not remember a time when someone had been so kind to her, said such wonderful things about her, or had even thanked her for anything of any worth. She had received nothing but criticism and reprimand from her mother regarding all she had done with and to Henry so long ago, to read this now was surreal. Though she didn't doubt his sincerity in the least or the intent behind it, she did believe perhaps he was being far too generous to her.

And so she wrote him back, thanking him for his words, showing gratitude of her own for his contributions to their courtship so long ago. A courtship that, as time went on and she began conversing regularly with polite and open Henry Bullock, she sometimes wished had followed through.

Chapter Three

1777

Katherine would often forget that she was writing to the same shy, soft-spoken boy from years earlier, until he would remind her of something from their youth and she had to recall him in her mind's eye. He was funny. He was articulate and clever, and for the first time she was informed of news going on in the world. He answered her questions regarding the conflict between England and America. When she asked about the Americans breaking the windows of his family home as she had understood it, he explained they in fact suspected it was a group of people loyal to the crown who had done it, since he and his parents had begun questioning which side of the conflict their own loyalties lie. He went on to explain his position to Katherine, worried that identifying as an American might jeopardize his relationship with her, as well as with her family, and relatives of his own that still resided in England.

It did nothing to sway her growing affection for him. Well over one year had passed, and the secret stash of letters grew. She would stow away to her favourite spot by the stream where she continued to pass the time with her old hobbies, but also found the same inspiration there to write her letters to him.

She enjoyed more and more the visits from her brother,

as they meant she would send or receive a message. Although sometimes neither, she grew to find she also enjoyed getting to know Edward as the witty, intelligent, capable man he was becoming. In getting to know both of these men in their adulthood, it was very clear why they became fast friends all those years ago and had maintained a friendship despite the distance.

And things were changing for Edward as well. While William had agreed to relieve Henry of the contract he'd had with Mr. Bullock, he had offered the same courtesy to the parents of Lucy Parker, who was arranged to someday marry Edward. While they accepted William's new proposal, they came up with one of their own, and a new agreement was made that they would not force marriage upon the couple, however they would still encourage the union in hopes that the children would grow together on their own. To their delight, once he was done with his studies and was fully employed, Edward did choose to properly court Lucy, and they fell very much, very happily, in love.

Katherine was happy for her brother, and truly enjoyed Lucy's company, but it seemed the more time Edward spent with Lucy, the less time he had to act as her personal postman. After a few more months Edward officially asked for Lucy's hand in marriage, and Lucy officially accepted. It was a hot and humid day in August. Edward and Lucy were visiting for the day with Lucy's parents and a few of William's business associates and their wives. They had just eaten a lovely brunch on the front porch when, in front of everyone, Edward knelt down. Katherine was surprised at his formality; it seemed to be very much rehearsed by him, however Lucy appeared to indeed be surprised.

William called for Rupert to bring wine, and once it arrived gave a toast the newly engaged couple, stating that he couldn't wait for the rest of their company to arrive that afternoon to share the news. Several people said a few words to congratulate them. And Fiona raised her own glass, stating how happy she was to see all their hard work finally pay off.

It may have been the wine, or perhaps the heat, but Katherine felt suddenly panicked. Something wasn't right. Everything felt wrong. She could feel the loneliness and emptiness within her, as Edward's already seldom visits would become fewer and farther between, and not only would she be losing her brother, the only person she ever physically talked to in the outside world, but she would also be losing her connection to Henry, the only person she spoke with besides her brother.

She excused herself and quickly walked into the house. She closed the door and leaned up against it. The house was cooler, but she still felt as though she were suffocating. She ran through the house, out the back door, and down the path. As she walked through the woods her instinct was to undo the laces of her dress, which were far too tight at this moment. She had removed the dress entirely by the time she emerged from the trees, wearing only her undergarments. She dropped her dress and pulled the pins out of her hair. She took off her shoes and waded into the deepest part of the water, which came up to her hips. She looked up at the sky, taking in several deep breaths, still feeling as though her lungs were being squeezed.

The sun was at its highest point in the sky. It was burning on her shoulders and the top of her dark head of hair.

Katherine lifted her arms straight out at her sides and fell backwards, letting the water envelop her. The current was light; she barely moved, except to sink to the floor, where she felt the rocks on her bottom and back. Her eyes were closed, but she could still see the sun's light as it trickled through the water and fell upon her eyelids. She let out the air in her lungs. She knew she would have to stand up soon...

Or would she? The idea of her future held her there

under the water. Loneliness and boredom until her mother chose some stranger for her to spend her remaining years with. Years that would likely also be boring and lonely, if her parents' marriage was any indication.

Her lungs screamed; her heart beat unbearably fast, then slowed down. She felt unconsciousness looming.

And then she felt it. A spark. A glimmer of… something. A pull; a warmth. A feeling she had felt before, in this spot, like something was on its way, soon, and she shouldn't miss it. It told her to put her feet down. It told her to stand up and breathe.

She did. She emerged from the water and inhaled deeply and moved her hair out of her face. She looked around her, waiting for her breathing to calm, and made her way back to the shore where her dress lay.

It didn't take her long for her shift to dry in the hot sun, and she wrestled back into the dress. Then she sat, for what seemed like hours, in quiet contemplation, eventually lying down on the soft grass. The past, the present, they were so bleak, and dreary, and the future looked absolutely no different; it brought tears to her eyes. Still, she felt the pull deep within her; it was weaker now, but not gone. What was it? Where was it? Whatever it was, whatever it was promising her, she wanted it right now. She needed it to explain to her that everything would be alright.

She hadn't realized she had drifted off until she was awoken by the sound of footsteps rustling through the grass. She opened her eyes to see a tall man standing over her. She wasn't able to make out his features as they were darkened with the sun's light at his back.

She sat up, startled.

"Oh, please Katherine, don't get up on my account," he said, taking a seat to her right, close beside her in the grass.

Katherine looked around, to see if anyone else had come with him, smoothing her hair as she did so.

When she turned back, he had laid down with his hands behind his head and closed his eyes. He was an attractive man. His hair light brown, several inches long. He had high cheek bones and a smile lit up his face. He looked to be close to her age, perhaps older, yet as Katherine did not recognize him, she took him to be another of her father's associates. Or perhaps her brother's? He should know how very inappropriate it was to be here alone with a lady, especially one who doesn't know him...

But then it occurred to her that he had called her by name as he sat next to her.

"Ha—Have we met?" she stammered, nervous at the situation.

He gave a few quick nods. "Oh yes. Several times, in fact." The smile on his face turned up into a grin— he was obviously enjoying this.

Katherine opened her mouth to speak, then closed it, then opened it again, and closed it again. She didn't know what to say. One hundred questions and comments were running through her mind, and they all wanted to escape at the same time, making it impossible for her to choose the right one. He said they had met several times, but she had absolutely no idea who he was, and she felt somewhat ashamed for not remembering. Her stomach flipped and her heart began to race as she worried about offending this handsome young man. "Forgive me, I..." she let out her breath, unable to choose her words.

He rolled his head in her direction. His face squinted in the sunlight as he opened his eyes.

She was taken aback at the blue that appeared from under his eyelids. She had seen those eyes before. It was so long ago. Where...?

She gasped at the realization. "Henry?" she whispered.

The grin returned to his lips, and he put his head back and closed his eyes.

She stared out at the water, not sure whether knowing who he was had made her more or less uncomfortable. His comfort, on the other hand, was quite obvious to her. "I thought you were in Philadelphia?" she asked, turning her head to him.

"I was. I still am, I suppose. I apologize for not mentioning it to sooner, I assumed someone else might. Did no one tell you I was coming?"

"No," she shook her head. "However, I am not made aware of most things."

"Oh?" he asked, opening his eyes to look at her again. They showed genuine interest. But Katherine didn't follow up on her statement, so he closed them.

She was anxious again. A part of her couldn't believe this was the same man she'd been conversing with, and still somehow the same boy from so long ago. When she'd imagined what he looked like now, she likely wouldn't have come up with anything close to this incredible form and face. She knew it was rude of her not to make conversation. Her mind was in a flurry to remember the things they had discussed on paper, or her time with Henry before, racing for something— anything!— to say. A thousand new questions fought to spill from her lips; one slipped through as she tried to determine whether to speak of the past or ask about the present.

"Do you still like boats?" It felt juvenile, and she hated herself immediately, closing her eyes, hoping to wake up from this awkward nightmare. She heard him chuckle.

"I do. I have been on a few and have yet to perish." He was teasing her, she realized. It seemed to take him a moment to do the same and come up with a question of his own. "Do you still like insects?" he asked, playing along.

"No. Or... well no less than before, I suppose." Again she became immediately embarrassed, silently wishing she had earlier let herself drown. She quickly realized that was something she hadn't gone in to details of in their more recent interactions since her mother told her a woman shouldn't have knowledge of such things, and it was likely to drive people away. She decided to follow up in a gentler, more lady-like tone, even though in his current state he didn't appear to have any desire for formality. "I don't seem to have as much time for such things as I did in my youth. And I haven't received any new books on them in a very long time. Most of my reading of late has been..." She trailed off, not wanting to divulge that her mother had encouraged her to read novels to explain love and affection and what was expected of her someday. Aside from that, all the reading she'd done had been written by him. With a sigh, she finished. "Entomology is for gentlemen, after all."

Henry's eyebrows rose though his eyes stayed shut against the sun. "Really? According to whom?"

Katherine hesitated. "My mother, among others. I have been told not to speak of such things with guests. Or friends. Or acquaintances. Or... anyone really."

Henry turned his head and opened his eyes again. "Well, I am a gentleman, and I do not know much about insects, Katherine. Since entomology is for gentlemen, I should be more educated! Please, teach me something," he said cheerfully.

She opened her mouth, somewhere between wanting to speak and utter disbelief. Part of her could have burst with excitement for someone actually wanting to hear of her interests in person; even her own family had never done that.

Another part of her wanted to run away and hide so her parents would never find out. She looked around, not sure whether she should speak or not. It had been so long she almost didn't remember anything about the topic at hand.

Henry sat up, resting his arms across his knees. "Go on."

"I-I wouldn't know where to begin... As I said, it has been so long since I..." she shrugged.

"Well, what is your favourite then? Still butterflies?" he urged gently.

She stuttered, looking at his face. She saw only genuine interest in his eyes. She glanced down at his lips, and it was then she realized how close his face was to her own, and suddenly she felt a small stirring in between her legs. She turned her head to look forward, trying to hide the blush she felt coming on. "Yes. Butterflies," she said softly.

Henry patiently waited for her to continue, never moving to increase the distance between them. "What is it about them that has captured your attention for all these years?"

"Well, they are lovely and elegant. And soft and graceful —."

Henry chuckled. "Everything a lady should be."

Katherine smiled a pained smile. Perhaps that is what a lady should be, but she was a lady, and she was convinced after a lifetime of anger and criticism that she was none of those things. "I suppose."

Henry watched her for a moment, noticing her face seemed thoughtful but sorrowful. "Is something the matter?"

She inhaled, coming out of the sad place in her mind, and turned her head. "No," she said with another quick glance down at his lips, again noticing the close proximity of him.

"Alright," he said, giving a nod as he turned to look forward. "What else?"

"I admire their freedom." It fell from her lips before she had a chance to stop it.

Henry looked back at her, but she was looking at the water. He smiled. "From a scientific standpoint?"

She felt herself grin. *What are you doing?* she thought to herself, only her inner voice sounded like her mother as it reprimanded her. What was it about this man that, for over a year, and even more so now, made her feel like she wanted to bear her soul? Perhaps it was his angelic appearance and demeanour. Perhaps it was that she had just come close to ending her own life and the lack of oxygen was affecting her brain. Or perhaps it was that no one ever talked to her and asked her questions, and now that someone was, she was overindulging. Either way, she had never been this comfortable around another human being in her entire life, not even around Henry himself as a young boy.

"Perhaps," she finally answered. "They are free to float about. To London, or to Paris if they choose. They are often alone, independent, but every once in a while, I watch two of them meet and float around one another as though they are part of some glorious dance and have known each other their entire lives. And just as suddenly they can be alone again and completely content."

Henry continued to smile as he listened to her. And when she finished, he continued with his questions. "Have you ever been to Paris?"

Katherine shook her head, feeling embarrassed yet again. "No, sir. The places I have *not* been greatly outnumber the places I *have* been."

His smile changed to an amused smirk. "That was... very well said." He let out a small laugh. "Well, dear Katherine,

I have been a great many places. And if you would be so kind to tell me about the insects you are so fond of, I will happily tell you of the places I have been."

She looked at him. He was again being so attentive. She remembered him hardly saying anything to her all those years ago, and she had been the one to put in the effort and make the conversation. Now things were flipped on their heads entirely, she realized. But unlike the earlier times between them, none of it seemed forced. It all was quite easy for him. He actually seemed to mean every word that had come from his attractive, distracting mouth, just as his sincerity had come through the words he'd put to paper. "That would be lovely," she said softly with a nod, finding that her eyes were drawn once again to his lips.

"Ah-ha! There you are!" a voice called from behind them.

A startled Katherine turned to see Edward approaching.

"To which *you* are you referring?" Henry asked as he turned—if he was as startled as she, he hid it well.

"Both," Edward chuckled. "Just like when we were boys, Henry!" he smiled, looking out toward the water.

Henry nodded. "Indeed! Only we did not allow girls to come here all those years ago," he said, nudging Katherine with his elbow.

"Hmm. Not much of a girl." Edward looked down at his sister with a grimace. "Good lord, woman. You look a fright! What is the matter with your hair?" he asked as he reached down and pulled a few wayward strands away from her face.

Henry didn't give her the chance to answer. "I fear may have interrupted her kip," he said with a wry grin.

"Well, I was sent to find you," Edward said.

"Which you?" Henry repeated. He began to stand.

"*You,*" he said, looking directly at Henry.

"Of course it's you," Katherine murmured, looking at the ground all around her for a place to put her hands. "No one would bother ask about me." Her angry growl sharply reminded her of her mother's own similar loathe and she internally scolded herself for it. She had planted her hands at her sides to push off the ground, when she noticed Henry's hand in front of her. She took it and looked up at his beautiful, sympathetic face as he opened his mouth to speak.

"How could someone not wonder where a lovely lady such as this has disappeared to?" He pulled her up, noticing her pale cheeks redden at his words.

She pulled her hand away like she had been burned and rushed ahead of the men so she could pick up any more articles of clothing she'd discarded along the way. Upon their return to the house, William informed them he was planning an impromptu engagement celebration with those who had been arriving throughout the day and having them stay for dinner, or even overnight should they so choose.

"Good God Katherine!" Fiona all but shouted once William had stopped speaking. Her eyes became angry and her brow nearly met in the middle. "Go and clean up at once! How dare you show yourself to our guests in such a manner!"

Katherine didn't speak. She dropped her head and slunk back toward the stairs, then bounded up them as though she were being chased. In her mirror she was finally able to see herself, and her brother and mother had been right, she looked ghastly. As she had slept out in the grass, her hair had dried, and what wasn't in one giant mat on the side she'd laid on was standing nearly straight up and then falling awkwardly back down, creating a sharp peak a few inches from her scalp. There were wayward blades of grass in her hair, and several creases still in her cheek that she could only assume had been created by lying on her sleeve. She was horrified. Years had gone by since the last time she'd seen handsome Henry Bullock, and this was how he had seen her for the first time.

She shouldn't focus on such things, she realized. She should be thinking less about Henry and more about her mother's approval and her newly engaged brother. She brushed her hair and pinned it up in the only way that it would cooperate. She changed her clothes. And then she sat on her bed, not wanting to return downstairs. She was ashamed that she'd considered ruining her brother's happy day by staying in the water. She was ashamed of what her mother thought. She was ashamed of what Henry thought. She realized how very different the two were. Henry, always kind and caring, seeming to accept her for who she was. Fiona, always harsh and bitter, and never accepting of Katherine in any way.

She turned her head in the direction of the secret place she had hidden Henry's letters, then got up to retrieve them. She flipped to the first one he'd sent, noting the tone of it, and how it had never seemed to change throughout the rest. Even when he had written of other things, harder times, difficult decisions, he was always cheerful when ending the letters, most of the time stating how he eagerly anticipated the next time he would receive a response from her.

It still seemed odd, surreal, that the man responsible for the words that had made her stomach flutter at times was here, downstairs. And that he was Henry Bullock, from so long ago. It was still nearly impossible to put together in her mind, like trying to sew a table to a tapestry.

Why is he here now?

She put the letters away again and ran her hands down her dress to flatten it out. She would go downstairs and talk to him. She would ask him questions and reference these letters, as though the man downstairs were some sort of imposter, or perhaps that the writer was the imposter and they were two different people. She needed to make it real for herself. If she could find the courage, that is.

It was quiet in the house, save for the familiar sound of the staff working in the kitchen. She felt compelled to help like she usually did and, thinking it would be a timely distraction as a means to avoid the new guest that was making her knees weak, she made her way toward the noise. Eleanor was cooking and instructing Rupert and a new employee called Peter as they arranged food and dinnerware on two large trays.

"Will there be anything you need me for?" Katherine asked, startling the others in the room.

"What are you doing, child?" Eleanor snapped in her heavy Irish brogue, waving her spoon at Katherine from across the room. "Get outside with the others before your mother comes back in with her guests and they see you in here! We will all surely be whipped if it appears we can't perform our duties, and you'll be flogged for acting below your stature."

"They're outside again?" Katherine asked for the sake of clarity.

Rupert nodded this time. "Your father thought it a shame to waste this weather, so he arranged a picnic near the trees," he elaborated, and used his hand to gesture to the platter in front of him.

"Alright," Katherine said quietly, taking a step back. "Thank you." The sun was still bright and hot but had moved somewhat and pushed the shadows with it. Katherine wasn't sure how long this picnic was to last— whether William had thrown away formality and would forgo a dinner to remain out here.

Fiona was never one to do the same, and proved it now by delicately holding a parasol to block out the sun, while a fan lay close by her in case she would need it. She did seem somewhat relaxed, Katherine noticed. Likely truly happy for Edward's engagement, her permanent scowl was gone, and her fake laugh could almost be mistaken for a real giggle now and then. One could blame alcohol for a relaxed manner and jovial spirit, but not Fiona. She was likely sober as a shoe, and just as engaging.

However Katherine knew she would never be so at-ease as her mother, especially *around* her mother and the company here, and chose to stand off to the side like she usually did. She observed as guests came and went and wandered. She smiled when she was smiled at. She watched Rupert and Eleanor and Peter serve food, lay a blanket, take a blanket away, refill wine glasses or teacups. She wasn't paying attention until she was startled by her brother, who was suddenly beside her.

"Are you enjoying yourself, sister?" he asked before taking a sip from whatever was in his cup. "This is my engagement party! A joyous occasion! Smile!"

She did. "Of course," she insisted, raising her eyebrows as she tried to convince him.

Edward narrowed his eyes at her. "Liar. You must be ready to fall over, standing for so long in this heat!"

Katherine shook her head. "I'm fine, thank you."

"Well, I suppose you did have a rest earlier," he smirked, and was rewarded with a sheepish smile from Katherine underneath narrowed eyes. "Come," he said quickly, grabbing her hand and not giving her a choice. He led her to the blanket farthest from Fiona, where sat a lone Henry Bullock. Edward sat and pulled her down with him. "Eat something," he told her, grabbing the plate and again not giving her a choice.

Katherine was confused by her brother's actions. He wasn't usually so forceful. Perhaps he'd had too much to drink, she thought. She took a small piece of bread to appease him.

"My dear sister," he said loudly. "This is my celebration. And I will not be content until I feel all our guests are well happy—."

"She's not a guest," Henry remarked through a grin, noticing as well that Edward seemed somewhat inebriated.

Edward wagged a finger at Henry and grinned. "You are right. She is family. And family..." He inhaled and lifted his eyes up to the heavens, then let out a sigh and gave a look of disappointment. "Bugger I forgot what I was to say."

Henry burst into a fit of laughter.

Katherine chuckled quietly to herself, not willing to risk losing composure. She found it amusing how much Edward's drunken mannerisms resembled their father's.

"No matter! I'll think on it and when I remember I'll return," Edward proclaimed, stumbling into a standing position. "Excuse me, I must fetch my beloved."

After a few quiet moments, Henry filled the silence. "I'm quite happy to see Rupert and Eleanor are still employed here after all this time. Edward mentioned in his letters it being quite difficult for your father to find and keep help."

She smiled politely, thinking it best to steer clear of criticizing her mother for now, and instead to focus on her own happier thoughts and feelings. "Yes. Well I cannot speak for others that may have come and gone, but as for Rupert and Eleanor, my father and brother and I love them as though they were family. I can't imagine having grown up without them." She looked away, trying to find something else to say to fill the silence, but could come up with nothing and lowered her eyes to the ground.

"Forgive me if I'm mistaken," he said quietly, "but you do not seem entirely happy, as one would be on such an occasion."

Katherine turned and gave him a glare. "You are quite forward for a man I've only just met." She had thought so from the moment he lay down in the grass next to her. He seemed to lack formality in every way, which Katherine found mostly appalling, but also slightly intriguing.

"It's the American way," he chuckled. "Perhaps you *have* only *just* met me as a *man*, but we were friends once long ago. And as a friend I am simply making an observation about another friend."

"Were we friends, Henry?" she asked, her voice dripping with irony. "If I recall, you and Edward were friends, and you lads did all you could to avoid me."

Henry smiled. "Perhaps. It was easier to be a young lad around other young lads, I admit. But I do remember times when it was just you and I, Katherine. I recall a shy boy being forced into a dreadfully awkward situation, and a young lady who understood that situation and tried to make the best of it for the sake of them both. Inviting him to play countless games of chess and go for walks and trying desperately to make conversation with the silly fool. And it was all for naught in the end. That poor, poor girl..." He shook his head dramatically, raising his eyes to the sky.

Katherine looked up at his face, grinning at the memories as much as his playful manner. The feelings that had emerged when she had read the letter he'd written thanking her for her efforts were present again within her. They caught her off guard and she shook her head to bring herself back to her senses. "Ah yes. Well obviously that poor girl's attempts failed, and she was an absolute bore."

"What makes you say that?" he asked, turning his perplexed face to look down at her.

"Well, that *shy lad* ran off at every meeting," she teased, "eventually sailing across the sea just to escape her."

Henry laughed out loud at that. "What a fool he was indeed!" he exclaimed.

Katherine watched Henry nod to where Edward stood smiling at them, and then she looked away, once again not sure what to say. The long moment turned into an even longer moment.

Henry took a drink from his cup and then spoke again. "Strange, isn't it?"

Katherine looked over to him and raised her eyebrows to show him he had her attention. "What's strange?"

A smirk flickered across his face and quickly left. "How we are able to write so many words to one another from so far away, and yet sitting here at your side, I can hardly think of a thing to say."

She smiled. "Indeed. It is as though you're reading my thoughts, Mr. Bullock."

Henry held her eyes for a moment then looked down into his cup. "Your mother seems just as... charming as I remember," he said before tipping his head back and downing what remained of his drink.

Katherine cast a glance in Fiona's direction and once again chose to stay gentle on the matter. "Yes, well, I'm not entirely sure she's ever truly forgiven your father."

Henry's brow furrowed and his head cocked to the side. "My father? For what exactly?"

Katherine's eyes scattered and blinked nervously. She thought that perhaps she shouldn't have mentioned anything. "For taking your family across the sea and ending our... arrangement." She hesitated before the last word, not certain how to address their situation, but content with what she'd come up with.

He made a small sound, a "Hmm," and Katherine thought it was perhaps a chuckle. "I don't believe any of us realized we had upset her so."

She looked down at the piece of bread that had yet to reach her lips. Then she inhaled and spoke very quietly. "It does not take much to upset her, Mr. Bullock."

"So I've heard. Nevertheless, I am here now. Perhaps I can change her opinion of us in the coming weeks."

She lifted her head to look at him, suddenly remembering what she'd been thinking about before descending the stairs. "Why are you here, Henry?"

"Ahh, that's better," he cooed with a smile.

"I beg your pardon?"

"You've been calling me Mr. Bullock and making me feel like the most pompous and cold of fellows." He drummed his fingers on his empty cup. Her eyes grew wide with surprise and she inhaled sharply to speak but he interrupted her. "No, do not apologize, Katherine. Just promise you'll not do it again."

She snapped her mouth shut and nodded. She suddenly felt like the cold and pompous one for causing him any discomfort. She was instructed to be a lady, welcoming and hospitable—a far contrast from her mother, though her mother had been doing the instructing. To hear she had failed in any capacity made her fearful she would be punished.

Suddenly his eyes lit up. "Over there," he said, smiling and pointing past her to the right.

She turned her head, expecting to see more guests arriving, but instead she saw two small yellow butterflies twirling around each other.

"Just as you said," he whispered softly.

Chapter Four

Katherine had gone to bed long before anyone else and awoke the same way to a quiet house. The lateness of the previous night had everyone lying in late the next morning. She chose to take a bath, as she hadn't yet had a chance to wash since her impromptu swim the day before. After, she wandered about the estate as she usually did while she waited for someone to ring the bell for breakfast. Many people had slept the night in their home, and a large group was at the table in the dining hall when Katherine walked in for the morning meal. This time there would be no resentment to her appearance, as she was fresh and clean and perfectly made up.

Since she hadn't said much of anything to him the rest of the evening, she was relieved to see Henry was not among them. She was also slightly amused to see how many of them, including her father, appeared ill after their overindulgence the night before. Henry's absence was brought up by another guest however. Edward explained Henry had gone into town to visit his aunt and wasn't sure when or if he would return. She soon excused herself from the remaining company and went about her day normally, helping with chores and sewing, only stopping now and then to smile up at a guest who caught her eye. By supper the only people remaining in the house were the residents, and when Katherine woke up the morning after, she felt as though life were back to normal.

Until Eleanor burst into her room.

"Up child! Your mother wants you ready for church..." the woman trailed off as she quickly crossed the room to pull out Katherine's dresses.

Katherine moved her hair from her face. "What do you mean?"

"Mrs. Whyte says you must go with the family every Sunday from now until your brother's wedding to be in good standings with the church."

Katherine was still confused but knew that she must follow orders. She chose from the dresses Eleanor laid out and let the woman fasten her hair into a braid, wishing someone had told her earlier so she would have more time to prepare. Her appearance satisfied her parents and the ride into town was uneventful and as silent as every other she could remember. Her parents had long ago run out of things to talk about with one another and hardly ever conversed unless they were in the presence of company or shouting about their differences in private.

Edward was waiting and smiling the moment they stepped out of the carriage. *And why wouldn't he be,* she thought, *with his lovely Lucy is at his side.*

Lucy had always greeted Katherine with a hug, and today was no different. "Sit beside me!" she insisted, pulling Katherine by the hand.

Katherine could only nod in agreement, as she felt distracted. Something deep within her stirred. It made her lightheaded, and the right side of her body and face tingled as a warmth spread. Her body followed the group as they moved toward the front of the church while her mind raced for a reason this was happening. The weather wasn't particularly hot, and a noticeable breeze was blowing. She hadn't heard of anyone within the household or their recent guests falling ill, nor was she regularly around anyone else that made illness a possibility. Perhaps her excursion into the water the other day had caused a chill…

She sat beside Lucy as promised at the end of the pew—Edward on the other side of Lucy and both sets of parents to his left, filling it to the other end. There was no room left in this row, save for the one to the right of Katherine, and unless some vagrant wandered in off the street, she was all but certain no one would fill it and felt her upper body relax into the space.

So she was stunned when she was alerted to the movement against the right side of her body as someone did in fact take the empty seat. By the time she turned her head she was staring at a villainous grin and a stunning shade of blue.

"I do hope this seat is not taken," Henry muttered quietly, never releasing her gaze. "I've come seeking absolution and this pew contains the only people I recognize here."

She was nervous suddenly. "Absolution from what?"

"From what we awful Bullocks did to your family so long ago. Perhaps if God forgives me, your mother can as well."

She smiled and didn't realize she had breathed a small sigh of relief until it was making its way through her lips. She looked forward, and around, but not in her mother's direction. She hoped Fiona was distracted by Lucy's parents or perhaps someone else, but Katherine still didn't want to chance making eye contact and receiving a scowl for sitting so close to Henry again.

"Are you still not speaking to me?" Henry continued in his low tone.

She looked back into his eyes. "What makes you think I'm not speaking to you?"

"The fact that you're not speaking to me. We've had a few opportunities for conversation and they've all been dreadfully silent. You have me so very confused, Miss Whyte."

She was dumbfounded, and though she didn't know what to say, she felt the need to speak to prove him wrong. "Confused?"

"Yes. Was it not you who wrote me all those times?"

She gave a small nod. "It was."

"Then I suppose what I find confusing is our current lack of communication. As I said during our lovely picnic days ago, it is so strange that we can speak so many pretty words on paper. I said it in hopes that we might remedy the situation, Katherine, and I feel as though *I* have tried." He smiled lightly and lifted his eyebrows, indicating he was done and wanted her to speak now.

She opened her mouth to speak, then stopped herself. After a brief moment to gather her thoughts she inhaled to speak again. "Forgive me. I don't often find myself in the company of... well, anyone, I suppose." She glanced in her parents' direction but again avoided any possible eye contact with her mother. "I thought I had offended you with my formality, as you had alluded to, and I suppose I have been trying to avoid any further offense."

Realization flickered across his face. "Katherine, I was teasing you. If it is more reasonable for you to call me Mr. Bullock then you are free to do so. You may call me by whatever name you like, as long as you speak to me. It was all in jest but if *you* were in some way bothered by it then *I* am the one in need of forgiveness. And indeed, absolution."

"You never gave me an answer," she said out of the blue, recalling more about the last time she'd seen him.

"An answer to what?" he repeated, signalling she had

his attention.

"I asked you why you're here, in England, and you never gave me an answer."

He cleared his throat. "To celebrate my dearest friend's engagement, of course. If any other blessings happen to befall me during this time, then I will accept them."

She inhaled to speak again but the service began, signalling for everyone to rise, and they did, except for Henry and Katherine, as she was still spellbound by his eyes and the grin that had found its way to the right corner of his mouth.

She caught herself looking at him throughout the service. At first he would notice and meet her eyes, and she would turn away quickly after being caught. After a while she held his gaze, and when the corner of his mouth flicked up, she found herself smiling as she turned her face back to the front of the church. As the minutes ticked on she became aware of everything about him—the warmth radiating in the small space between them, the way he smelled, how he tapped one thumb on the top of the other when he appeared to lose focus.

She was caught up in her thoughts and was surprised when suddenly the service was over and everyone around them stood to leave. He waited to join the wave of people as they moved to the door, then took a step back as any gentleman would to allow her to walk before him. She did, though she wasn't used to making decisions, and as she walked she was worried: she was going too fast, or too slow. Should she stop and let someone else in? Once she passed through the door, should she go down the stairs, or wait for her party to join her? The options before her led her down the stairs and to the left of the crowd. Henry was immediately behind her, though her family had fallen back somewhat. Lucy and Edward were the first to join them and cut the awkward silence.

"Lovely to see you again, Mr. Bullock," Lucy said through

the smile she always wore as she extended her delicate hand for him to take.

"You as well, my dear." He smiled back and took her hand to give it a small squeeze. "And please, as I've already stated to Miss Whyte here, you *must* call me Henry from now on."

"Of course," Lucy said with a nod. "My parents will host supper tonight and I absolutely insist you join us."

Henry raised his eyebrows in pleasant surprise, glancing down at Katherine before replying to Lucy. "Why, yes of course. Thank you."

"Have you the direction?" Lucy continued even though Henry had taken a breath to speak. He snapped his mouth shut and shook his head. "You can ride with us!" She turned to Katherine. "Both of you! Come!" She yanked on Katherine's elbow.

Katherine turned the way she was directed and came face to face with her mother.

"What's going on here?" Fiona asked loudly.

Edward spoke up. "Lucy would like Katherine to ride with us to her parents' home."

"Oh?" Fiona chirped, her head cocked like a curious bird. "I don't believe she will be joining us. She accompanied us for the service, and that was all that was expected of her."

Katherine felt something she'd felt before at times like this. It was a mixture of crushing disappointment and anxiety of solitude that caused her stomach to drop and her face to flush and her hands and legs to tingle for a brief moment before going almost completely numb. Her gaze fell as she bowed her head and her breathing became shallow.

"Why would she not join us?" Lucy asked, looking from Fiona to Katherine with genuine concern.

"Yes, Mother. Why?" Edward asked, his voice containing both a chill and a challenge. And he made his voice loud, as though he was daring her to speak her insane words in front of all these people and God himself, here at church.

"Rupert will be bringing us to the Parker's and then taking Katherine home."

"Nonsense," Edward said with a bit more force. "The horses should not be made to make two journeys. Nor should Rupert since it'll be raining soon. It's been settled. Katherine will ride with us." He stepped in to take Katherine by the arm and guide her into the carriage before Fiona had a chance to protest.

Lucy was next, moving quickly, heavy fabric rustling as she settled in the carriage. Edward followed her and took his seat beside her, and Henry took the open spot beside Katherine. The carriage was moving within a minute of Edward uttering his last words to his mother, and it was all so swift it nearly made Katherine's head spin.

Again she was aware of how close Henry was, but she didn't dare look at him in such close quarters, especially with her brother sitting right across from them. She watched as Edward settled his hand on top of Lucy's, which were folded in her lap. Not daring to be caught with her eyes lingering on that or anything else in the carriage, she forced herself to look out the window at the buildings as they passed.

"Isn't this cozy?" cheerful Lucy chirped. When no one bothered to respond she continued. "Are you not feeling well today, Katherine?"

Katherine turned to look at her and shook her head. "I feel fine, thank you. Why do you ask?"

Lucy dropped her eyes. "Your mother wanted to send you home—."

"You know why," Edward snapped in a low tone.

Henry spoke up. "Well I do not. Enlighten me."

Edward sighed. "Fiona once again found an opportunity to exclude her daughter from something. Lucy was hoping that perhaps it was Fiona looking out for Katherine's welfare, but she knew better, did you not?" he asked, turning to look at Lucy.

She nodded, though she didn't meet his eyes.

Edward continued speaking to Henry. "God love 'er, she wants to see the good in everyone. She wants to believe Fiona is not as wretched as she is. And she is always surprised and disappointed when Fiona treats Katherine like a burden." He shook his head. "The old sow should be jumping at opportunities like this. If Katherine went to more suppers and events and dances, perhaps they could marry her off and be done with it all."

Henry cleared his throat loudly. Too loudly, Katherine thought. She'd seen men do it before as a signal to end a conversation, usually when someone was approaching.

"Oh, come now!" Edward shot back, and then made eye contact with Katherine. "Have you suddenly become unaware of the life you've lived, sister?"

She was stunned to be called upon, but she managed to shake her head.

"Precisely," he finished with a satisfied nod.

The rest of the ride was quiet. By the time they stopped, Edward's prediction of rain had come to pass, and a light drizzle had started. Edward got out first and helped Lucy down the step. Henry followed and turned to do the same for Katherine.

"Thank you," she said politely.

"Of course, my lady." He kept her fingers clutched in his hand and moved them to hold his arm as he walked beside her into the house. "I do hope you'll continue to sit with me throughout the rest of the day."

Katherine smiled politely but didn't feel it reach her eyes. She took a few steps to follow the rest to the doorway but he held her back.

"Will you tell me what's the matter?" he asked in a low voice. "Was it your brother's words or your mother's that seem to have taken the joy from you?"

She shook her head. "Edward spoke the truth. And he's right. I *am* aware of it. I'm not meant to be here—."

"Nor am I," he interrupted her. "So we must do our best to keep one another company throughout the entire experience. Remember Katherine, your mother views me in the same way she does you. And perhaps the best way to ruffle her feathers some is to enjoy ourselves in plain view of her." His smirk brought a smile to her face. "See, it's working already." He squeezed her hand and turned to lead her in the direction the others had gone.

She watched him throughout the afternoon, fascinated with how well-spoken he was. More people arrived at the house, and he could make everyone in the room smile without any effort whatsoever. He made sure whoever was speaking knew they had his full attention, asking questions or responding appropriately no matter the subject. He always held eye contact, she noticed, except for the times when she found him looking in her direction. When she caught his gaze he would grin ever so slightly, and she would need to look away lest her face become flushed. Nevertheless, she was both surprised and delighted when he chose to sit next to her after dinner had been announced.

"I've never met anyone like you, Henry."

He furrowed his brow and gave a perplexed laugh. "What do you mean?"

She paused for a moment. "You have an answer at the ready, always. You never falter. Your wit is absolutely remarkable."

He grinned again. "Should I thank you or is it a quality you find atrocious?"

"No. In fact it's... refreshing. In a world full of uncertainty, you always seem so certain. I understand entirely now why you and Edward get on so well. And how you've maintained your friendship through these years."

She was horrible at conversation, and she knew it, but she now knew how skilled he was, so she looked away and searched her brain for a topic, in hopes she could hold his attention the way others had throughout the day. She thought back to the day they sat at the water's edge and inhaled to speak. At this, Henry turned to look at her, and she felt a flutter within her core. She'd felt it a few times, and each time Henry had been the cause. Whether it was his gaze or his voice or his smile, he created a feeling within her that began in her belly and radiated out into her limbs.

"Yes?" he asked, waiting for her to say what she'd inhaled to say.

She'd forgotten. He'd made her forget. She blinked and was thankful to quickly recover. "The other day," she said softly, "you said you would tell me about the places you have been."

He smiled, and gave one, deep, slow nod. "I did indeed. Where would you like me to begin?"

There wasn't much she knew about his past, she realized. "Would you tell me of arriving in America? And of the journey?"

"Of course," he smiled.

He spoke softly and clearly, to her and only her. His smile made her smile. Katherine had never been on a ship, but his attention to detail, using his finger to draw on the table before them, had her imagining the voyage as though she had been there herself. She forgot they were in a room full of people. She forgot there was someone else to her right or sitting immediately across from her. She forgot she had food on her plate until he asked if she was going to eat. She picked at it slowly but continued to pay close attention to every word that spilled from his lovely lips.

And then he stopped. "It would appear dinner has ended," he told her quietly, glancing around.

She followed his eyes and noticed that people, including her parents, were indeed standing. It caused her heart to sink. She didn't want it to end. She didn't want to leave his company. And it must have shown in her face. She caught a glance from her mother and knew she was being instructed to follow. She stood and walked toward the entrance to the house, not realizing Henry was right behind her— until he was right in front of her. Her parents and their hosts were saying their goodnights at the door, but Henry stopped her in her tracks before she was able to leave the dining hall.

"Perhaps I should visit tomorrow," he suggested in a low voice.

Her face lit up and she gave a small gasp. "Would you?" she asked, searching his face to be certain he was sincere.

He took her hand and squeezed it. "If you want me there, Katherine, I will be."

His touch made her dizzy. And when he brought her hand up to his lips to kiss her knuckles, she lost feeling in her knees. He gently let go of her hand and took a step back and turned to leave out the door as Edward held it open.

"Come," Edward gestured to her with his hand.

Katherine stumbled toward him and took a deep breath after realizing she had momentarily forgotten how to breathe.

Had that really happened? She wondered on the ride home. And what did it all mean? In just a few hours she suddenly felt as though she couldn't be without Henry Bullock. The thoughts of the day consumed her and the anticipation of seeing him the next day kept her up throughout the night.

And so she waited, driving herself mad. The morning passed. The afternoon dragged on as she looked for anything to keep her mind occupied. She made note that it would be improper for a bachelor to visit a household without the master present and assumed Henry would not arrive until after William came from work. She wondered if perhaps Henry might even join her father on the journey home, but those hopes were dashed when William arrived unaccompanied. As the sun moved west in the sky, she wondered if perhaps he would be joining them for supper, but that too came to pass without the presence of Henry Bullock. Her emotions ran amok within her, everything from sadness to worry to anger.

Her frustration brought tears to her eyes, which she fought to control, as she was sitting at the table with her family and did not want to explain the inner dialogue that was causing them. Again and again she swallowed the lump in her throat. She excused herself from the table before anyone else and found herself outside, once again seeking the cool air and calm of the stream behind the house.

The sun was low and distant, and the sky above her was pink as she found her destination. As she stood there watching the shadows grow long she thought perhaps she shouldn't be angry with Henry. She should be angry with herself. She had likely read too much into his words and actions when he was simply trying to be gracious toward her. She had let her mind wander and created girlish fantasies.

Then again…

He *had* engaged her and only her throughout the previous evening. He *had* promised to visit the house. He *had* taken her hand and kissed it when no one was looking. No, this anger should rightly be directed to Henry Bullock. And after all the lovely things he had written her. She thought the chances of him having written or spoken similar words to other young women who fancied him were great, so there and then she decided she would do away with the letters, all of them. She would start a fire in the hearth in her room and watch them burn when she returned to the house.

She spun on her heel in the now dim lighting and marched several yards back through the trees when a moving, solid mass startled and stopped her.

"There you are," it called out through the distance in between them. "I've been looking everywhere. What on earth are you doing out here?"

"I live here! What are *you* doing out here, Mr. Bullock?" she snapped back while he quickly closed the distance between them.

"Looking for you," he said softly and he gazed down at her. He set his hands high up on her arms, near her shoulders. "I am sorry, Katherine. So very, very sorry. I tried all day to get away, but more people arrived as the day went on and I didn't want to be rude… I so hate to be rude…" He stared off to his left for a moment, then inhaled and found her eyes again. "I am here now. Your brother and father were kind enough to offer me a room for the night. And if you can accept my most sincere apology, I shall take that room. And I'm yours. Tomorrow, the entire day. And I'll tell you anything you want to know. About ships or Philadelphia or Paris—."

"You've been to Paris?" she asked, stunned.

"No," he smiled, "but I would invent stories if it means I

get to spend an extra moment in your presence."

Something about his voice, the desperation, made her suddenly forget she was on her way to her bedroom to burn the letters he'd sent her. His eyes and face were a mixture of timid and terrified, and for the first time since he'd arrived, she saw the young boy she'd known so long ago.

"Forgive me, Katherine, please," he whispered.

Every sense in her body was overwhelmed by him—except taste. And she glanced to his lips as she had so many times before this moment, wanting to remedy that. Instead, with her hands still down at her sides, she balled them into fists and dug her nails into the palms of her hands to help bring her wits back to her.

She inhaled sharply and sighed. "Of course," she chirped through a light smile and took a purposeful step back so his hands were no longer holding her. "Now if you'll excuse me, I am on my way to bed, sir. Goodnight."

More flowery words and promises, she angrily thought as she made her way back to the house and straight to her room. She could hear him padding through the grass behind her as they walked but neither of them spoke a word.

Yes, she thought, there was likely a woman back in America who he'd made sincere promises to as well. Maybe even more than one, and they had found out about one another and their angry families had driven him out of the country! Oh yes, she would indeed talk with Henry Bullock tomorrow. She would find out all about Philadelphia and his philandering ways.

But first, she would spend another night trying to sleep.

Chapter Five

Her arrival downstairs for breakfast saw her parents already long eaten and gone into town. This was nothing new; by this time she was well used to being forgotten. Her mother going into town was slightly unusual but not entirely unheard of.

What was unheard of, however, was the table being entirely empty of food. And plates. And cups. And cutlery. The absence of everything was what first caught her eye. The second thing she noticed as she came around the corner was her brother, sitting in their father's seat at the head of the table, leaning back, with his feet up and crossed, ankles resting on the arm of their mother's chair. The sight stopped her.

"What are you doing?" she asked him, confused by everything before her.

"Waiting for you. Are you feeling rested, sister?" he asked as he dropped his feet to the floor and sat up.

She wasn't sure. She'd been up late with the thoughts running through her head, but when she did finally fall asleep she slept well, explaining the lateness of her rising and emerging from her room. "I suppose," she answered honestly.

"Good then," he said with a nod and rose from the chair. "Shall we?" he asked, gesturing to the door Katherine had just come through.

She stared blankly at him, waiting for instruction or explanation.

Edward sighed and dropped his hand. “Let us go for a walk, sister.”

“Why have you not left for work? Or your own home for that matter?”

“I’m feeling dreadfully under the weather,” he told her, his cheerful tone an outright contradiction of his words.

She still felt compelled to ask, “Then should you be out for a walk?”

He spun her by the shoulders and practically shoved her out of the room. And down the hall. And out the back door. “What a lovely day,” Edward said as he looked up to the bright blue sky. “The sunshine and fresh air are precisely what I need.” He walked along the path babbling on about the birds that flew overhead and how he wished Lucy were here to appreciate this day with him.

Katherine walked along with him, confused by his behaviour, and even more so by the words coming out of his mouth.

Halfway through the trees he quickly spun to face her. “You must be so hungry!”

It was so abrupt and loud it startled her. And just as swiftly he spun back around and swept through the rest of the trees. Katherine had to pick up her skirt to keep up, and she was breathing heavily by the time she reached the clearing.

Edward quickly veered to the left and up a small incline where he immediately sat down— on a blanket, beside Henry Bullock.

Henry, however, stood when he saw Katherine

approach, and again she caught a glimpse of his younger self within his eyes. She waited for him to say something. She watched him swallow and inhale and open his mouth to speak but he never did. He even released a nervous laugh at his own obvious speechlessness. It caused her more confusion, for seeing Henry like this made her scold herself internally for the things she'd thought about him the night before. On top of that, his lack of articulation itself was bewildering. She'd watched him speak with such charisma and confidence only days earlier. Now, his silence in her presence made her nervous.

"Oh, bugger all!" Edward growled from below them, breaking the silence and once again sounding very much like their father. "Sit down Katherine and eat!"

The likeness to her father's commanding voice had her immediately on the ground as she'd been instructed, trying to arrange her legs and her dress in a ladylike fashion once seated.

Henry joined them on the ground and handed Katherine an apple. She thanked him quietly, and no one spoke again for a long time after that. Katherine looked around herself, up at the sky, toward the stream, until she heard her brother sigh and shake his head.

"I thought this would be far more entertaining," Edward muttered, shifting and then standing and walking away from them toward the stream. After tossing a few pebbles into the water he strolled to his left along the water's edge, toward where the river forked to create their stream.

Her anxiety crept up again. She was less than amused with Edward's leaving them there as she had never been great at conversation, and would now have to wrack her brain—yet again!—for something to say. She decided against bringing up the letters exchanged between them, choosing instead to revert back to more recent conversations they'd had in person. "You have *not* been to Paris then, Mr. Bullock?" she asked, once and for all.

He turned his head to look at her. "No. No, I have not. Our vessel stopped for four days in Ireland, then continued on around and didn't stop again until we reached the colonies."

He seemed to relax, which brought relief to Katherine. "Go on," she prompted, and then took a bite of her apple, which was really her way of avoiding having to speak.

And within a few minutes she had again become lost in the tales he told of his arrival, picking up where he'd left off at the Parker's dinner party. He'd told her in his letters that he now resided in Philadelphia. He went on to tell her how his father's royal business as a banker moved them from London to Boston for the first two years before they settled in, then Philadelphia for good in a different house that his parents found more appropriate for their stature. As he went on, she remembered the angry thoughts that she'd had before she'd fallen asleep, and she waited patiently for him to finish his thought.

"We *are* friends, Henry?" she said, lowering her chin to her chest and looking up under her lashes at him to gauge his reaction.

"Yes," was all he said from under a furrowed brow, somewhat curious.

She tucked a strand of hair out of her face. "May I ask you something then? It may seem bold..."

He nodded his head lightly though his eyes had drifted to Edward in the distance. "Anything you would like."

She hesitated slightly as she figured out which words to use. "How is it you are not married?"

This brought his eyes back to her, surprised. This was bold indeed, but also amusing in a way, his face told her. "What do you mean?"

She pressed her lips together nervously now, wishing she hadn't brought it up, and not exactly sure where she was going with it. "Well, you... are... obviously..." she stammered, "a handsome man. And you are intelligent, and a gentleman. And lovely company. I just find it... odd that you haven't yet found a wife. Or perhaps I am wrong? And there is an American lady whom you intend to make a wife someday, you just have yet to speak of her..." she drifted off, opening the conversation for him to once again take over, trying desperately to control her voice... And her face should the answer be a let down.

He did a splendid job of hiding his grin at her comments, though his eyes gave him away. "How am I lovely company?" he asked, rather than answering her question.

She wasn't expecting that. Her cheeks were red already, and it was spreading. "Well, you are charming. And well spoken. And kind. And you make me laugh." His eyes changed as they moved back down to the stream. They looked somewhat thoughtful, almost sad. Katherine thought perhaps she had offended him. "What is it? Are you alright?"

He remained quiet for a moment. "I am glad I can make you laugh, Katherine. Even smile. It does not seem like you do either very often."

Katherine was at a loss for what to say, and he must have sensed it for after a few seconds he continued.

"I am content, Katherine. In my life I am simply content, but I am not *happy*. I have enough money to keep my own home. And to be honest I have fancied a lady or two, and while the rising tensions have made me weary, if I had wanted to marry, I probably would have found the occasion to do so. To answer you, I do wish to marry someday and make a life with a woman and children. But I have yet to find someone who can make me *happy*, and until I do..." He shrugged.

"I don't understand," she said, tilting her head to the side and furrowing her brow.

He shook his head and held her eyes. "In truth, Katherine, I believe you do understand, perhaps more than most."

"How so?"

"This life of yours," he said with a wave of his hand. "You cannot be happy. I would think you cannot even be content. Perhaps *you* are simply... existing. Being ordered around by your mother now, and in future by whatever scoundrel she places before you with the intent of marriage. Think of how it would feel to be completely happy. To feel pure joy every day. Like your brother and Lucy. And still feel that way when you've grown old with them, like Rupert and Eleanor. *That* is what I want. *That* is why—." He stopped himself abruptly and cleared his throat. "That is why I have yet to marry."

She hated that he was right about every word he had just said. And to hear him speak so passionately about the happiness he sought made her want it as well. She swallowed the anger she had felt and replaced it with shame. He wasn't the scoundrel she'd believed him to be last night. Quite the opposite. He knew what he wanted and wasn't willing to settle for less. It was admirable. All she could do was break her eyes from his and give a nod, turning her head to stare out toward the stream.

Another long pause followed. Henry again took it upon himself to fill the silence. "Perhaps we should join your brother," he suggested, looking past her up the stream to the distant dot that was Edward.

Katherine followed his eyes to her brother, then looked directly into them and feigned a smile. "If you would like to."

He squinted at her for a moment, then smirked. "I

suppose we could wait for him to join *us* again."

She smiled back at him and gave a small nod.

He answered with a nod of his own. "Good then! However, I believe, my dear, it is your turn to hold up your end of our arrangement."

Her stomach jumped into her throat, as the first *arrangement* that came into her brain was their long-forgotten marriage. "What do you mean?" she stammered.

He remained unfazed. "Well, twice now I've told you about my journey to America. Now I expect reciprocation in the form of knowledge." He moved, lying on his back with his hands behind his head, similar to his first arrival in this exact spot. "The insects, Katherine. Tell me about the insects."

***

She told him about butterflies, their life cycles, the differences between butterflies and moths. She told him how she was long ago able to identify a caterpillar and what butterfly it would become. She expanded his knowledge on the different types of bees. At times she felt as though she was talked out or slightly embarrassed by her knowledge, but Henry would ask her a question, lighting her fire anew, and she would start up all over again. She didn't even realize that Edward had long gone from sight and not returned. The sun had moved across the sky to the other side of the stream and all the food had dwindled and disappeared before it occurred to her that they had been out here for hours.

Henry took notice when she started to acknowledge her surroundings. "Perhaps we should return to the house," he said with a small smile. He stood and again held his hand out to assist her to her feet. He allowed her to lead him through the trees, only dashing ahead of her to ascend the stairs to the house to open the door for her.

"Ever the gentleman," she murmured through a smile as she crossed the threshold. She led him to the study, where she was surprised to see Edward already sitting in a chair flipping through a book. "How did you get here?" she asked, stopping in her tracks.

Edward looked up from his book. "By way of my own two feet, of course. The sun became too much for me in my delicate state," he said, setting the back of his hand on his forehead, still feigning illness. Then he dropped his hand and looked past her to Henry. "Did you have a nice chat? I trust my sister was a most gracious hostess."

"Of course," Henry nodded, then stepped forward and sat in a chair identical to Edward's a few feet away. "It was the most pleasant morning, or rather, the most pleasant day, I've had in years." He turned to look at Katherine and bowed his head while holding her eyes. "I thank you, my dear."

She shook her head. "The pleasure was all mine, sir," she said, mostly out of habit, though as the words came from her she realized that she did, in fact, mean them. She forced herself to turn and walk to a window. Her eyes looked through it to the scenery outside though she didn't really see any of it. Instead her mind returned to how she could have been so angry with Henry last night, leading into this morning, and how she could feel so very different about him in only a few hours.

When she turned back the men had begun a conversation—another one about current world events beyond her realm of knowledge, so she left the room, feeling she would not be missed, and found her way to the kitchen to help Eleanor as she usually did in the afternoon.

Eleanor smiled as she entered the room. It was a smile Katherine had never seen on Eleanor's face before. And it didn't go away. "Did you enjoy your morning?" Eleanor asked.

Katherine's brow furrowed in confusion. Her heart began to race. If Eleanor knew that she'd been left alone with Henry, then the news might travel back to her parents, and surely she would receive some form of reprimand. "What are you talking about?" she stammered, not willing to incriminate herself in any way.

"The picnic your brother and his friend laid out for you. It was nice of them…" Eleanor trailed off, the smirk on her face not giving an inch.

"Oh. Yes, it was very thoughtful of them," Katherine played along, also not willing to budge. "They know how much I enjoy the sunlight near the stream. We all had a lovely time." Katherine was sure Eleanor would have seen Edward come back to the house alone at some point, but again the fear of her parents kept her coy.

It had been so long since Katherine had been in any sort of trouble. Really, with the life she lived, there was not much trouble to be found. And because of that she wasn't sure what potential punishment she could receive. Long ago she would feel the sting of a hand if she misspoke or stepped out of line. Early in her teens, when she had displeased her mother by reading in front of company they'd had, her mother had later thrown her book into the hearth in a fit of rage. But being alone with a man, out of sight of anyone, was something much bigger than anything she'd done before. And she expected a punishment to suit such an act of indecency would also be bigger. What could they possibly do?

She thought long and hard as she cut vegetables, her hands shaking at times. In truth, she wasn't sure her father would have a problem with it. William trusted her, and he respected and trusted Henry as well. William knew Henry was a gentleman who would never accost a lady in any way. But Fiona would let her mind wander and repeat every inappropriate thought that came to mind until she believed it.

And then she would scream them at Katherine and William until something was done about it. She would burn every single book they'd ever bought Katherine. Or send Katherine somewhere to learn what it means to be a lady.

Katherine didn't really think of the latter as punishment. She could get by, she thought. Perhaps even make a friend. She believed herself to be well mannered enough that she wasn't likely to find too much trouble. They, whoever they would be that owned the wayward home in her imaginations, would likely find her far less offensive than Fiona did. She would miss her father and her brother, but she would survive. And she would miss Lucy as well. And Henry...

Henry, she thought. Not seeing Henry would be sentence enough. The realization stilled the hand with the knife in it. She remembered how she had felt the day before, longing to be in his presence—*longing!* What had he done to her?! What was this effect he had on her? After dinner at his side the other night she felt... exhilarated. Without him yesterday, she felt empty. And today, sitting with him exchanging words and interests and stories, she felt complete. And yet she was ashamed of it, as she'd never felt this way about anyone before, and wasn't entirely sure whether it was right or wrong.

Witchcraft, she thought with a shake of her head.

It was wrong, she decided, moving her hand up and down to continue chopping. Definitely wrong, as she wouldn't feel shame if it was right...

But why *did* she feel ashamed? She pondered for a moment. Her parents *had,* at one point, thought Henry good enough to marry her. Not much had changed for Henry Bullock. He was still the same lovely, respectable person he'd been when he'd left for America...

Her hand stopped again. *America.* That was it, she

realized. Henry lived in Philadelphia now. And he would return soon. And that was the reason she should try to stifle any feelings she might have for him. Because he would soon be a memory and she would be forced to continue on with the life she had here, chopping vegetables and dodging judgement, across the ocean from him...

Her heart sank and she set the knife down. She had to leave the room before the ache within her spread and caused tears to fall as she knew they would. She chose, however, to avoid her bedroom, full of letters from Henry, as the thought struck her that soon writing would once again be their only means of contact. She could hear the men still speaking in the parlour as she passed it. She chose to slip out the back door and hide in the shade of the house while she waited for her emotions to calm. She was both surprised and relieved by the small amount of tears she shed, as it meant her red, swollen face would take less time to recover. She resolved to no longer allow herself to be alone with him, and promised she would no longer allow herself to care deeply for him.

It was far more difficult than she could have anticipated. She found him making conversation with her at dinner again that night, continuing conversations they'd begun that morning. The next day the three young people rode into town to meet with Lucy, who insisted they walk together and dine at an inn. Their manner of walking, Katherine realized, made she and Henry look as though they were also a couple, though she was satisfied when Lucy led the conversation and engaged Henry as well as Edward.

In the days that followed Henry was again invited by his aunt and uncle to town, and he obliged, taking leave in the morning and presuming he would be gone for a few days.

Katherine felt torn. Her heart hated to see him go that morning, but her mind was glad for the reprieve, as every minute that passed in his handsome, polite presence she felt more of an attachment. She set about her normal routines, and found herself missing him within hours, though she convinced herself she ought to get used to it, as when he set off for Philadelphia once again there would be no expectation of him.

His return to the house Sunday was in time for dinner.

The entire Whyte family had come back from church and tea at the Parker home, though Fiona, exhausted from her trip to town and the heat, had excused herself for the day as soon as the front door was shut. And very soon after, the bell rang to tell the family of an approaching carriage.

When she looked out the window, Katherine felt the warmth spread again from her stomach to her limbs, and she scolded herself for it. Instead of following her father and brother to meet Henry at the door, she dashed to the kitchen to busy herself by helping Eleanor make supper.

Fiona's absence brought from the three men at the table a more jovial attitude, as Katherine could hear laughter before she'd even opened the door to the dining room. Henry stood as Katherine entered the room, which received a snicker from the other two men. It didn't stop him from pulling out her chair as she approached. "Thank you, Mr. Bullock. I'm glad to see your journey was a safe one."

"I'm happy to be back, my dear," he told her. Once they were both seated the men continued their conversation. Katherine ate and listened but could not fight the tightness in her chest. She avoided Henry's eyes, which she could feel falling onto her repeatedly, for fear she would lose control of her emotions.

"I do not believe I have yet asked you how long you intend to stay," William said, turning his head to Henry.

"A few more weeks if you will have me. I would like to stay for the wedding."

"Of course!" William assured him. "You are welcome to stay for as many weeks or months or years as you wish."

"Do you ever miss England, Henry?" Edward asked.

"At times. There is a formality here that I enjoy, the bowing and such. Manners are far less cordial there, sometimes lost entirely. And the smells take me back to when I was a boy. Especially returning to your estate, sir. The little things like that, I miss. And the people."

"Oh come now," William cried out. "You've been there long enough to have made friends. Surely a handsome and well-spoken man like you would have lots of friends! And prospects, I'm sure," William finished with a wink.

Henry grinned. "Yes, sir, I have many friends. But having many friends leaves me little time for *prospects*."

Edward laughed.

"Oh I don't believe that!" William cried out on a loud, gasping laugh of his own. "There must be women queued up at your door. And I'm sure you would be a gentleman and oblige them on the lonely nights." William brought his cup to his lips after lifting his eyebrows knowingly at Henry.

Katherine suddenly lost her appetite, at the topic as well as the display. She pushed her plate away slightly and gave a small sigh while her eyes looked for anything else to look at.

Henry spoke quietly. "There is one. She is lovely and elegant and soft. But also intelligent, more than any female I've encountered. And I dare say she consumes more of my thoughts than I should care to admit."

Katherine was brought back to their conversation, the one they'd had only earlier that week, where he'd told her why he hadn't yet married. But hearing this now brought forth both sorrow and anger, as she felt he'd lied directly to her earlier. Or perhaps not, if in the days he'd spent in town with his aunt and uncle he had become acquainted with a lady and had come to fancy her. Though she found herself again wondering if she should be glad for the distraction, in the moment, jealousy prevailed. “And does she make you happy, Mr. Bullock?” Katherine snapped across the table, unable to control herself.

Henry stared back, challenging her. “I have yet to find out, though from what I know of her, she is entirely capable.”

She avoided him for days again, although this span of absence felt easier to do as it was guided by rage and hurt. She would see him only at meals as he still found reason to stay here at her home, though she was scarcely spoken to. Henry still tried to include her in conversations, but these efforts which she had found endearing had since become irritating, and her answers were swift and without elaboration. She couldn’t bring herself to burn the letters as she’d promised, mostly since she refused to go near them lest she feel her heart break over again. She was invited by Henry and sometimes Edward to play a game of cards or chess, or to accompany them to town, which she would politely refuse with one excuse or another. She instead went for long walks alone, going farther past William’s property lines than she’d ever had the nerve before to pass as much time as possible.

Until one evening more than a week later, to Katherine’s secret delight, he announced he would be leaving to visit an uncle and aunt who lived in Bedford. She wished him a safe journey, as she should have, before retiring to her room to finish up some sewing before bed.

When Eleanor came to wake her the next morning, she handed Katherine a sealed letter. It had Katherine’s name on it in writing she knew very well to be Henry’s.

Katherine set it on her night table beside her bed. Eleanor, having no patience for the girl’s silliness, sighed and opened it herself, unfolding it and placing it in Katherine’s lap.

"I did not raise a fool in you," she scolded.

My dearest Katherine,

I have not been blind to your indifference toward me of late. I wish I knew what I've done to cause this, as I so enjoy the pleasure of your company, and I was certain you did mine. If I knew, I would move heaven and earth to make it right. However I am not one to linger where I am not wanted and as you so blatantly wish me gone from your presence, I have made it so.

As for any offence I may have caused you, trust me it was done entirely without my knowledge. My only inkling is that perhaps I misspoke when I told your father of my fondness for you over dinner. If that was in fact what caused you upset, forgive me, Katherine. My only intention was to suggest my affections are singular, belonging to you and you alone.

My uncle has invited me to stay for as long as I wish. If it is your intention to continue to avoid me, I may stay until I leave again for Philadelphia, only returning for Edward's wedding.

Yours always,

Henry.

Chapter Six

She read it three times before she truly understood it. She had been so blind, so naïve. She'd let the negative voices in her mind win. They had always convinced her that she was less than. They told her she was pretty enough, but she needed to remain humble. They told her she was polite enough, but one wrong look could be her downfall in society. They told her to only speak when spoken too, but even then she was never articulate. Now they had led her to believe she had been anything *but* enough for Henry, and that any other woman in the world was more worth his time and efforts.

She jumped from her bed and ran down the stairs in her nightdress to the study. She wrote with haste, making something of a mess, before pulling out a new sheet of paper and rewriting neatly, choosing the words carefully, as though it would somehow disguise her urgency.

Mr. Bullock,

I've been a fool. You must understand that until receiving your letter I was unaware that your affections toward me were anything more than friendship. I have indeed been avoiding you. I believed you were courting another and to save my own heart I made myself distant from you.

It is I that require <u>your</u> forgiveness, as my innocence has *blinded me to your advances. I am not a worldly person. I am very much still a stupid young girl in many ways. Therefore you must allow me to make it right, please, and I ask that you return at your earliest convenience.*

She signed it only with her name, once again unsure of herself. Eleanor agreed to send it out straight away.

Katherine chastised herself for having wasted these past several days, choosing to be alone instead of happily in his company.

One day passed.

He would still be here had I not acted as I did...

Two days passed.

She read the letters again, wondering if there was something in them that she had missed, but they were indeed all cordial and respectful, nothing within them would suggest that he cared for her.

So it must have been after his arrival that he developed these feelings, she thought.

Three and four days passed.

She inspected herself closely in her mirror, trying to see herself anew, trying to find what it was that brought about his attraction, and wondering how she might enhance it.

Finally on the dreary fourth day, just as Katherine thought she might go mad, Eleanor rushed into the study where Katherine was seated and closed the door behind. She was wide-eyed and pressed a finger to her lips. She crossed the room quickly and without a sound—something she'd perfected after so many years in this house. She handed folded paper to Katherine, then continued on to the door on the other side of the room and slipped out—just as the door she'd come in flew open and Fiona entered.

Katherine slid it under the book in her lap, then looked up at her mother, startled.

Fiona stared at her; her brow furrowed in confusion. "What are you doing?"

Katherine blinked, giving her mother a moment to see for herself. "Reading."

Fiona's eyes flittered around the room, to her daughter, to the book, and everywhere else. "Is Eleanor in here?"

Again Katherine took a moment before stating the obvious. "No," she said with a quick shake of her head. "Why do you ask?"

Fiona looked to the window. "I saw a man come to the door. I want to know who he is and why he was here. And why I didn't hear the bell."

"I'm certain if it were important she would have come to find you." Katherine closed the book for effect. "Last I saw she was on her way to the chickens. Shall I fetch her?"

Fiona seemed to think about it for a moment, never relaxing her stern chin. "No." With that she turned on her heel and left the room.

Katherine waited until she could no longer hear her mother's footsteps before standing. She hid the letter in her skirt and left out the back door of the house. Her strides were long and her pace quick as she felt again the mysterious warmth and compulsion usually associated with her interactions with Henry Bullock. It pulled her, even in the light mist of rain that fell, to the place by the stream where they'd spent so much time in each other's company.

My dear Miss Whyte,

You are indeed forgiven for your part in our misunderstanding. And I am quite surprised to hear of it, as I thought in all my efforts, perhaps I was in fact being too bold in my words and my actions. If you will allow me, I shall save us now from further confusion. I delight in your presence upon every meeting we have, and I think of you often when we are apart. And in the rare moments you are not foremost in my mind, I instead wonder at the possibilities had I remained in England so many years ago, and those possibilities lead my thoughts back to you.

As for my returning to you, I intend to be at your side Sunday next when you arrive for service.

Yours,

Henry.

She took a deep breath, and she counted the days—exactly one week. She passed the time every day in the way she always had, taking walks and reading, anticipation rising within her with every dawn and every sunset.

When Eleanor woke Katherine on Sunday it was a rainy morning, but Katherine's spirits were high. She dressed quickly and ate quickly. She normally didn't care for bonnets but fastened her prettiest one in place to keep her hair dry; it was important for her to look her best on this day. Her mood lifted evermore when Fiona announced she would not be joining them at church as there were few things she hated more in the world than a cold rain. Katherine and William rode alone in the coach, quiet as ever. William knew how to carry on a conversation with women he knew little about, as there were questions to ask and much to learn. He knew almost everything about Katherine and her daily life and had no questions or comments that would suggest otherwise. Instead both father and daughter brought books to keep them entertained, though Katherine's wandering mind didn't allow for many words to be absorbed.

Upon arrival Katherine left the coach and climbed the stairs, looking all around the dreary crowd for Henry, but not finding him. Inside she did the same and was again disappointed to not find him. She stood by while her father chatted as he usually did, watching the door as people entered until the doors finally closed.

William sat. Katherine sat beside him.

Moments later her heart fluttered as someone sat beside her but stopped just as abruptly when she realized it was Edward. She hadn't been expecting him, but at the same time it wasn't odd that he be here. What was odd was the look in his eyes, staring her down, trying to say something without actually saying it. And then she noticed the subtle movement: his arm and hand moving ever so slightly to reveal something white and square pressed between his hand and his thigh.

Another letter.

Katherine's breathing quickened, and she turned her head to look forward, trying to focus on the sermon to no avail. All she could think about was the letter and its contents. She looked to her left at her father, who didn't much care for church and was instead having a quiet, drawn out conversation to his left with an associate of his. Katherine held out her hand, and Edward, after a brief hesitation, handed it to her. She waited until again she was sure she wasn't being noticed and broke the seal, then was forced to stand for a hymn. In the bustle of everyone once again taking their seats she slipped the paper into an open bible which she then placed in her lap.

The writing was hasty and there were spots of ink throughout the page, reminding Katherine of days ago when she had written her own letter with such quick desperation.

Katherine,

I once again find myself surrounded by company I cannot leave out of duty and respect and I am once again asking for your forgiveness. I shall leave first thing in the morning, which means that by the time this letter arrives for you to read I shall be well on my way to you.

Please wait for me.

Henry.

She felt her heart swell. Yes, there was slight disappointment, but she knew how important it was that he make and keep new friends and acquaintances. *"I so hate to be rude..."* she had heard him say not long ago. And her fanciful mind hoped perhaps if he were successful in his social interactions here, he might stay in England...

She looked over to her brother, whose eyes were turned up to the rafters, focused on nothing in particular. "Where did you get this?" she whispered.

"Same as all the others. It arrived at my home this morning, along with a note for myself hastily explaining the situation and a request that I bring it to you here."

"The situation!" she hissed.

Edward's eyes widened and his lips pursed, signalling with his face his irritation, and that she need not bring attention to them in this moment. "Katherine, while you have perhaps been blind to Henry Bullock's feelings toward you, I most certainly have not. I have encouraged several opportunities for you to be alone in his company in hopes you might enjoy it as I do."

Katherine's face did little to hide the astonishment she was feeling.

Edward paused, allowing her to respond, but when she said nothing he continued. "You know Bullock has been a dear friend of mine for a great many years. I care for him as I would a brother, and nothing—save for perhaps my own marriage to Lucy—would make me happier than to call him thus. He is a good man, Katherine, among the best I've ever known. You know of his character, as do I, and I know yours, and I believe there is not a better match for you in all the world."

Katherine turned her head to look forward and leaned back. She was not naïve to Edward's attempts, blatant as some were, though she believed it more to be for his own amusement at seeing her uncomfortable. She would never have assumed his intentions were serious or considerate. She handed the letter back to Edward and allowed him to tuck it inside his breast pocket for the moment.

She leaned her head and whispered after several minutes of silence. "When do you expect he'll be back?"

"If he left when promised, without knowing how swiftly he travels, I would say at any hour tomorrow."

She gave one nod and listened to the last few minutes of the sermon. They stood back as William continued to socialize afterward. "Edward, my boy! You were late today. Where is your darling Lucy?"

"The weather has given her a chill. I only came to learn this when I stopped at her home to retrieve her. Hence my late arrival today."

Katherine had to hide her smirk. Though they were expected to attend every service leading up to their wedding, Katherine knew the couple had no intention of joining them today.

Before leaving, their father invited several couples to join them for dinner that evening, and informed Edward he was expected to be there as well, to which Edward agreed.

After their arrival home, upon learning that they would be expecting company, Fiona suddenly and miraculously recovered from her rainy-day headache and began shouting orders to the servants as to what should be made for the meal. She also ordered the parlour be set up for cards and Katherine change into a different dress, for there was a chance Mr. and

Mrs. Granger could bring their son, Harold.

This was the first Katherine had ever heard of him. She'd met the Granger's several times now, but was unaware they had a son, and was unsure of why his presence called for her to wear a nicer dress. She watched through the rainy window as the first of their guests arrived, then was shuffled into the drawing room to entertain them as they waited to greet others. The Granger's did arrive thirdly, and they brought with them their son, tall and young, and though he appeared to already be losing the hair toward the front of his head, he was not unattractive.

Fiona introduced Katherine to Harold and made loud mention to her daughter of Harold's stature and education and accomplishments, thoroughly embarrassing both young people.

Edward caught his sister's eye, just as perplexed by their mother's behaviour.

When dinner was announced, Katherine was ordered by her mother to sit beside her, and persuaded Harold Granger to sit on Katherine's other side. It was around this time that Katherine became wise to what her mother was ever-so-subtly suggesting, and it caused her to become suddenly, awkwardly silent. While she had found the words to politely ask questions and answer the ones asked of her until then, she found her mind racing and her throat dry and her eyes unable to meet Harold Granger's. She fought to elaborate on her mother's prompts but gave only short answers. She felt her face flush and grow warm, and assumed it was of shyness.

Until she heard the bell ring from the front of the house, and suddenly she felt that warm feeling she'd come to know in the pit of her stomach. She looked to the entrance of the dining room and waited only a moment before her eyes were satisfied.

A soaking wet Henry Bullock strode into the room.

The men stood in acknowledgement, and William voiced his surprise to see him, but Henry's eyes held Katherine's firmly, knowingly, for a long moment before turning them to his host.

"My apologies for my lateness. If you would all excuse me that I might go and change my clothing," he said, "I shall return shortly."

"Of course! Of course!" William told him. "Do as you must, my boy."

Henry bowed his head to William, then met Katherine's eyes again before turning to leave the room. She heard his boots quicken down the hall to the stairs.

Fiona tried to continue the speech she was making to Harold Granger; Katherine paid less attention now than she had before Henry's arrival at the house. It made for difficulties when Katherine was asked to contribute to the conversation.

While Henry was gone Eleanor set a place for him at the only empty spot left at the table, and Katherine's pulse quickened when he came through the door again. His clothes were now different and dry, his hair still damp and pushed back. He was sat on the other side of the table, five spaces down, and though he was at something of a distance she felt a calm run through her body, replacing her anxiety and longing.

Katherine now had far more trouble trying to focus on the things her mother and guests were saying, as she found her eyes being drawn to her right, where they would meet Henry's for a moment and then one of them would look away before doing it all over again.

Dinner ended and the crowd moved to the parlour. Katherine was surprised when Harold pulled her chair out for her to stand, and politely thanked him, but she chose to walk more slowly behind the crowd, where Henry came to her side. His presence, so close—his arm and hand brushing up against hers, causing her head to spin in ecstasy.

Through the door they could see two tables set up for two different games. They stood still together, waiting for the other to decide where to go so that they might stay together. Katherine's choice was made for her, however, when a demanding look from her mother compelled her to veer to her left to take the empty seat beside Harold. To her relief, Henry remained at her side, though he was forced to sit across from her.

The entire table laughed throughout the course of the game and made conversation. Katherine sat silent, only wishing to speak to one person, though as per usual, she could never work up the courage to do so or think of what she should say. And she knew from previous experience that her attempts to make conversation on her own brought about stammering, which displeased her mother and herself. She thought for a long moment. She was always able to find the words when writing them...

She looked down at her hands. "I trust you had a safe and pleasant journey, Mr. Bullock," she said before lifting her head to look at him.

"Thank you," he said, holding her eyes. "Safe it was indeed. And pleasant, yes, until I returned in the rain."

"I hear you're from the colonies," Mrs. Granger asked, turning her attention to Henry.

"Yes, ma'am. Though I was, in fact born here."

"How long have you been back in England?" she inquired.

"I am in my fourth week," he informed her with a nod.

"Are you here on business?"

"No, ma'am. Mr. Edward Whyte informed me of his intention to become engaged to Miss Lucy and I wished to be present at the wedding of my dearest friend. I have also taken the opportunity to visit other members of my family in the country."

"He must be dear to you for you to make such a journey!" She seemed pleased with him, smiling and nodding. "You just returned from Bedfordshire?"

"Yes, ma'am."

"And how much longer do you anticipate you shall stay in England?"

"Likely a fortnight, ma'am, perhaps longer," he said, casting a quick glance at Katherine. "I have yet to find a ship on which to arrange my return to Philadelphia."

Mrs. Granger suddenly appeared perplexed. "Philadelphia?"

Henry nodded.

"When did you leave, young man?"

"The twelfth day of July," he answered, looking upward as though trying to see into his own brain.

"Oh! You are lucky to have missed the battle!" she proclaimed.

Henry paused and tilted his head slightly. "I beg your pardon?" The conversation brought forth the attention of everyone in the room.

"Yes, sir. We have only learned of it this very morning! Philadelphia has been taken, and most of its residents have fled!"

Edward spoke up then, concern forming a crease between his eyebrows. "From whom did you hear this, ma'am?"

Mr. Granger spoke for his wife. "There was talk of it among the officers who attended church this morning. Word has been slow, having to cross the sea, after all. They said their garrison was involved in the siege on eleven September—."

Henry sat breathless, shock visible throughout his face and body.

Mrs. Granger continued to speak, while her husband filled in the details he knew to the guests at the other table.

Katherine wasn't listening. She was watching Henry, knowing he was no longer listening either. Her eyes went from Henry to Edward, who was also watching Henry carefully, and back again.

After a few moments Henry stood and excused himself. Soon Edward followed to check on his friend. Katherine desperately wanted to be with Henry as well. He'd only just returned. They had only had a few moments together, none of which had been spent discussing anything of worth. She wanted to know what he was thinking, whether he was alright. She weighed her options and knew her mother would likely bring down the sky if she left the table.

And still that was the choice she made. Katherine stopped outside the parlour door, listening for a sound that would indicate where in the house Henry and Edward had gone. She heard nothing, and the crowd behind her was far too loud, but she felt the warmth within her pulling her to the right. As she walked through the hall, she could hear their voices in hushed tones as she approached the study. It was well dark, save for the few candles one of them would have to have lit and brought in with them, and Katherine used it to her advantage, hiding in the doorway to listen as they spoke—but their conversation seemed to have ended. She watched Edward come toward her. He was temporarily startled when he noticed her but gave a quick nod as he passed and continued on down the hall.

She watched Henry sit at her father's desk and begin

writing. After a few moments he stopped and sat back in the chair, looking up toward the roof.

She stepped into the room. "Mr— Henry?" she stammered quietly. "Are you alright?"

Whether he had known she was there or not, he didn't appear startled. He didn't move at all. He simply sighed, and then he lifted up his hand and held it in the air.

Katherine crossed the room without a thought and gently placed her hand in his. She gave a small yet reassuring squeeze. "You must be worried about your parents," she whispered. "I wish I knew what to say..."

He shook his head, then brought their hands up to his face, and rested his nose and lips on the back of her fingers. It wasn't a kiss, but wasn't *not* a kiss—an intimate gesture nonetheless. He held it there for a while, and she did nothing to break away, feeling the breath from his nose as he inhaled and exhaled. Then he sighed again, and though he didn't move his face away from her hand he spoke softly.

"There is nothing you can say, love. Your being here with me now is enough." He did then place a firm kiss on her knuckles, and he let her hand go. "I'll be going into town at first light to send a letter to my father, as well as one to my uncle in Bedford to ask if he's received any word on the welfare of my parents. Then I will go to my aunt and ask her the same in person, although I'm certain had they any word from my parents they would have messaged me straight away."

"Katherine!"

They were both startled at Edward's hiss toward her as he scurried back into the room.

"Mother insists you return to the parlour at once," he said coming to her side.

Her eyes were still fixed on Henry's, and he tilted his

head quickly toward the door. "Go on, my dear, duty calls. I have much to do in here on my own."

She nodded. "Goodnight," she whispered before turning and sweeping out the door.

Back in the parlour Fiona continued to induce conversation with Harold Granger, though Katherine's mind and heart were with Henry more now than they ever had been before.

The next day was as miserable as the previous two had been, and William offered Henry the carriage to use for the day. Edward accompanied him to town to be of any assistance he could. The evening came without their return, and William surmised they must have chosen to spend the night at Edward's home rather than spend another moment travelling in the rain.

The following morning Katherine was happy to see the rain had stopped, though it was still a cold and cloudy morning. She kept herself busy until Eleanor called out that the carriage was coming, and she dropped what she was doing and hurried to the door, where her father met her.

When Rupert closed the door behind Edward and Henry, William spoke.

"Have you any news? Have your uncles received any word?"

"No," Henry said, and then cleared his throat. "No the first they heard anything of it was upon my telling them."

"Mr. Granger said he expected it to be in the newspapers by now. Perhaps that will offer some new information," Katherine added, as though it would offer some comfort.

"Hmm," was Henry's response, coupled with a nod. "Not much can be done," he said as he walked slowly toward the back door. "I've sent a letter to my uncle in Bedford and one to my father, though it will be months before it arrives. If it has anyone to receive it..." He opened the back door and walked through it, leaving the three Whytes to watch him make his way down the steps to the path and across the paddock toward the trees.

Edward sighed and spoke softly. "After we sent off the letter to his parents and spoke with his aunt and uncle, we moved on to find any militia men of high rank who might know of the events in Philadelphia. There was not much they could tell us that the Grangers hadn't already. Civilians had loaded carriages with what they could carry and fled to the hills out of town. I've tried to reassure him his parents would have done the same and are likely in good health, but he is still worried sick—."

"Of course he is!" William agreed. They were all thoughtful for a moment before William continued. "You ought to keep him occupied today, Edward. Take him up to the river, do some fishing. Keep him from thinking about it."

"Yes. Yes, of course," Edward assured him. "Katherine should join us. He does enjoy learning what she knows about insects and animals."

"Good then. Edward, gather your tackle. Katherine, prepare some food," William told them, turning around to return to the study where he had been before the other men arrived.

Once their father was out of sight, Edward lowered his voice, as well as his eyes to his sister. "I'll gather everything. You go," he said with a nod toward the door.

Katherine, feeling unprepared to be outside protested. "I need my bonnet—."

Edward nodded. "And a shawl, yes. Go!" he instructed.

She picked up her skirt and dashed out the door toward

the trees. She slowed to a walk at the treeline, out of breath and careful of her footing. Once through, she looked to her left to see Henry sitting at the shore of the stream watching the water. She was compelled to sit with him and was silently grateful to have put on a dark coloured dress that morning. She sat, close enough to have his arm against her own, giving her some warmth—it had been colder in the trees, and just as brisk here near the water where the chill and moisture from the days of rain remained. Henry was still, continuing to watch the water and whatever visions were moving before his eyes. Her mind raced with words, but she could choose none. "Tell me what to say," she whispered. "I don't know what to say."

He sighed after a moment. "I was indifferent to sailing to America. I was upset to lose my friends, and you. Even as a young boy I was drawn to you. Once we were settled, I asked my father if he would send a letter I had written to Edward, which he did, and I was quite pleased when Edward wrote back. I enquired about his family, and you of course. Throughout all of it I wondered about you, Katherine. Had another marriage been arranged for you? Was Fiona still an awful wretch? Every time I saw a butterfly or a ladybird, I would think of you, though I would never write such things lest I give my heart away. Years passed and I rejoiced when you wrote me. I felt as I had when I was young and in your presence. Soon I was told of Edward's wedding, and how happy he would be were I able to make the journey. We planned together that he might offer his hand to Lucy the day of my arrival. When I came upon you lying here in the grass my heart leapt. It was as though I'd found a fallen angel. And dare I say the fun I had teasing you while you fought to recognize me. You are always sweet and polite and have genuinely made me laugh though I know you hadn't meant to. I went to church not seeking God, but seeking only you. I watch the fire that lights in your eyes when I challenge you. I would offer you my arm out of mere friendship, but have never felt so comfortable and complete as when you are near me. I wanted to decline my uncle's invitation to stay with them, so I might spend every possible moment with you." He stopped. His eyes looked all around his mind as he wrestled with the conflict of thoughts. Then he inhaled deeply and sighed again, giving in. "I've loved you since I was a boy. A day has not passed in my life where I did not think of you. And I was prepared to stay in England if you would have me." He finally looked at her.

She couldn't breathe. She couldn't move. She didn't want to do anything that would interfere with this moment. Right now— before the negative she was sure was coming—was perfection.

He moved his face back to look forward again, having run out of words perhaps, or no longer knowing how to put them together for what he had to say now, and so he was silent for a long time. "I suppose there is nothing can be done until more is learned. However..." He looked to her again. "I must know, Katherine, would you marry me if I remained here?"

A small smile came to her lips. "I feel as though my heart would not allow me any other choice."

A similar smile, small and wistful, found his mouth as well, before he turned his attention once again to the stream. "I would make it right, Katherine. I would speak with your father this instant if I knew what's become of my own parents."

Katherine nodded. "There is still time," she insisted, trying to sound appropriately cheerful.

Henry seemed to agree. "There is. If I receive word from them..." He sighed again and hung his head for a moment. "If they are well, I would plead with them to come to England. I would ask them to return to celebrate our marriage."

Katherine's voice was still soft. "I would like that very much."

The sound of rustling through the trees brought their attention away from the topic at hand. Edward appeared, jostling Katherine's shawl as well as a basket of fruit and bread and his fishing essentials. With his hands full, he chose to wear her bonnet, bringing a much-needed laugh for his sister and their companion.

Chapter Seven

The saving grace that came with the uncertainty of Henry's situation was that Katherine suddenly became his constant companion, along with Edward of course, though Edward had his own agenda and felt completely confident leaving them alone from time to time. Edward chose to stay at the house instead of returning to his own home. Throughout the next week they made four trips into town to see Lucy. They spent one day walking for miles, as it was the only sunny day, and the rest were spent in one another's company within the confines of the house, though it seemed neither boring nor depressing, a stark change for Katherine.

Sunday came about again and the entire family attended church with their houseguest. Before and after the service Henry was met with well-wishers who informed him that they were praying for him and his parents. They were once again invited for tea with the Parker's, to which they agreed, though Katherine had recently become aware of Mrs. Parker's growing distaste for Fiona, which did not hurt Fiona's feelings in the least. It was silently known that these meetings were only temporary and would end soon after the marriage of their children. It suited the women just fine. The bride and groom's fathers, however, got on quite well, and Katherine felt they would likely find another avenue in which to enjoy one another's company, perhaps making arrangements for hunting or fishing together.

Katherine happily sat beside Henry to converse with the younger people, when after a while she noticed her mother speaking feverishly, which was something she did not do often, raising her voice so the whole of the room would hear. Fiona was talking of Harold Granger, going on about his amiable qualities, his fortune and rank, and speaking of how any young woman would be lucky to accept him. Katherine listened, knowing these words were meant for her ears, but she did not turn her head to meet her mother's eyes, instead she looked from Henry to Edward to Lucy, all of whom had knowing looks similar to Katherine's and were doing their best not to smile.

Lucy raised her own voice, as though to continue a conversation they weren't actually having. "I often wonder if wearing the dresses I have in the French fashion would be considered treason now with what's happening." Her companions shared thoughtful and exaggerated looks and nods as though they were entirely enthralled in the conversation as well.

"I suppose it is worth considering, and being mindful of," Henry agreed, keeping the grin in his eyes from reaching his lips.

Although Fiona continued sharing her point of view, it was temporary and soon the topic changed among the older company. A short time later, the bell rang to signal someone was at the door. The Parkers' maid entered the room to interrupt the gathering and handed a note to Henry.

Henry paused. Katherine noticed he was hesitant to open it and seemed to be holding his breath. The others in the room remained silent as they waited for him to decide what to do.

He inhaled deeply. “It is from my aunt…” he said quietly. He turned it over in his hands and again hesitated. Then he broke it open and read it. He sighed. “She says they have received news about my mother and father and would like me to come to the house immediately.” He looked around at the faces staring at him. “If you will all excuse me,” he said, standing up and taking a few steps.

“Shall I join you?” Edward offered.

“No, thank you,” was all he answered, not bothering to turn around before he walked around the corner and out of sight.

Katherine wasn’t sure why she suddenly felt empty. Perhaps because she had spent so many days in his constant presence. Perhaps it was the way he left, and she pitied him. Perhaps because, even though her brother was there, she was suddenly vulnerable to Fiona’s intrusive matchmaking. Whatever the reason, she became uneasy, and wondered how long he would be gone.

It depended on the news, she figured. If it was bad news he could be gone for days, perhaps even leaving for America ahead of schedule, though she still hoped that no matter what the news, he would keep his promise to come to Edward’s wedding on Wednesday.

The atmosphere was somewhat solemn after his departure, and it all but ended the afternoon tea. The Whyte family left soon after for their own home, and the mood continued this way throughout the ride, as not one word was spoken from anyone the entire trip. Again Katherine tried to focus on her book but found her imagination wandering away from the story on the pages.

At home Katherine felt she needed to help Eleanor with supper, hoping it would take her mind off things like it usually did. She boiled potatoes and carrots and cut up the bread. She helped set the table. She ate quietly with her family, while her father and brother made small conversations, avoiding the topic on everyone's mind.

They hadn't heard the bell ring, so all were surprised when Henry Bullock swept into the room, breathless, taking long strides. He came to stop near the head of the table beside an astonished William Whyte.

William looked up at him. "Henry! My boy! What news from your family?"

Henry looked worriedly to the rest of the family at the table. "My apologies for interrupting your meal, but I request a private audience with Mr. Whyte, please. It cannot wait another moment."

Fiona, who had never shown a moment's compassion in her entire life, surprised them all by standing. "Yes, of course." She looked to her grown children so they would follow suit. Fiona's pace was quick and she was nearly out of the room before the others had stood, likely more of her continued avoidance of Henry than a sympathetic gesture.

Edward and Katherine looked to Henry with concern, and while Katherine gave a small curtsy and turned to leave, Edward hesitated for a moment before following.

Katherine stopped outside the door, not sure where to go, and before long Edward joined her. He grabbed her arm and pulled her to the side of the door and around the corner, then put his finger over his lips, signalling her to be quiet. She was appalled at the notion of eavesdropping on the conversation but did as she was told.

The first thing they heard was William ask again of his parents, and then the voices were hushed, and for a long time Katherine felt as though standing here was indeed as pointless as she'd expected. Edward crept closer to the door, as did Katherine. Tones formed into words now from this vantage point.

"This is a happy day then!" William exclaimed.

Katherine met Edward's eyes and gripped his arm happily. He set his hand on hers and squeezed it. Both smiled and exhaled a silent sigh of relief.

"Indeed sir. And before I left my aunt's house, I sent word to them of my intentions," they heard Henry say.

"Your intentions?" William repeated.

"Yes. With the fate of my parents no longer of such concern to me, I now find myself entirely at your mercy."

There was a pause before William's response. "What do you mean, boy?"

Henry cleared his throat. "Mr. Whyte, you know I have the utmost respect and admiration for you and your family. You have all been so gracious toward me, both in my youth as well as now. And while the affections I feel toward you are that of another father and Edward as a brother, my affections toward Miss Katherine go far beyond those of an extended family. I am in love with your daughter, sir. And while I am a man of no great fortune, I believe you to hold me in as high a regard as I do you, and I ask that you allow me the honour of following through with the original agreement you had made with my parents so long ago."

William was a man never at a loss for words, which made the long silence that followed all the more unnerving. Katherine was afraid to move, or breathe, or think. She'd left the room thinking Henry was about to break awful news regarding his parents, but now she was listening to him bear his soul to her father and beg his permission to marry her. *Her!* She was beside herself at this moment. She once again found herself clutching her brother's arm, as though convincing herself she was awake. She knew her mouth was agape, and her eyes were wide— she could only imagine how shocked her father must be as well, the poor soul.

"I must say," William began slowly, quietly, "that this comes as something of a surprise, Henry. I was entirely unaware of any of this. Might I ask when you first became aware of this affection?"

"Long ago, before we left London," Henry told him, reaffirming what he'd told Katherine days earlier. "We wrote each other at times, as old friends, of course, but upon my return I..." He paused to take a breath and gather his thoughts. "She is as lovely and intelligent a woman as I've ever known. And I am not certain I can live another day without the promise of her hand."

They heard William grunt, something Katherine and Edward knew him to do that would be paired with a thoughtful nod.

"And you girl," William called out, "would this make you happy?"

It took a moment for Katherine to realize that she was the girl he was referring to—and that it meant he knew she was there. She swallowed hard and took a breath to steady herself, then stepped into the doorway— and into view of the two men. She took another step, crossing the threshold into the dining room and then nodded. "Yes. Very much."

William appeared stern yet thoughtful, giving a nod as he stared into the space before him. After a moment he spoke again. "I have one condition."

Katherine felt her stomach flutter and her breath catch in her throat.

Henry's face remained unchanged. "I'm listening."

"I would like you to stay in England," William said, "so that I may know my grandchildren before I die."

"Mr. Whyte, while I consider myself an American, I cannot bear the thought of living in a country on the verge of war. My intention is to sail to the colonies to collect my belongings, find my parents and return with them to live out the remainder of my life here in England."

This brought a smile to William's face. "Then I believe it is settled." He stood and gave a nod. "If you will excuse me, Mr. Bullock, I must go now to inform my wife of this happy news."

"Mmm," Henry said with a serious look. "Best of luck to you then, sir."

William nodded again and sighed, patting Henry on the back and then walking across the room and out the door. Katherine wasn't sure if Edward was still there.

Once William was gone Henry exhaled a long breath. "I'm sure Harold Granger will be well disappointed." He was rewarded with a grin from her. "I was afraid he would reject me."

Katherine continued to smile. "Why did you not tell me before you came to him?"

"There was no time. I received a message from my father and—."

Her eyes went wide and she inhaled sharply. "Your father! Your mother! What news, Henry?" she interrupted.

"They are alive. They fled to the hills as we had hoped. There is much uncertainty..." He looked at her now and shook his head. "No, my dear. Now is not the time for such talk. Now there is only talk of weddings. Edward's is days away, and then our own..." He watched her eyes move away from his and her face change. "Is something the matter?"

"You told my father you intend to leave again for America before we are wed. That would mean our wedding must wait."

He sighed and took her hands. “Yes. I understand your urgency, and I share in it entirely. However I have not here with me the money I would need for a wedding or a home. And I wish my parents to be a part of it. I cannot be happy, or even content on the day until I know they are well and safe and here with us to celebrate. And I cannot begin a life here with only the clothing I brought for my short stay. You must understand —.“

“I do,” she said. Then she put a smile on her face. “And I shall be happy to welcome them upon your return. Forgive me. I am being selfish in my desire.”

He brought her hand up to his lips and kissed the back of it gently. “You are forgiven. And you are welcome to be as selfish in your desire as you wish, forevermore. However, I have yet…” He dropped her hands and surprised her by pulling her into his arms and setting his cheek against her head.

Katherine felt every fibre of herself vibrating and buzzing. Her stomach was fluttering and every hair on her body was raised up. She wasn't sure how or when, but she suddenly realized her arms were tucked under his and her hands were gripping the backs of his shoulders.

A whisper came from within him. “Marry me, Kather —.“

“Yes,” she whispered back before he had the chance to finish.

Their embrace ended abruptly when from above them they heard a loud thud, followed by escalated shouting from Fiona. They let go and Henry took a step back as both sets of eyes lifted to the ceiling. Then after a moment Henry grinned and looked at Katherine again.

“After hearing such magnificent things about young Mr. Granger, I would expect nothing less.”

Katherine laughed.

Despite Fiona's objections, things became settled very fast that evening. Henry stayed with his plan to return to America after Edward's Wednesday wedding. The morning after they became engaged, Edward chaperoned Henry and Katherine into town so Henry might make arrangements for his departure. As they walked, Henry made sure to stay close to her, keeping her hand tucked into his elbow every time they left the carriage.

Once he acquired a ship to sail him back to America, he directed the carriage to his aunt and uncle's home, where he formally introduced Katherine as his fiancé, and informed them he would be leaving Saturday. He thanked them for their hospitality while he had stayed with them, as well as for informing him when they'd received word from his parents. After promising to write them upon his return to America, he bid them farewell.

They met up with Lucy for lunch, who was thrilled and delighted to be told of their engagement. She'd of course known of Henry's designs, as Edward shared most everything with her.

At seventeen, Katherine had never felt so grown up as in this moment, sitting with her grown brother and his fiancé, days away from their wedding, and a handsome fiancé of her very own. Though she knew she was likely a year from her own wedding, she couldn't help smiling the entire afternoon at the pleasant company and the possibilities before her.

Chapter Eight

The wedding ceremony of Edward Whyte and Lucy Parker was in the afternoon and was very brief. It included only the bride's parents, the groom's parents, Katherine and Henry. They had tea at the Parker's home again to waste a bit of time before the ball they had planned at a public assembly hall.

Henry doted on his new fiancé, dancing with her until she was exhausted. They ate chicken and drank wine and received congratulations from the few people who knew, though they were quite content to keep it something of a secret between themselves.

Katherine wasn't entirely sure what time she arrived home with her parents and Henry, though they all slept well into the morning. When she opened her eyes, it took a few long moments for her to come to her senses. She remembered the joy she'd felt all evening, but now realization was setting in. She'd been so looking forward to Edward's wedding. But it was over, and now the only thing she was expecting would be painful.

She and Henry ate together, then spent several hours playing chess and enjoying one another's company. They reminisced about the night before and the party and the people and discussed the things they liked and disliked, and what they would do or not do with regards to their own wedding.

They dressed warm and went for a long walk in the afternoon.

"Look here!" he called to her and bent down.

Katherine took a step toward him and watched as he moved his hand behind a large rock and pulled out a small, purple flower.

"Is purple still your favourite colour, my lady?" he asked as he rose again.

"It is," she said with a smile.

"Incredible how it has survived the frost thus far," Henry noted, and Katherine agreed. He held the flower out for her to take, and then thought again and pulled it back toward himself. "I have an idea," he told her.

The sun was beginning to sink and turn the sky orange. Henry suggested they return to the house. Katherine's heart sank slightly, realizing that she would now only have one day left with him before his journey, and as per his decision, he would be leaving the estate tomorrow at sunset to say goodbye to the new Mr. and Mrs. Whyte, and then board the ship for its departure early Saturday morning.

Inside the house Katherine followed him into the study and watched him scan the shelves until he came across what he knew to be her favourite book. He opened it to the middle and placed the flower inside the pages, then closed it. "You shall think of me next time you read this book," he told her with a grin. "You'll remember this day and the time we had." He set the book back on the shelf and then set her hand in his elbow to lead her to dinner.

Their final day together was spent much the same as the day before had been, indoors conversing throughout the morning, walking the grounds in the afternoon. Whether by choice or not, Henry refused to speak of dismal things. Though Katherine felt her solemn mood was obvious, he spent Friday looking only forward—to his return, to their wedding and marriage and life together. He spoke of the children they would have someday. He wondered aloud at what kind of house they would live in and insisted he would only make a decision based on the size of the library he felt she deserved.

Edward and Lucy joined the family for dinner, as they would take Henry to town with them after. The conversation was carried on by Lucy mostly, as she spoke of newly married life. She turned it now and then to other things, and asked questions about Henry and Katherine's wedding, to which they would hear Fiona snort or sigh her own silent response. She eventually excused herself.

Dinner ended, and with the setting of the sun so did the conversation. After a pause Edward suggested they should leave before it became too dark. Henry excused himself to retrieve his things. When he returned, he thanked William for his welcoming and hospitality these past months, while Lucy and Edward insisted Katherine see them off to the carriage. Henry followed, and while he loaded his things onto the carriage Lucy convinced Katherine that she must come to their home after church on Sunday. Edward helped Lucy into the carriage, then bid farewell to his sister and climbed in himself.

Katherine felt Henry take her hand and she turned to look at him.

"Come," he said quietly, gently tugging on the hand he held.

She gave way, allowing him to lead her away from the carriage back to the steps of the house. He spun her to face him, and upon looking into his eyes she felt every emotion possible, every ounce of blood as it coursed through her, every nerve throbbing. He continued to hold her hand and took the other to hold her full attention. He opened his mouth to speak, then closed it and looked away. Then he inhaled again, and to her surprise he let out a small laugh.

He brought his eyes back to hers. “I should have married you yesterday. You would come with me and…” He sighed. “This is dreadful. I haven’t any idea what to say.”

Katherine understood completely. Not only was she at a loss for words, she knew anything she said would give way to a flood of emotion, sobbing, heaving, that would make them both feel even worse. All she could do was swallow hard and nod her head.

“I shall make every attempt every minute of every day to finalize the conditions of my return. And I shall write to you the moment I step off the ship. You have my word.”

She nodded again.

He grinned suddenly, bringing a weakness to her knees, and let go of her hand. He reached into the pocket of his overcoat and pulled out a small package which he placed into her free hand. “I will still be on board come Christmas, so I will give this to you now.”

She looked up and shook her head. “I haven’t anything to give you—.“

He interrupted her with a whisper. “You have given me everything,” he assured her. “You have given me everything.” His head quickly moved, and his lips met the skin of her cheek below her temple, and just as swiftly he let go, turned and was up in the carriage.

Katherine’s body let out an involuntary shiver, as though a part of her soul had been ripped away. She watched the carriage leave, and it was halfway down the drive before she remembered to breathe again.

The next day she waited, as though she expected him to have changed his mind overnight. When she awoke Sunday, it was later than she’d expected, but she was convinced he had boarded the ship, and resigned herself to the lonely waiting she would have to do. She went downstairs to ask Eleanor why she hadn't woken her for church. Eleanor explained that Fiona had decided Katherine no longer needed to attend church regularly, as Edward's wedding was now passed.

Though Katherine momentarily wondered if her mother would force them all to attend in the weeks leading up to her own wedding, it didn't bother her much. In fact, it almost made sense. Without Henry or Edward around for protection, Fiona was bound to revert to her old ways of locking Katherine away from the world. And William would allow it now that she was engaged, seeing as the only reason a woman would be out in society would be to capture a husband. It did dawn on her for a moment that, if Fiona still had designs of her marrying anyone but Henry, she might put an embargo on Katherine's isolation. She shuddered and hoped her mother wouldn't have the same idea.

She was disappointed though, having promised Lucy she would come for tea after church. She had been looking forward to it in fact, knowing Lucy's gift for conversation would take her mind off Henry. She wondered if her parents would still be going for tea, and if they did, she knew her mother's jealous streak would be the reason; having not been invited herself, she would force her presence on them.

Thus began again the past for Katherine. Things were as they had been prior to Henry's arrival, and as Fiona refused to acknowledge the union, Henry was rarely spoken of, just like before. Katherine would try to break the monotony, but with these winter months she was once again mostly confined to the house. However, a small miracle came to her now that Edward and Lucy were married— William would allow Katherine trips into town to spend a day or even a week at their home, and Katherine tried to convince her family to allow these trips every month. She was quite happy to join them for a party they had at Christmas and stayed the night there again. She was so caught up she forgot to bring with her the gift Henry had left but remembered it on the ride home as she thought about him spending the holiday in the middle of the sea, without loved ones.

She left the carriage without waiting for the door to open or for her parents to follow. She went immediately up the stairs to her room, to the panel where she'd hidden his letters — and now the gift he'd given her. She'd hidden it the night he left and hadn't looked closely at it. Now as she sat on her bed, she noticed that he'd taken the time to wrap the tiny box with purple silk ribbon tied into a bow. She undid the bow and opened it. There was a small note in it.

Happy Christmas, my darling.

I wish for nothing more than to return to you as swiftly as I can, to see what it looks like upon your hand. Until then, when you wear it, I hope you will think of me and the unwavering love I have for you.

You are in my thoughts always.

Henry.

She was slightly puzzled by the note, not sure what "it" he was referring to. She picked up the box and peeked inside, then emptied it into her lap.

A ring fell out, small and delicate, made of gold with a dark stone at the top. She got closer to the window to see it more clearly. The stone was an oval sapphire, nearly half the size of the nail on her little finger. It was a beautifully crafted ring. She slipped it onto her hand and vowed to not take it off until Henry was at her side once again.

The ring did not go unnoticed by her parents at dinner the next evening, with William asking about it and thus bringing it to Fiona's attention. Katherine explained its origin, bringing a smile to her father and a scowl to her mother.

More time passed before Katherine felt joy enough to genuinely smile again— weeks, then a month. On a rare Sunday when Katherine was invited to church by her father, Edward mentioned Henry's ship should have reached shore by now, and it was likely he'd already sent word back to her. This made her grin from ear to ear, and as Edward had been watching the papers to make sure no ships had capsized recently, a new kind of waiting began for Katherine. It became anticipation for a letter, a note, anything to calm the anxious fire that threatened to overtake her lately. It became restlessness, and the next time she spoke with her brother she told him of it, babbling excitedly, reminding him of how Henry had promised to return as soon as possible.

"Do you think he could have found his parents and boarded another ship already?" she asked him and Lucy over lunch.

Edward flicked his eyebrows up. "I suppose anything is possible. Though I'm certain by now he would have located his parents and perhaps returned to Philadelphia with them. I believe removing and preparing their belongings and arranging their affairs would take some time as well." He watched her face fall with disappointment. He pitied her then and felt as though he needed to pick up her spirits, as he had just stepped on them. "Perhaps you could write him instead? We could send it out immediately. I'm sure he would be incredibly happy to receive a letter from his true love."

Her face didn't lighten as he had hoped. Instead he watched her brow furrow. "You believe he will be there that long?" she asked, knowing it would take months for a letter to arrive.

"Perhaps. I cannot be certain. We shall find the fastest ship in the fleet!" he suggested cheerfully. "And if Henry boards a ship and returns to you before your letter arrives across the sea then so be it."

Katherine nodded and put on a smile to show she agreed. Later Edward allowed her to use his library to sit in privacy and write her letter. Before they left town, they made a trip to the harbour to speak to some of his connections. They found a ship leaving for the colonies in the next few days, and as Edward had promised, it was faster than most.

The weather began to warm, and the trees began to bud, and this time of year usually brought Katherine joy as it meant soon the insects would return. This year however it hardly piqued her interest. As time continued to pass the only thing that made her happy was when Lucy, soon followed by Edward, began calling her Mrs. Bullock in secret.

And then it came to pass in May, Katherine heard the bell ring at the door, though she was reading near the garden behind the house and didn't see who had come or left the property. A minute later movement caught her eye, and she looked up to see Rupert scurrying down the back stairs and walking quickly toward her, a look of urgency on his face. Katherine closed her book and stood as he approached.

"Miss Katherine," he said with a nod. He handed her an envelope.

Katherine looked down at it in her hand. She recognized the writing and gasped. In her excitement she grabbed Rupert and hugged him unexpectedly, doing all she could to stop herself from jumping up and down with excitement. She let him go and turned, picking up her skirt as she ran through the trees, not stopping until she was in their spot near the stream.

She sat and sighed as she stared at it.

My love,

As promised, I have written and sent this within my first hours of arrival. I am sure you would like to know of my welfare, as I wish to know of yours. I am well, and quite happy to once again be on dry land.

I feel as though ten thousand years have passed since I was blessed to be in your presence and look upon your face. Every minute has been torture. Every day, an eternity. I wish for nothing more than the day I return to you, never to part from you again.

I shall write again very soon, as my soul is bound to yours.

Always,

Henry.

She decided she would write him again when she returned to the house and send it tomorrow. She stared out at the water, as she had done so many times before in this spot, with him at her side. In the field across the water she watched two small yellow butterflies dance around one another in the air. Deep in her heart she felt this was a sign from the heavens. Katherine immediately felt contentment, knowing that this letter was sent months ago, and that there was a chance he was already on his way back to her.

Another letter arrived just over two weeks later, letting her know he had found his parents and that they were both ill with smallpox they had contracted while staying at an army camp. Due to this, among other circumstances he hadn't made clear yet, his return to Philadelphia had been delayed.

Katherine was disappointed, then she hated herself for being selfish. If she were there with him, she would be understanding and sympathetic, so that is what she strove for. His devotion to his parents made him all-the-more endearing to her. And again she held on to the hope that, in the months that had passed since he'd written and sent this letter, his parents had recovered and they were well on their way back to England with him.

Weeks passed, then a month, without word, until finally another letter was handed directly to her, this time by her father, who had met the post carrier at the door as he was waiting for some letters of his own. This letter apologized for the time that had passed. Henry explained that he had become ill himself and was then quarantined with a group of soldiers and civilians. When he had recovered, he returned to find his mother had succumbed to disease and infection and had been buried nearly two weeks before he had ever been informed.

Katherine's heart broke for him. She wished she had been there with him, to hold him and help him through his grief. She scolded herself again for her selfishness, but also for not realizing the severity of the disease, as she'd come to in the time since his first letter, through her father and brother. Though Katherine had no loving maternal relationship of her own, she knew the tenderness and care he held for his mother. Katherine herself remembered his mother Anne as a kind, engaging woman who smiled a lot. She informed her parents and wrote to Edward, not certain whether Henry had sent word to him as well. She then sent Henry a letter telling him of her sadness, knowing how much they both wanted his parents at their wedding, and giving her family's condolences to Henry and his father.

Less than three weeks later another letter arrived to tell her he would be leaving for Philadelphia the next day, though he was having trouble convincing his father to come with him. He didn't explain why, but Katherine assumed it was due to the grief of having recently lost his wife, and perhaps not wanting to leave the site where she was laid to rest. His letter once again declared his love for her and his hopes of being back on a ship headed east within a fortnight.

Her heart skipped a beat when she read this, as it meant he was certainly on the water already. *He could be halfway across the ocean by now!* she thought with excitement that reached the corners of her mouth. *He could arrive any day!*

Day after day she floated through her world on these hopes. Every time the bell rang her heart leapt and she nearly jumped out of her skin. After a month of waiting she returned to her normal demeanour, setting aside excitement and expectation. After two months she began to doubt herself. She hadn't received another letter, though she was convinced it was likely because he was aboard a vessel. Under this impression Katherine felt there was no use in sending anything back to him as it would arrive to an empty house, or to a new tenant who would have no idea who she was and care not for the sentiment within it.

Three months passed with no word and no Henry. *Perhaps it was a very slow ship...*

She hated these days as they passed. Though she was still determined he was on his way back to England, the lack of communication was enough to bring her to tears now and again. At least when he was on dry land, he could send word to her and she to him— she had something tangible to hang on to, and she knew he thought about her as much as she thought about him. But now the emptiness was pulling at her, taking a piece of her with every day that passed.

The weather was turning cold again when on a Thursday night Edward stepped into the dining room as the family ate supper. Her brother, usually so full of life and flare appeared solemn and pale.

William noticed as well, after greeting him with his usual boisterous cheer, paused to study his son, and then he stood. "Is something the matter, my boy?" he asked.

Katherine wasn't sure whether it was a white cloth or a paper in his hands, but he appeared to be wringing it nervously. She watched his eyes search in front of him for the words he wished to say, and he licked his lips more than once.

"I—." he began, then stopped and cleared his throat. "As you know I have several friends and acquaintances in the militia, and those at the harbour with whom—." Again he stopped to clear his throat. "I was asked about my relationship with Henry Bullock today." He paused and looked away.

Katherine felt her insides turn to ice and her breath stop.

"What of him?" William urged.

"At the market, a man I know from the harbour informed me of some news he'd heard from the naval officers. Immediately thereafter I rode to find my friends within the militia for confirmation..."

He was shaking now, Katherine realized, in his hands and his legs. His jaw was twitching and he blinked a lot, something she knew him to do when he was very upset or nervous.

"What news? What of Henry?" William demanded.

Edward looked at his father, avoiding the eyes of his sister. "Henry Bullock and his father were captured by the British army and charged with spying on the English."

At last William was speechless, and he sat back down in his chair stunned.

"George Bullock has been imprisoned," Edward whispered. "Henry Bullock was hanged for treason."

Chapter Nine

Katherine hadn't heard the last two words as she had immediately fainted at the word *hanged*. Consciousness came back to her in blurry bits and pieces. She remembered hearing the sounds of things crashing down around her and the thud as her body hit the floor. She remembered seeing her brother's face at her side through the blackness.

She regained consciousness in her bedroom. She wasn't sure how long she'd been there. It was dark and the hearth had only a few embers glowing. She didn't feel cold, but she pulled her covers up under her chin and tucked them tight around herself. She remembered what had occurred immediately after she woke, and it continued to repeat itself inside her head over and over. Tears filled her eyes and spilled over, running past her temples, into her ears and her hair as she stared up at the ceiling.

So many emotions arose, but above all she felt confusion. How could this happen? How long had it been since he'd been hanged? How is it they weren't informed sooner? How had she not known, somewhere deep within herself, that he was dead?

How?

How?

How?

She lay there, falling in and out of consciousness. She was aware of the things around her—the sun rising, Eleanor entering her room and speaking to her while leaving food on the table near her bed—but she didn't move. She couldn't move. She could still see his face before her eyes, and if she moved an inch these things might be torn away from her, fading like memories do with time. If she moved, she would have to continue living. If she continued living, she would meet new people and create *new* memories. If she created new memories, they would take the place of the old ones she held so dear, the faded ones, and she would lose him forever.

It didn't seem fair that she would continue living when he would not.

But none of this was fair. Henry had been accused of spying on the English, something she knew very well he had not done, and it had cost him his life. If she knew anything about the subject, it was that Henry and his family had chosen to side with the Patriots—his only reason for returning to England was Katherine. His father was now locked away in a prison for his association with his own son. George had lost a wife, and now a son, and Katherine wasn't sure how long a man of his advanced age could survive in such a place. Edward had lost his greatest friend. And Katherine had lost her love, a part of her, her salvation from this wretched life.

Thinking of her brother's pain caused her to finally weep, but the realization that she would remain alone here gave way to her despair and broke her down into heaves and sobs and gasps.

She would never be Mrs. Bullock.

***

William would come to her room once a day. Fiona made her only appearance with him on the second day, though she said nothing and stood near the door, and had Katherine not glanced toward the door for a moment she would not have known Fiona was there at all. During his first visits William would try for words of comfort, but after the fifth day he had nothing more to say; he would simply come sit with her for a few moments, and satisfied with the fact that she was still breathing, he would offer her an awkward pat on the hand or the leg and then see himself out.

Fiona never returned, though this was not surprising to Katherine, and truthfully she was grateful. Her mother was never much comfort to her, and Katherine was more than certain that, should Fiona spend an inordinate amount of time watching Katherine grieve, she would only make things worse somehow.

Edward came every day as well. He explained the first day that Lucy sent her condolences and love to Katherine, but that she was so woefully heartbroken herself that Edward thought it best she stay away for the time being. Edward said very little, as every time he tried to comfort his sister his own emotions would get the better of him, causing him to choke on his words and tears to form in his eyes.

For Katherine the days bled into one another and she lost track of them. Tears came without warning, and she wasn't entirely sure what caused them as all her thoughts and feelings were the same and constant from one minute to the next. Some days she had the strength to move to the window, other days her body was wracked so hard with her sobbing that her muscles became weak and sore.

Having lost all concept of time, she wasn't sure how long she'd been in her room before she finally felt steady enough to walk through the door into the hallway. She lifted her eyes to see the door to the room that housed Henry during his stay here, and she felt the air being sucked out of her lungs. She stumbled back into her bedroom and closed the door, gasping. She pulled herself back onto her bed and covered herself up to her chin like a child who'd just awoken from a nightmare.

Days later she tried again, this time refusing to look at the door to her left as she passed it. She made it down the stairs where she was bombarded by the smell of food. She had nibbled on the things Eleanor had brought her now and then, but this was the first time she'd been aware of herself and her surroundings enough to feel how hungry she actually was.

She could hear people in the dining room as she passed it; more than just her parents, she deduced from the noise. She knew she likely looked a fright and had been wearing the same nightgown since she'd received the news, but her carnal craving for whatever the smell was coming from the kitchen pulled her along with little to no regard for her appearance.

Eleanor turned when she heard her enter the kitchen and looked as though she'd seen a ghost. "Goodness child!" she cried out, dropping the large spoon she was holding and raising her arms in fright. "Are you trying to stop my heart?" After a moment she regained her wits and the realization hit her that Katherine was out of her room for the first time in almost two weeks. "What are you doing down here?"

"I was hungry," Katherine managed to croak. Her throat was dry with the cold weather, though she was sure after all the crying she'd done there was likely not much fluid left in her.

Eleanor scurried around the kitchen putting food onto a plate. "You go and clean up before your mother sees you and kills us all!" she demanded with her back turned. "I'll bring this to you. Go!"

Katherine did as she was told, leaving the kitchen and making her way back toward the stairs when she was met in the hall by her father and brother and three other men. She was quite startled, though muscle memory took over and she gave a quick curtsy as she'd done thousands of times before.

The men stared, stunned to see her in such a state, pale and unwashed and in her undergarments. Edward inhaled sharply and took a step forward to shield the sight of his sister and remedy the situation, though not soon enough, as a shriek from Fiona filled the silence.

"Katherine! What on earth?!"

Edward grabbed Katherine by the elbow and swept her into the closest room, the study, and quickly closed the door. The sun had sunk low, and in the dim, orange lighting of the room they listened as their mother apologized to their company loudly for the spectacle, explaining Katherine had recently suffered a great loss and the grief was causing her to lose her senses.

Edward shook his head and closed his eyes against Fiona's flippant regard for her daughter's current state and complete disregard for Henry's loss of life. They listened to the men give words of forgiveness and continue on, making their way to the parlour. They waited in silence, letting enough time pass as to safely return to the hallway unnoticed, but soon they heard footsteps coming back toward them.

The door was thrown open and through it flew Fiona, her nostrils flaring with every angry breath she drew in. "Have you no shame?!" she hissed, approaching her daughter with an air of intimidation.

"Have you no mercy?!" Edward shot back, though it did nothing to slow Fiona's charge, and she continued.

"This is inexcusable Katherine! Absolutely inexcusable! Surely you must have known we had guests coming to supper!

I cannot believe—!“

“How is she to have known when she’s been in her chamber for weeks now?” Edward growled. He put himself between the two females and stared his mother down. “You have not made your presence or intentions known to her, as you happily told Lucy at church, and it has seemingly brought you such peace not having to vex yourself with where Katherine is or what she is doing or how she will embarrass you simply by existing. Oh yes, Fiona,” he responded to the look on her face having gone from rage to shock, “my wife has been so kind as to share your sympathies with me and I must say they are disgusting. Completely and utterly disgusting. You may have had no regard for Henry Bullock but clearly you also have no regard for your family who loved him so dearly as a son and a brother and a husband. Are you truly so severe in your disdain?”

Fiona set her jaw and stared at him, lifting her chin slightly in defiance though she said nothing.

Edward took Katherine by the wrist and walked to the door. “I have yet to meet someone so evil as you,” he grumbled over his shoulder, turning back to once again make eye contact with his mother before reaching to close the door.

Edward led Katherine to her room and promised to return soon. Eleanor had already stoked the hearth and brought food, though Katherine had since lost her appetite. As promised, Edward returned a few hours later. Katherine was surprised, as it was quite late and she’d thought perhaps he had forgotten and gone home. She was even more surprised when William followed him into the room. Edward moved to sit on the bed near her, while William stood at the foot of the bed.

William spoke first, seeming to fumble as he searched for the gentlest words to say. “Katherine, your brother has made a suggestion, and we think you will find it most agreeable. While we all cared for the Bullocks, your affection and commitment to Henry was... of course, far greater than any of ours. And it would appear... your grief has become more than we can manage here, your mother especially. So Edward believes... and I agree... that it might be best if you live with him and Lucy for a while. We can all agree that Lucy is great company, far more understanding than your mother could ever hope to be. And living in town will provide... many great... opportunities and distractions when you are feeling like yourself again, dear."

Katherine had been looking at her father when he'd begun, but somewhere in the middle of his speech her eyes had wandered to the nothingness beside him, though she was still listening and considering his words. Her lack of attention must have been concerning for Edward as he reached out and took her hand. She looked down at it for a moment, and then away again when Edward began to speak.

"You seemed so happy when you stayed at our house in the time before, Katherine. I know it will take time, for all of us it will. But no one understands what you are feeling more than Lucy and I, and if you are nearer to us we can all help one another."

Katherine closed her eyes for a long moment, then opened them again to stare into the abyss before giving such a faint nod that William and Edward had to look at one another to be sure the other had seen it as well.

William's nod was far more defined. "I shall send Eleanor to pack some of your things, and anything else you feel you may need you can most certainly send for." He reached out and gave her ankle a squeeze, which was more awkward than comforting and caused Katherine to once again look at the hand that was touching her. With that William left the room.

Edward stayed with her, though he said nothing as he sat, continuing to hold her hand, giving it a reassuring squeeze now and then.

Eleanor's face was solemn as she gathered Katherine's belongings and clothes. Katherine watched her but said nothing, not knowing what to say, as was usual. She knew she would see her soon enough—Edward was here several times a week, and Katherine was sure she would be forced to join him. So to Katherine this was not a goodbye moment, and she was sure Eleanor knew it as well. Still deep down beyond the fog Katherine felt she should say something, she just didn't know what, and her indecisiveness kept her quiet throughout the entire encounter.

Eleanor brought Katherine her boots and coat and helped to dress her for the journey. Edward helped Katherine down the stairs and into the carriage. Her parents didn't bother to see her off, though Katherine hadn't even noticed.

"Lucy will be well happy," Edward insisted once the carriage was moving. "We've talked about this for quite some time now, and we are both convinced it will be best for all of us. Her only regret will be that it had taken *this* long to bring you to our home. Oh yes, she will be well happy indeed."

Katherine was unmoved by his cheerful reassurances, and the rest of the ride was silent.

The women hadn't seen one another since they'd received the news about Henry, and Lucy was surprised it had actually come to pass, but was indeed happy, nonetheless. She welcomed Katherine with a hug and when she pulled back Lucy's eyes were brimming with tears.

Katherine took to the room they offered her and fell into a deep, dreamless sleep. She awoke the next morning to a light knock on the door and lifted her head to see Lucy come through with a tray.

"I've brought tea," she told her, smiling to give the impression of cheer though it was missing from her voice. "When we are through here I shall have a bath drawn for you."

Lucy did what she did best, chattering away about the lives of friends and acquaintances, gossiping about the neighbours, and even finding a way to work in the politics and scandals she had read in the newspaper recently. Katherine listened and sipped her tea, and though she made an effort to smile now and then, she found herself thinking about the insignificance of the conversation Lucy was having with—herself, really. These people had the smallest of problems, and yet Lucy went on about them for what seemed like hours.

Katherine thought she knew Lucy well enough, but she'd never been so irritated by her. She wondered whether Lucy had always been so insufferable and she'd never noticed it before. Then it occurred to her as she watched that every now and then Lucy would stop momentarily to look her over: Lucy's eyes moving from her head to her shoulders to her hands and her tea cup, taking it all in before continuing on with her verbal observations of the world. Katherine realized Lucy was keeping an eye on her, literally— keeping her company rather than leaving Katherine alone like she'd been for days, or weeks, or months, or however long it had been. Lucy's incessant babble was in fact a strategic distraction from Katherine's own mind.

The odd thing was that it was working. Though she'd caught on to their scheme and had been upset moments ago, she quite suddenly loved her brother and his bride for taking the measures they had. She couldn't be certain how long they'd perhaps been planning to bring her to their home, whether it was an impulse only recently brought forth, or if they'd thought of it as far back as before they'd received the news. Whatever the case she loved them for it, and she felt loved by them in return.

Katherine bathed, and then Lucy was with her again throughout most of the day, making sure Katherine ate or drank, suggesting Katherine read the newspaper or a book, playing the piano and encouraging Katherine to join her or sing along. Katherine ate supper with Lucy and Edward and soon after excused herself for the evening. She told them she was exhausted, and she actually was, as she'd done more talking and thinking and walking on this day than she had in a long time. But she also felt lighter, as though something had broken through the stone that had been weighing her down and she could see sunlight through the cracks. It was a nice feeling, and as she fell asleep a small smile adorned her face.

Chapter Ten

Katherine still lived with Edward and Lucy. She was twenty now. Everyone was careful in their words and actions in the first year, avoiding talk of the war, and it became so that Katherine herself avoided the subject whenever she could. Edward's efforts limited Fiona's time with (and access to) Katherine, and while Katherine was certain William bore the brunt of it in private, she was never made aware of it.

Katherine stayed in the house most of the time and was never forced to leave as she might have been at her parents' home. She was invited to join guests at dinner, never commanded, and there was an air of understanding when she declined. However, as time went on, she would sometimes accept these invitations for company within the house and outside of it.

All this time no one spoke of Henry to spare her feelings, until Edward and Lucy became pregnant. And when a baby boy was born, Edward asked for Katherine's blessing in naming the boy Henry. Katherine was indeed momentarily stunned, though soon a smile spread across her face and she nodded her consent.

Another year passed with Katherine still in the young Whyte home, helping with baby Henry when she could, and soon another home was acquired, larger, on a property just on the outskirts of the ever-growing city.

Another year passed, and another boy was born to Edward and Lucy, this one they called Matthew. With Lucy unable to join Edward at balls and parties, Katherine began to accompany him on a regular basis, finally finding a new normal, and able to once again enjoy the company of others. And while Katherine had never been a vain person, a part of her did indeed enjoy being told how lovely she was by people other than her mother.

She was quite content to sit at most functions and simply observe. More and more Katherine would adorn the drawing rooms of friends and neighbours. She watched the ladies fan themselves and hide their faces while they blushed or giggled. She watched the men stand together and check their pocket watches or adjust their vests or jackets. She watched as the women would approach the men to begin a conversation, or the men approach the women and ask for a dance.

Katherine was often asked to dance, though she never did. The women around her would tell her that she would never get a husband that way, and Katherine would inform them that she did not want a husband.

"That is what I tell people as well!" one young lady told her through a giggle. "It makes them try that much harder to get my attention."

These conversations caused her to be bitter over time, as she was not saying it in an effort to be ironic. She meant it with all that was inside her. She knew she would never find someone as kind and witty and handsome as Henry. She knew there was no one else in the world that would cause her body to ache with wanting as he did. She remembered the feeling of warmth that came over her when he was near, before she even knew he was there, as though her soul could sense the presence of his. It was a feeling she hadn't felt since his departure, and one she knew she would never feel again. Therefor the idea of seeking out another man to marry was foolish. She was only twenty-one, far from being a spinster, but content enough with herself and her life to say no to the advances of men without regret.

She did not like what others came to think of her. The men would become angry that such a beautiful woman would reject them. And the women thought her foolish and ridiculous. They would call her a prude and a snob and a tease. Sometimes when more drink was involved, they would call her worse things, and after a while these things no longer bothered her. She would be reminded of her mother, and would set her jaw, stare them down and turn up her chin in defiance as Fiona often did. Soon most knew of Katherine, the loveliest of all with no desire to marry, and though it took some time, her wishes were realized and she was left alone.

There were, however, a select few that enjoyed Katherine's company, and they were usually introduced by Edward, or on some occasions William, should he and Fiona attend. They would announce Katherine's interest in reading and books, or her fascination with insects and animals, or speak highly of Katherine as a painter. Although Katherine still considered herself quite fond of these things, she found the frequency with which she enjoyed them had dwindled significantly. She hadn't painted a thing since she was fifteen. She hadn't discussed entomology with anyone since Henry. And she couldn't remember the last time she picked up a book for leisure. The proclamations made by the men in her life made her feel like something of a fraud. Still, more and more, she found she could hold a conversation, taking suggestions about the things she should read and the artists she should become familiar with, and it made Katherine, who had grown up with no formal education or governess, feel scholarly. She was most gracious during these situations as they were among the few things she truly enjoyed, and the others involved seemed to return her sentiments.

It was during one of these conversations Katherine noticed her mother approaching her group of friends with a man on her arm who wasn't her father. Katherine had seen this man before at church and in a few settings similar to this one. Fiona was smiling at this man and would lean in to whisper something every now and then while they paid attention to the conversation, though they didn't contribute. They waited for a break in the conversation and some of the crowd to disperse for a dance before they got closer to Katherine.

"My lord, this is our daughter Katherine Whyte," Fiona began. "Katherine, I would like you to meet Lord Arthur Thacker, Baron of Brandenburg. He is a cousin of His Majesty."

Katherine noticed a look in her mother's eyes but had no idea what it was or what it meant, pondering it while she curtsied.

Arthur smiled. "Second cousin, actually," he corrected Fiona. "But we did spend much time together as young boys."

"And you are one of his most trusted ambassadors, I hear!" Fiona laughed. It was obvious to Katherine that she was putting on a show, as she rarely smiled, let alone laughed.

"I fancy I was at some time, but no longer," Arthur nodded. "I am now a simple lawyer, though nearly half of the business I do is on behalf of His Majesty."

He was somewhat handsome, but he seemed older than Katherine, and wasn't much taller than her. He had dark brown eyes that matched his dark brown, shoulder length hair, and he had a pleasant smile.

"Oh?" Katherine asked, noticing her mother beckoning her to speak with her eyes. "What is it that you do in law?"

"I specialize in land and property."

"Ah. Well... Lovely to meet you, sir," she said giving a quick curtsy.

"You as well." He held out a hand for her to take. "I have heard many things about you, Katherine Whyte. I must say, you are indeed as lovely and elegant as I have heard. If not more so." His eyes traveled down and then back up and held her own eyes for a long moment.

This caused Katherine to look away and sigh, as it was something she was used to but cared nothing for. Katherine watched Fiona continue to make conversation with this man, amazed. She had never before seen her mother this enthusiastic and charming. Fiona kept her arm linked in Arthur's elbow, and they turned to walk. She gestured for Katherine to follow behind them.

Katherine obliged for the sake of her own curiosity at her mother's behaviour but wasn't able to follow along with the conversation. Some of it was too quiet for her to hear, and the bits she could hear she didn't understand. She heard them make plans for Arthur to visit her parents' house later in the week, and then Katherine smiled as she watched him walk away.

Fiona was also smiling. "Katherine, he will be coming to supper in two days and would like the pleasure of your company. You will join us, and you will be on your absolute best behaviour." Fiona turned and left her there, standing in the middle of the room, without waiting for a response.

"Of course she walked away. She knew you would protest," Edward explained to Katherine later after she'd recounted the story to him at home.

"Do you think I should join them?" she asked.

Edward gave his head a wag from side to side. "If you do not, you risk insulting a distant member of the royal family. If you do, you risk pleasing Fiona. I would not be comfortable with either."

Katherine nodded and thought for a moment. "Will you come?"

Edward let out a laugh he seemingly hadn't meant to. "I will not. I am a devoted family man," he said, his voice deepening with sarcasm. "And I want no part of this."

"Family man indeed!" Katherine cried out, "Sending his own sister to the wolves." Though her words were as playful as his own, her nerves were real. She chastised herself for having spent months gaining this haughty confidence only to have it ripped away, and by Fiona of all people. It made her feel sick. But she barely had time to stress about it, because two days later her parents' carriage was sent for her.

Arthur made good on his plans to join them for dinner. He brought no one with him, arriving on horseback. Katherine was seated across from him at the table. He would ask her questions in an attempt to open conversation, as one would, but for the most part Fiona took it upon herself to answer them.

After dinner they all went for a walk so William and Fiona could show their guest the grounds and the gardens. Through the front door, they walked around the house and past the gardens and stopped at the dirt path. Katherine realized she hadn't been past the trees to the stream in years. She felt herself yearning for it, the tranquility of the babbling water, the feel of the cool, moist air, especially now, in this awkward and uncomfortable situation. She momentarily fought the urge to break away from the others and scurry into the woods. But she remembered what was beyond the trees, that place and all it meant to her, and feeling her heart break all over again, she dutifully followed as they walked back up the path the way they came.

When Arthur took his leave, William left the women

alone while he called for the carriage that would take Katherine back to Edward's, and Fiona, who had been prattling on throughout the day, felt the need to continue.

"Lord Thacker is a handsome man, is he not? So highly educated and well spoken—."

"And old," Katherine added coolly, picking a piece of lint off her skirt after sitting back down at the table. "Much older than even Edward. I suspect he is nearer to your age than mine —."

"Enough!" Fiona barked. "I'll not allow you to speak ill of him, Katherine! He is a good man with a good reputation. He is royalty! You will show him respect!"

Katherine had been suspicious but understood completely now. "Do you wish me to marry him, mother?" she asked, cocking her head to the side, being sure to keep her tone even.

Fiona turned to her daughter and sighed. "Yes. You will marry him, Katherine. He has come to your father and I on more than one instance asking about you. He is royal by blood and his rank is sure to rise through his loyalty to His Majesty. We will never want for anything again."

Katherine pondered the information she had just received. *We* will never want for anything, as though Fiona were also to marry the man. "I wish to marry no one."

"You will do as you are told!" her mother shouted.

"Sit down!" William's voice boomed through the room, rattling the teacups on the saucers that were still on the table.

Katherine was startled to her core, as her father had entered the room from behind her. She closed her eyes and breathed deeply to calm herself. She was already sitting, so William could only be shouting at Fiona she realized. She opened her eyes and lifted her chin to look at her parents.

Fiona was doing what she typically did—staring William down, the whites of her eyes visible and large. She stood still, defiant as ever.

A furious William gave no ground, his chest heaving as he breathed. "She is a grown woman who can make her own choices. Who she wants to marry, or whether she marries at all is none of your concern, hag!"

Katherine had to bite her lips between her teeth to keep from laughing.

William sighed deeply and walked to stand across from her at the table. "I have no expectations, Katherine. The choice is your own. Thacker has shown interest, and your mother has spoken quite highly of you—for the first time in her life," he added, turning his head in Fiona's direction. "He is a fine gentleman. He has many amiable qualities aside from his family and rank. My only suggestion is that you take the time to know him better before you decide anything. If nothing else, we'll have gained a new friend and companion of high rank."

Katherine turned to look out the window, as stone-faced as her mother. "A good many men show interest, but as I have said a thousand times, I have no desire to marry—."

"I understand, girl. It is a great burden you bear. I only ask for your consideration on the matter. It might bring you some peace. It might bring *us all* some peace," he finished, casting another glance in Fiona's direction. Then his tone and gaze softened, and he leaned over a chair, lowering himself and holding Katherine's attention. "In truth, while I'm sure Edward and Lucy would allow you to reside with them forever, it would ease my mind in my old age to know you are taken care of, Katherine. Settled on your own, in good standing with a blessed future before you." He nodded and then stood upright again.

Katherine was never one to deny her father in times like this, when he showed her such respect. She *would* consider it, though she was certain her feelings toward marriage would not change. Such displays as were exchanged between her parents that day were the reason she had always cringed at the idea of marriage. She knew people had happy marriages — Edward and Lucy were proof of that—but without Henry she knew there would be no possibility of her sharing in such joy. Any other marriage would be one of convenience or settlement, like that of her parents, and she was not willing to live the life she'd been witness to all these years. And by the time she arrived at her home with her brother and his family, she was once again opposed to the idea, royalty or not.

She was, however, still a lady, polite and demure, and days later at church when Arthur approached her, she was cordial when he was friendly. He spoke of Fiona's invitation to supper at their home again that evening, and Katherine felt her eyes shoot her mother a damning glance, which was returned to her.

"Then I suppose I should apologize in advance for my absence," she told him.

"Whatever do you mean?" Arthur asked.

"I no longer reside in my parent's home, my lord. I have been in my brother Edward's home for nearly three years now."

He furrowed his brow and cocked his head to the side, contemplating her words for a long moment. "Then perhaps I should inquire about becoming a guest in *his* home this evening."

Katherine had no time to protest as he turned quickly and moved to speak with Fiona. And then Fiona led Arthur to William and Edward and Lucy. As she watched them speak, she slowly came to feel pain in her hands, not realizing she had been balling her hands into frustrated fists and pressing her nails into her palms.

Lucy was never one to be rude and seemed genuinely delighted at the idea of having someone so regal in her home. Edward however knew the meaning and held his sister's eyes while the conversation took place before him. Katherine watched him follow along, smile politely, nod now and then, and raise his eyebrows to her in a look of subtle submission.

Katherine sighed. It would happen this day, but she was certain her brother would support her in the future. If anyone in the world understood and shared Katherine's reservations, it was Edward. He'd spoken of them to her before. Yes, anyone chosen by Fiona would likely be less than appealing, but his father's confidence in the potential match had swayed her brother ever so slightly.

And if Edward could be convinced, then perhaps William was right, and she should at least get to know this man that could open up the world to her.

Chapter Eleven

Arthur returned after that day. Every week after church he would make the journey to Edward and Lucy's home, or invite the entire family to his home for dinner, followed by a walk or a game of cards or dice or simple conversation in the parlour. As time passed, Katherine found herself able to speak for herself more, with some guided prompting from her parents and brother. One evening at her parents' house she was asked to show Arthur her needlework as well as some of her paintings— the ones Fiona found acceptable, of course. Arthur seemed in rapture of her paintings, going on and on about the queen's grand art collection and how Katherine's were as good as any of them. He even stated how he would tell Their Majesties of her talents.

This was strange for Katherine. She was used to men falling over themselves for her, but usually the compliments were directed to her beauty or the clothes and jewelry that adorned her. So to hear a man admire her efforts out loud was indeed flattering.

After two months, the visits became more frequent, changing from once a week to twice, sometimes more. Katherine did find she was enjoying herself as time went on, finally having someone else to talk to. She enjoyed listening to his stories of the king as a young boy, and tales of Arthur's travels to the colonies before the rebellion. And Arthur seemed like he enjoyed her company as well. Although he continued to show interest in her paintings, he seemed less interested when she spoke of her inspiration for them—the insects. Katherine, while slightly disappointed, noticed his disinterest and quickly changed the topic as not to receive a tongue-lashing from Fiona, who had been spending more and more time with Katherine since Arthur had come along.

This continued for months. Now and then Arthur's visits would be postponed when he would leave for business trips. Sometimes he would send letters to Katherine. Her mother would instruct her to return a letter to him, though she was never able to create the flare and flowery words that Arthur did, nor could she find the ease in writing she had done long ago. With Henry, she'd been genuinely curious about his life and would ask about it. With Arthur, he volunteered the information about himself even before she would ask, and she found herself struggling to come up with even the most basic sentences.

Eight months into the courtship, Katherine noticed something—her mother hadn't scolded her in ages. Katherine honestly couldn't remember the last time her mother raised her voice or scowled in her direction. Fiona was content, perhaps even pleased with Katherine, and the progress she was making in her relationship with Arthur.

But upon this realization, Katherine also noticed that she was still somehow miserable. At first it was that she wanted nothing to do with Arthur and felt pressured by everyone in her life to try harder. Then as time went on, it was anxiety and fear of her mother that effected her mood. But now that her mother was calm, what could it possibly be that was causing Katherine such melancholy?

It was Arthur again, she realized after a time, coming to terms with the circle of events. She was bored of him and found herself becoming frustrated. The more he continued to speak, the more Katherine realized he was speaking mostly of himself, still perhaps trying to convince her of what a catch he was. At first when he would speak of his cousin the king, it was charming and impressive, but after a while, it seemed to be the same stories over and over. It was a rare occasion he would ask her opinion, but then it was a rare occasion *anyone* would ask her opinion. If she was indeed to become his wife someday, shouldn't that be different somehow? He was showing himself to be just as bored with her as she was with him, interrupting her often to change the topic, or walking away altogether, which caused her even more frustration, and to wonder what the point of their interactions were anymore.

He bought her a brooch for her birthday, which she politely thanked him for of course. It was big and gaudy and expensive looking—Katherine hated it. She got the sense upon fixing it to the bodice of her dress that Arthur now owned her somehow.

The next evening, Katherine was quite happy to be having dinner alone with her parents at their home. She had been thinking all day about her feelings, and whether or not she should bring herself to speak with her parents about them. She tried to find her father alone, but he was still a very busy man. So with knots in her stomach she pushed her food around her plate while they quietly ate, until she had enough wine to calm her and somewhat dull the physical or psychological pain that could potentially be inflicted upon her by Fiona.

She took a deep breath to steady herself. "Father?"

William looked up at her from his plate.

Katherine was silent for a long moment, gathering the words in the correct order before letting them out. "I was wondering, I suppose, as to your recent thoughts on Arthur."

William's brow furrowed above his wide nose. "What do you mean?"

"Some time ago, you encouraged me to spend more time with him. In my doing so, you have also come to know him more. Do you like him?" she asked, feeling rather inarticulate and hating herself for it.

William looked thoughtful. "I suppose I do. He is a good man. Well educated and well-traveled. And of great wealth, of course."

These to Katherine felt like the same things he had stated before, as though he hadn't really come to learn much more about Arthur as a person in the months that had passed, but she chose to keep that to herself. "And your intentions remain for me to marry him?" she asked quietly. She felt her mother staring at her, but never took her eyes off her father.

William glanced at his wife and then nodded. "It would be ideal, indeed. He hasn't yet asked for your hand, but I'm sure he will in time. We have discussed this before, Katherine. Why are you asking me again?"

Katherine swallowed hard. "Would I have any say in the matter at all?"

"In the matter of your marriage?" William clarified.

Katherine nodded.

"It is *your* life, so I should think so," William said, ignoring the noises of protest his wife had made. "Do you *not* like him?"

"I am not certain," she answered. "I still feel as though I hardly know him. He is often away. He speaks mostly with you two, not me. He is loud, and his personality is… quite loud as well, I suppose. And he is much older than I am. He is a nice man," she nodded, "but I—I do not love him."

William nodded and took a few bites, chewing and

staring forward while he absorbed her words.

"None of that matters!" Fiona finally spoke up loudly.

Katherine was suddenly reminded of another dinner long ago where Fiona had lost control. It had also been in reaction to Katherine's future, and the loss of Henry Bullock as a suitor. Katherine found it strange how day to day, her well-being wasn't all that important to Fiona, and yet somehow the matter of Katherine's marriage could drive Fiona to fits of rage and madness.

"You will marry Arthur, Katherine. It has already been decided. You will bear his children and secure—."

"Decided by whom?!" William shouted. "And what should she do were she to marry him?! Become a raving lunatic like yourself?! You have made it no secret how your parents never allowed you the choice and how you despise them for it! And me! You would have your own flesh and blood suffer that same fate?!"

Fiona said nothing.

Katherine took a breath. "I understand how... very important... this is to you. I am not saying no. I am simply asking for time, and for the chance to make the decision without repercussion, whether I choose to marry Arthur or not."

"You've had time!" Fiona shouted, at which point William slammed his hand down on the table to silence her.

After taking a long moment to regain his composure William nodded. "Your request seems reasonable. Perhaps some time alone without prying eyes and judging ears and ever-wagging tongues—," he shot a look at his wife, "would help you and Arthur better know one another. No rash decisions should be made on the part of either party."

Katherine smiled at her father; it was a genuine smile.

He was listening to her. Though this was not her first adult conversation, it could very well be her *most important* adult conversation. Katherine was firmly holding her own. William was softly standing his ground. And yet they understood one another. "That sounds wonderful," she said, giving him a nod. "Thank you."

"How dare you!" Fiona shouted across the table at her husband. "I am your wife and you will show respect..."

In a flash Katherine's mind wandered back to a similar instance where her parents were fighting and Katherine jumped to her father's defence, on the streets of London. She felt the same urge emerge within her in this moment and she spoke loudly over her mother. "It is *you* who will show respect! It is my choice to marry Arthur, or not to marry at all. And my mood being what it is in this very moment I refuse to do anything that would bring you any pleasure! If it eases my father's mind then yes, I may marry Arthur, but on my word Fiona you will reap none of the benefits that would come with such a decision."

Fiona's mouth fell open in shock. William's mouth curled into a grin. And Katherine's posture straightened up as the feeling of power overtook her. She hadn't felt in control like this since the times she sat alone at parties and men fell over themselves, vying for her attention. She found it intoxicating and it momentarily ebbed her anxiety.

Very soon after that, Katherine excused herself for the evening. She knew her mother and father would need to be alone to shout at one another, and she didn't want to be there for that. The sun was still up, and a full moon was rising in the distance. She was grinning. She couldn't stop grinning the whole way back to town, at the stars and the moon and the setting sun.

The next meeting with Arthur was weeks later as he had been away on business again. Katherine still wasn't sure she could be happy with him as things stood, but she would be giving him an honest chance to redeem himself, without interference from Fiona. Katherine would be speaking for herself, asking questions for herself, making judgements for herself. There was a chance she wouldn't like the answers she was given. There was a chance she wouldn't like Arthur himself, without Fiona's gushing over him. There was an equally likely chance that Arthur wouldn't like her without Fiona's constant 'observations' of Katherine's likes and dislikes and skills and beauty.

Arthur came in the early afternoon, and Katherine invited him to join her for a game of chess before dinner.

Once they were seated Katherine began her quest to learn more about this man. "I trust you had a pleasant journey." She moved her first pawn out.

"Yes. The journey was pleasant indeed. I won't bore you with business speak. It is not anything you would understand. The trip there was pleasant, however. The stay was blessedly uneventful. And the journey home took longer than it should have, but I did arrive, nonetheless."

It was a vague response. She wasn't sure whether she should be offended by it or not. Sure, she may not understand the business aspect of it, but he could *try* to help her understand. He could have described the scenery, or explained why his return trip was delayed, but he chose not to. Perhaps he was indeed trying to spare her what he thought would be boredom.

Or perhaps he genuinely didn't care enough to share with her. Either way, Katherine would continue pressing him as the game went on.

"You have never told me in detail what it is you do, Arthur. I know you often leave on business, but I have yet to fully understand. Perhaps you could enlighten me."

"You would find it dreadfully boring, I'm sure," he told her with a flamboyant wave of his hand coupled with a shake of his head.

So he *was* in fact trying to spare her the boredom it seemed. Katherine thought this momentarily charming.

But then he continued. "I've yet to meet a woman who understands it, or seems the slightest bit interested as I explain."

Katherine felt herself instantly irritated and hoped he would notice the emotion in her face.

He didn't. He stared at the board between them.

She inhaled deeply, letting the feeling subside before speaking again. "I am quite certain I could follow along. If you would be so kind..."

He glanced up at her and briefly raised his eyebrows, making the decision to indulge her. "I am a lawyer. I deal mostly with the sale and possession of land. In fact, I first met your parents years ago when I was an apprentice. Your father came to possess his land and estate from your grandfather and chose to sell off the bulk of it to the farmers, keeping only the house and a small parcel. I do, also, act as an ambassador for His Majesty from time to time."

The smile on Katherine's lips did not reach her eyes. "Yes, you have told me that much before."

"Mmmm," he mumbled from behind the hand he had set his face into as he studied the game. "Well, I did simplify things for you."

The smile fell from her face. Katherine never thought she would wish her mother were in the same room, but she did now. Her awful mother had somehow made this hideous man endearing through her pressing. All this time Katherine thought Fiona was ashamed of her and had wedged herself between Katherine and Arthur to spare embarrassment of her daughter. But maybe she was in fact trying to save Katherine from learning that this man was a dreadfully boring and selfish person. There was a tender thought toward Fiona, but it quickly faded with the realization that Fiona was set to send Katherine away with this man for the rest of her life. No, Fiona wasn't trying to spare Katherine, or save her in any way. She was in fact trying to make Arthur tolerable until they were married and it was too late to change anything.

Her heart sank and her face fell. She chose not to ask any more questions, as he obviously had no interest in answering them. She played her next six moves in complete silence.

Arthur became aware of it. "Is anything the matter?" he asked, cocking his head to the side after finally looking up from the board.

"What are your intentions with me, my lord?" Katherine suddenly didn't care what his opinion of her was. She would be forceful, if need be, and make her point. Whether or not he found it offensive or endearing was of no consequence.

He blinked up at her, stunned. "Why, I intend to court you until a proper amount of time has passed to ask for your hand."

"Hmm. Interesting," she said thoughtfully. "Do you speak with such arrogance to all women, or just the ones you intend to wed?"

"I beg your pardon?"

"You are pardoned," she said, glaring into his eyes, a signal she wanted him to leave. Then she gave an exasperated, albeit exaggerated sigh. "I have been nothing if not polite and engaging, sir. And of late you have shown me nothing but pomp and utter disrespect. I care not for any arrangement you have made with my mother if it means I am to spend my life being ignored and disrespected. I will not stand for it, and neither will my father."

His face softened, but only slightly. "Miss Katherine, if I have caused you any offense, I apologize." He paused and thought for a moment. "Perhaps you are correct. I should be more considerate of the thoughts and feelings of my intended —."

"How old are you, sir?" she interrupted, her face unchanged.

He took a moment to size her up, not understanding the relevance of it. "Thirty-five years."

She glanced down and moved her bishop. "How is it that you are not yet married?" she asked, feeling like she already knew the answer. Maybe this was all very forward, but she no longer cared. If he left here and never came back, she would be content with that.

He stammered. "I… I am a busy man, Miss Whyte. I haven't found the time. Or the right woman yet," he told her, meeting and holding her eyes.

Katherine glanced away, pondering what he had said. "What makes you think *I* am the right woman?"

He didn't speak for a long time; so long it made Katherine uncomfortable. "You are a beautiful woman. I have yet to meet a man who hasn't heard of you or your great beauty. You are…" he raised his eyebrows briefly as he forced the words from his mouth, "…well spoken. You are young enough to bear children. And… there are people, your mother included, who speak of…" Again, he seemed like he was choking on the words. "…your quiet obedience. I find all of these qualities desirable in a wife."

"You would base your judgements on the opinions of others rather than trying to discover the true quality of my character? That seems ill advised, considering you are to spend the rest of your days making a life with me, and not the people with whom you have been consulting."

He cleared his throat. "Yes, well, perhaps I've never... looked at it that way before."

A housekeeper quietly came in to interrupt and inform them dinner was ready. The rest of the evening Katherine said very little. She was lost in thought at the idea of marrying this man. She would overthink it and under-think it. For Arthur, nothing would change. He would still come and go as he pleased in his life. Only now he would have shiny a new accessory. And, according to him, a quiet, obedient one at that.

She knew now what he expected of her. She was to make the home and bear the children. She was to dress up for balls and smile. She was to be seen and not heard. She would spend days alone, with only the servants of the house. It seemed a miserable and lonely existence.

But then she was stunned to realize it was nearly the same life she had here with Edward, and with her parents before that. This life she was used to. This life offered her certain freedoms; life as Arthur's wife would offer her more freedom. Her mood lightened the more she thought about it. In the times of his absence, she would have the home to herself, and *she* could come and go as she pleased. She already enjoyed the pleasure of her own company. She could read her books without interruption. A full staff to take care of the rest, that would be waiting on her hand and foot. Decisions made would be hers and hers alone while he was away.

These thoughts brought her comfort. Perhaps this life could be salvaged.

Chapter Twelve

The more Katherine seemed to accept her fate, the more Arthur accepted the things he may have found undesirable before their conversation. Katherine spoke more of her own accord, and Arthur made the effort to engage and enlighten her. Over time Katherine and her family began accompanying him to more and more events, big ones and small. He introduced them to nobility near and far. He presented her parents with silverware and fine china and trinkets from his travels.

And it was becoming obvious that Arthur desired her. He would touch her hair or come in close to breathe in the scent of her. While these actions from Arthur would make Katherine uncomfortable, they happened on such rare an occasion that Katherine would often forget about them until the next one happened. She mentioned it to Eleanor once, but Eleanor said it was a sign that he was falling in love with her, and that she might was well become used to them, for they would be married soon enough.

Eleanor and Rupert seemed genuinely happy for Katherine, and to really like Arthur, which was more important to Katherine than the opinion of her parents. Perhaps the hardest part of living with Edward and Lucy was that she missed Eleanor and Rupert. She missed the way they were always there to help her through her nervous bouts and guide her in decisions. She missed helping them with their work. She missed the food they cooked. She missed knowing what Eleanor was thinking just by looking at her. Therefor these moments and conversations were precious to Katherine. And though her feelings for Arthur were lukewarm at best, being able to please those she truly cared for kept Katherine content in the choices she had made.

And so, when on a rainy September day Arthur asked that she marry him, she said yes.

They were at her parents' house for tea when he did it. In front of her parents and a handful of other guests Arthur mentioned having already spoken to William and that he had also received the appropriate blessing from his cousin the king. He presented her with yet another large piece of jewelry — a necklace made of gold with blue and purple jewels— that received a gasp from the crowd gathered around them. He professed his love for her and his intention to make her happy once they were wed. He told her she could travel with him should she ever have the desire to do so.

He spoke for a long time. Katherine noticed her ever-animated father, behind Arthur, roll his eyes and then sigh after several minutes. Fiona, however, was entirely enthralled by Arthur's performance, and Katherine thought she could see her mother's eyes glistening. Though she was confused by this, Katherine's thoughts returned to Arthur kneeling before her, and she smiled politely and feigned enthusiasm as she always did.

When he finally concluded his speech Katherine looked around the room and noticed something she hadn't until this moment: a new servant was tending to the guests. She was young with pale white skin and dirty blonde hair pulled tightly back. While Katherine wasn't entirely surprised by this— Fiona had talked of taking on more staff to keep up appearances with the new crop of nobility entering the house— Katherine did find it odd. Most who were hired worked outside or out of sight. Eleanor was usually the main housekeeper and cook and server. At this time Katherine realized she hadn't seen Eleanor or Rupert since she'd entered the house that morning and wondered if they were ill, as she highly doubted Fiona would allow them the day off otherwise, knowing they would be entertaining.

She left Arthur's side and approached her parents but avoided her mother's eyes. "I do hope you are pleased, father." He gave a nod and pulled her in to kiss her cheek, and then she moved on with her purpose. "Where is Eleanor?"

William glanced around the room, as though he was expecting to see Eleanor within it, but Fiona answered. "She is working in the garden."

"In the garden?" Katherine asked with a furrowed brow. This was indeed out of the ordinary.

"Yes. We have been blessed with an abundance of vegetables this season and the staff have fallen behind in their work. She and Rupert are assisting the others today."

"Ah yes," William nodded as he suddenly remembered this information to be true.

"What do you need that Miss Walker cannot get for you?" Fiona asked Katherine, gesturing to the new young lady in their employ.

The way her mother held her gaze increased Katherine's suspicions. "Not a thing. I was only curious." After a few minutes passed Katherine excused herself. Initially she had wanted to find Eleanor to take her mind off things, but something about her mother's actions she found odd and she was curious to know what it meant. Knowing Eleanor would be in the garden she went to the back door and opened it, when she realized something: she hadn't walked out this door since

Henry had died. She hadn't walked the path, passed through the trees, been near the stream at all. It was approaching five years since his passing.

She swallowed hard as emotion hit her. For years now, she had controlled herself, if for no other reason than to keep up appearances. She had taught herself to be as stone-faced as her mother most of the time, smiling only when it was appropriate. She was unaffected by most things that went on around her as not to waiver in the calm, unfeeling countenance she strove for. She'd heard the things people said. She knew they now compared her to her mother, and it did not bother her. They left her alone, which was all she ever wanted. Therefor anyone she wanted in her life remained there, and anyone she didn't stayed away.

But here looking through the door toward the trees, she felt herself choke and tears spring to her eyes. It wasn't just that she missed the place where she'd been so happy, or that she missed Henry, which she did from time to time; it was that she'd just accepted the proposal of another— a man who was the opposite of Henry in every way. Where Henry was humble, Arthur was pompous. Where Henry was witty, Arthur was dull. Henry had been interested; Arthur was generally conceited. She felt as though she were somehow betraying Henry. What would he think of this? What would he think of *her?*

Her eyes moved down to the ring on her right hand. She had promised herself she would never take it off, and she hadn't. But she thought now she might have to. She could not wear the ring given by one man when she was set to marry another, could she?

She closed the door and turned around, slipping up the stairs to the bedroom that was once hers. Nothing had changed within it, as though her parents and their servants expected her to come home someday. She pulled out the drawer and moved the panel where she'd hidden Henry's letters so long ago, and they were still there. She was somehow surprised to see them there, though at the same time she was the only one who knew they were there, unless Eleanor had stumbled across them while cleaning. Eleanor would never dispose of them though, knowing how much they meant to her.

Katherine pulled a letter out. She wasn't sure which one it was, but she couldn't bring herself to open it either. She lay back and held it to her chest, and let the tears flow as though she'd gone back in time, as though Edward had just told her Henry was never coming back to her. She cried. She sobbed. She rolled onto her side and cried some more. She cried until she had no more to give.

Once she felt composed enough to return, she checked her reflection in the mirror. Her hair was damp with tears and her face was pale in some places, red and swollen in others. She put the letter back where she'd found it, replaced the panel and closed the drawer just as there was a knock on the door.

"Katherine." She recognized her brother's voice.

She looked up to see Edward and Lucy at the door.

"Father sent us to find you," Edward told her as they came into the room. "You are missing the celebration."

Katherine looked out the window. "Yes. I suppose I am..."

"Are you feeling alright?" Edward asked, showing a bit of concern for her lack of enthusiasm.

She sighed and nodded. "I am tired," she said.

"Perhaps it's the weather," Lucy offered.

"Nevertheless, you are to join us," Edward told her.

Downstairs she was informed William had organized an engagement celebration with those still in the house and had sent Peter into town to invite others out. Katherine felt immediate dread. She was certainly in no mood for such a gathering. She also quickly came to learn that the future groom had departed before Katherine had returned.

Fiona conveyed the message. "He is leaving on another long journey tomorrow and had to go home to rest and prepare for it."

Katherine furrowed her brow. "He did not make mention of anything this morning."

"Yes, well. He *did* say this morning, when he arrived here, he did not intend to stay late…" Fiona trailed off as she looked over her daughter.

Katherine didn't stay to listen to any more excuses, nor did she want to feel Fiona's wrath at her appearance. She knew she looked dreadful and was embarrassed about it as she passed so many guests in the house. But while the absence of Arthur should have added to her feeling of shame, she was glad he was gone, she realized. Yes, of course it felt odd throwing an engagement party for the two of them when only she was there, but she felt like she may as well get used to it. It wouldn't be the last time—this was the life she had chosen.

Officially.

She felt that same choking despair creep through her again. It plagued her as she wandered around looking for an empty room. It turned her stomach inside out and she was no longer hungry, as she had been upon re-entering the main level. She made her way into the study and sat down, letting it consume her. Looking past the floor and the walls, into places within her mind, she revisited conversations that could have gone differently, and imagined scenarios yet to come. She was pulled from her reverie by the sound of her mother's phony laugh, and it caused her to glare at the doorway. She didn't want to be near her mother right now. She didn't want words of congratulations from strangers and their questions of where her beloved fiancé had run off to.

Beloved, she sighed and shook her head.

She was able to put on a brave face and be civil to all those she encountered. Several people came—most of whom she didn't care for at all. She was somewhat surprised at the number of guests by the evening, but Fiona managed to make use of herself and explained Arthur's absence so Katherine didn't have to. And the evening became another opportunity for Katherine to perfect her stoicism.

As the wine flowed, the crowd became louder. Katherine kept quiet and to herself as she usually did. She picked away at her food and drank only water, wordlessly waving away the new servant, Miss Walker, when she tried to fill her cup with anything else. She saw the sun setting outside the window. Toasts were being made to her and her absent fiancé; she politely smiled, not lifting her glass. After a few unmet glass raises, an inebriated William took notice.

"Katherine child!" he slurred loudly enough for the room to hear, even though she was only one seat away from him. "What on earth is the matter? This is a joyous occasion! You must be joyous!"

"I apologize," Katherine said. "Perhaps it is the weather," she repeated Lucy's earlier words and cast a look in her direction to see her grin.

"Or perhaps, you miss your beloved!" William called out, raising his glass again. "To Arthur! May his journey be safe and swift!"

Beloved, she thought with a roll of her eyes, *there's that word again.*

The crowd called out a response to William's toast and sipped from their glasses. They continued making toasts, everyone around the table taking their turn.

When she managed to say her goodbyes for the evening, she was able to catch a glimpse of Rupert and Eleanor. They looked at her—something in their eyes followed Katherine for days. What was it? Fear? Urgency? She couldn't be sure. She decided she would ask them what was going on the next time she was at the house. Or perhaps at church if Rupert happened to drive her parents into town one upcoming Sunday.

She was happily left alone for nearly a month before Arthur came back, spending time with only Edward and Lucy and their boys. She was invited to several teas and suppers and balls, but knowing what her life would be once married, she felt she should cherish the life she had now and spend time with the people she loved.

She knew Edward and Lucy could sense her melancholy, but she said nothing when asked about it. She chose to focus on the present instead of the future, this being the happiest time in her life since Henry all those years ago.

Upon Arthur's return she became more attached to his side than ever before, though it was not entirely of her own desire. It seemed now that they were engaged, she was unable to go one day without him. He would take her to meet other rich people for tea. He would take her to the dressmaker of his choosing. He would take her to weddings of people she didn't know.

And then he took her for tea with the king and queen. Since her parents were present when he informed her, Arthur proposed she invite Fiona, but Katherine had brushed off the words, suggesting that her mother was far too busy with their abundant vegetable crop for such a thing. When Fiona tried to protest, Katherine simply walked away with her head held high. She had meant what she'd said before: after years of feeling Fiona's wrath, Katherine now had the power to turn the tables.

But the day was upon her and Katherine was terribly nervous until they arrived and she looked around. The room was full of people, mostly women. She was introduced. She curtsied. And then she watched Arthur leave the room with the king and the rest of the men.

Katherine listened to the conversations happen around her. She watched the servants, in awe of their attention to detail and how they seemed to anticipate every possible movement the queen made. She watched the queen's ladies. She had heard about them, these women whose only purpose was to adorn the room with their beauty and fill empty space with their presence. They stood for the entire event. They seldom made eye contact with Katherine or anyone else. The queen however seemed warm and engaging, appearing to take genuine interest in those around her.

When the men returned hours later Arthur excused them both, and it wasn't until he asked how everything went during the carriage ride that she realized she hadn't spoken a word the entire afternoon.

"It was... delightful," she said with a small smile. She felt it was an acceptable answer, as she didn't want to insult her fiancé or seem ungrateful for the privilege of having an audience with the queen.

He smiled and patted her hand. "Did you discuss painting with Her Majesty like I suggested?"

"I did not. She was rather obliging to her other guests, and I would have thought myself rude to interrupt her for something so silly."

A puzzled look came to his face. "You believe your paintings to be silly? Or my suggesting it?"

"No, my lord." She found her mind suddenly racing as she fumbled for words. A feeling came over her that she had not felt in a long time, a form of dread and panic that she hadn't felt since leaving her parents' house; a fear of repercussion that would all depend on the next words she spoke. She chose them swiftly and carefully. "I simply meant Her Majesty had other, more important matters to discuss, and I dared not interrupt."

"Mmm," he muttered with a nod. "How thoughtful of you. I suppose you shall have other opportunities. The king," he changed the subject without skipping a beat, something Katherine had become used to, "has asked that I return to Glasgow on his behalf. You don't mind terribly, do you?"

Katherine felt her heart leap and had to stop her body from giving a physical sigh of relief. "Of course not."

"It will mean putting off the planning of the wedding for a few more months."

What wedding? she thought before realizing he was talking about their own. She put on her best Fiona smile. "It will be well worth the wait, I'm sure."

He informed her he would be departing before church on Sunday, and she felt a weight lift from her body. In less than four days' time she would have her life to herself again, and this exhausting regimen would come to a stop, albeit a temporary one. Either way, she was grateful, and her phony smile gave way to a real, relaxed one.

A large part of Arthur's people-pleasing involved her parents, and he suggested they have supper at William and Fiona's home before he left town again. He made plans with her parents as he usually did and she would simply arrive with him as expected. She was told to be ready at three o'clock Friday afternoon and his carriage would come to get her.

Arthur was nothing if not prompt, and at three o'clock the bell rang. He made small talk on the ride out of town about people she didn't know in London and people he was expecting to meet on his journey.

Katherine listened, responding more enthusiastically than she normally would have, ready for the much-needed break from Arthur's world that was coming in the next few days. This jovial mood continued on throughout their visit with her parents. Fiona, however, usually so chipper and talkative around Arthur seemed quiet and reserved, even stern at times. Though Katherine noticed it, she paid no attention to it, and found that she was actually enjoying herself. She felt shame for relishing in Fiona's melancholy, but the joy she felt watching her father engage with Arthur made up for it in her mind.

The time passed far more quickly than Katherine had realized, and soon Arthur sent one of her father's servants to fetch his carriage— another servant Katherine didn't recognize. She looked around the room. She recognized Miss Walker from the last time she was there, and Peter had attended to the table throughout supper. There was a new woman, who appeared older than Katherine yet younger than her parents, and a tall, strong looking man closer to Arthur's age, neither of whom Katherine had ever seen before. This seemed to be a lot of strangers.

"Have you given Eleanor and Rupert the day off?" Katherine asked as she donned her shawl and bonnet and approached the door to leave.

William looked to the floor, while Fiona lifted her chin.

Fiona inhaled deeply and sighed, signalling she was already done with this conversation. "Eleanor and Rupert have worked for us many years, as you know. They worked diligently, with a generous wage might I add, and will forever hold a place in our hearts. However, they earned their right to move on, and did so with a handsome final payment as a thank you for all they have done."

Katherine felt the blood drain from her face, making her way into her throat, closing it off. "What? When?" she squeaked.

It was William now, who spoke up quietly. “Weeks ago, Katherine.”

“Weeks?” she cried out. She could feel herself about to lose control, so she inhaled deeply, squared her shoulders, and nodded before passing through the door without another word. Arthur was speaking to them about what a pity it was, as Katherine had always spoken so fondly of Rupert and Eleanor. She walked quickly toward the carriage. She couldn’t let them see her shed a tear, as yet another person— people— of significance had gone from her life without a proper goodbye.

Chapter Thirteen

Arthur joined her in the carriage after a few minutes but chose not to speak, understanding, for perhaps the first time since she'd known him, that this was a time for silence, and allowing her to simply stare blankly out the window. She did not sob but wiped away tears now and then, paired with the occasional sniffle. She was done crying before they were back in town, but was still lost within her own thoughts, so she did not notice where they were going until he helped her down from the carriage. She looked around and realized they were not at the home she shared with Edward and his family but were instead at Arthur's grand home. She looked at him with a furrowed brow.

"I would like to show you something," he said, continuing to hold her hand as he answered the question in her eyes.

He led her into the house, his servants quietly opening doors as they approached and walked through the halls. He took her up the stairs and down a hall and through another set of doors. Katherine was becoming somewhat unnerved, being alone with a man whose desire for her was evident, allowing him to lead her to a private and unknown room within his home. Yes, his servants were there, but she didn't really know any of them well enough to trust the situation entirely.

The doors before her opened and the sight stopped her. Before her was a room filled entirely with her paintings. Some hung on the walls, others stood on the mantle, some still lined edges of the floor. The room was well lit with the light of the setting sun from the two large windows on two walls indicating this was a room on the corner of the house. Set up directly in the corner was a small desk covered with brushes and jars of paints, and beside the desk was a large easel.

Katherine's mouth had fallen open slightly in awe of what she was seeing. "What is all this?"

"It's all for you, of course," he told her as he let go of her hand and watched her walk toward the corner to admire the easel and desk. "I had them made for you, my love. Both carved from Oak. They arrived from France only recently, in fact."

She turned to look at him, still stunned, perhaps even more so with the knowledge of what he'd said. A pang of guilt ran through her for her earlier thoughts of doubt as she searched his eyes and saw only sincerity.

"I know I shall be gone soon and for a while, Miss Katherine, but I am giving my steward instruction to allow you into this room at your convenience. And to provide you with whatever you might need during your time here." He allowed her some time to explore the room then he took a step back and gestured toward the door. "I shall have my footman take you home now." He walked her to the front door of the house, still allowing her the silence to absorb the happenings of the last few hours.

Finally at the steps she turned to him and spoke. "I do not know what to say, my lord. Or how to thank you. This is most generous, indeed."

"You are most welcome, my darling. And truly, no thanks are necessary. I only hope it has brought you some comfort." He took her hand and pressed his lips to the back of it. "I will take tomorrow to ready myself for my departure. Therefor I fear this shall be the last time I behold your beauty before my return."

"I wish you a safe journey," she said, giving a curtsy though he still held her hand. With that he let go and she made her way down the stairs and into the carriage.

The next morning she told Edward and Lucy what Arthur had done. She'd thought about it most of the night, still dumbfounded by it. She hadn't painted in years. It hadn't even been one of her fondest interests. She wasn't sure she still had any talent for it, nor that she would still enjoy it, but she found it to be a most touching gesture. She explained the appearance of the desk and the easel and what he had told her about them. She described the room, at which point Lucy remarked he must have spent a great deal of time and money on it, and had likely been planning it since before the day he had actually proposed and promised it to her, suggesting he cared deeply for her. Katherine hadn't thought about any of that. *He must have been quite certain then that I would accept his proposal.*

Edward commented on his acquiring her paintings from their parents' home. It was then she remembered the other news she'd received the previous evening, that of Eleanor and Rupert, and relayed it to her brother, who was just as stunned and hurt as she had been.

"I don't understand how we could not have been informed!" he told her.

"Nor I. I would have thought our father at least would have had the decency. He knew how we cared for them. He knew Eleanor was truly the only mother we've known. He should ha— ."

"Have you any idea where they may have gone?" he urged.

Katherine shook her head.

"Had I known I would have offered them to come here! Perhaps there is still a way! I shall do my best to find them, sister, fret not! If I have to wring the neck of the elder Mrs. Whyte, I shall find them, if for no other reason than to bid them the most gracious farewell."

The vision brought forth by her brother made her smile again. From the thought of him strangling their mother to the thought of him finding Eleanor and Rupert. If anyone could, it would be Edward. He knew many people of different backgrounds, and many, many friends in high and low places.

***

Her brother stayed true to his word. First Edward spoke with his father and came back to Katherine to tell her William had no knowledge of their departure until after it had happened. William had never been an observant person, and so in the abundance of new employees he didn't notice the missing ones until they'd been gone for days. William promised Edward he had all but beaten Fiona for having done it, and especially for not informing him, the head of the house, of her intentions. He assured Edward that he understood the sentiment of it all, as he also held a special place in his heart for the couple.

What bothered Edward the most was that Fiona had given no reason, and he wondered aloud to Katherine and Lucy about it at supper one evening.

"She made it seem to me as though they had served enough time in their home," Katherine said to him, though since then Katherine had wondered to herself if perhaps it were revenge for the choice she made aloud to shun Fiona and keep her from Arthur and his friends

"No," Edward said, looking down at the floor and

shaking his head. "We all know Fiona has not an ounce of giving nature within her. Most people would release a long-term employee for other reasons, but I would lay down my life before I would believe either Rupert or Eleanor capable of theft."

Katherine's head snapped in his direction, her eyes wide. She hadn't even considered that as a possibility. "Absolutely not!" she cried out.

Edward gave a nod in agreement, and after a long, thoughtful moment he nodded again. "I presume then, that she did it because of your marriage."

"What do mean, Edward?" Lucy asked from across the table.

Katherine also looked at him with question, narrowing her eyes as she waited for him to elaborate.

He cleared his throat. "Since Arthur began courting Katherine, William and Fiona have taken on new housekeepers and gardeners… to keep up appearances, if you will. They've had several guests of high rank and stature enter their home. It is my belief that Fiona relieved Rupert and Eleanor of their duties because they no longer meet Fiona's standards for the residence."

"Standards?" Lucy asked. "Do you mean they are no longer able to perform their duties up to the standards that Fiona wishes?"

Edward shook his head and exhaled through his nose. "Katherine, their age was visible. If you have noticed Arthur's staff or that of the palace, they are likely young, unmarried ladies and men." He paused and looked to Katherine, who nodded lightly to confirm what he was suggesting. "Some our age perhaps, but likely none so old as Rupert and Eleanor. And unless Fiona were able to hide them in the cellar they would be seen."

"True!" Katherine said, more loudly this time. "Their new hires have all been young people. In fact, when last we were there, Fiona had them in the garden. The garden!" she repeated, as though it seemed the most preposterous thing. With what she had witnessed and all that had transpired, her brother's words made sense. "Why would she not tell us? Or Father?"

"We would have objected. *He* would have objected. She knows that," he responded with a shrug.

"And you believe you can find them, husband?" Lucy asked.

"I am willing to try, my love," he said. "They are as dear to me as any family I have. Perhaps even more-so," he said with a grin and a playful wink to his sister.

Thus in his spare time he would draft a letter or make a trip to speak with his lawyer friends. He also spent one afternoon at the harbour asking anyone who would listen if they'd seen or heard anything. He visited the parts of London that truly scared him on the off chance he might run into them looking for a place to live.

Katherine, as usual, had spare time as well— time she spent thinking and praying, and once she'd driven herself stir-crazy she broke down and paid a visit to her future home. Arthur's steward, Mr. Burnley, was warm and welcoming. She'd never spoken with him or any of the other employees within the house, as usually Arthur was with her and did most, if not all, of the talking, but she was happily shown to the room that already belonged to her.

She didn't know where to begin, so she started by playing with colours on the canvas, mixing and swirling, hoping something would emerge. Her inspiration had always been insects, but so much had changed in her life since last she painted, and she no longer knew what inspired her. Arthur's gesture of this room had made her feel— something— toward him for the first time in a long time, though whatever it was, it paled in comparison to feelings she'd once known. The last time she felt truly alive was the night Henry had left her, when he'd kissed her on the cheek, and when she closed her eyes now, she could still feel it. She could feel it all; the warmth that radiated whenever he was near and beckoned her ever closer to him; the way her heart beat faster when he fixed his blue eyes on her; the ache that caused her limbs to throb.

Before she knew it, the sun had moved to her side of the house and began to blind her through the west window. She realized hours must have passed, and when the spots before her eyes dissipated, she tried to tidy up the desk and the brushes as best she could, feeling guilty that someone might have to clean up after her when she wasn't even their mistress yet. Once finished she turned to leave but glanced over to the canvas on the easel and her heart leapt into her throat.

It was Henry, or rather the outline of his face, his hair as she remembered it; the texture of his skin— though she hadn't completed his eyes, and while she stood there looking at it, she wondered if she ever could, as there was likely no shade of blue paint she could ever find that would do justice to their colour.

How had she done this? How had she become so lost in thought that she hadn't even realized what her own hands were doing before her face? And what in Heaven's name had possessed her to paint the portrait of her former fiancé within the walls that belonged to her current fiancé? As she closed the door behind her, she wondered if perhaps she had inherited some form of madness from Fiona.

She stayed away for days out of shame. She chose to spend her time reading and waiting for Edward to make ground on his search for Eleanor and Rupert. But after days of disappointment and insufferable confinement she returned to her new painting room. The likeness of Henry stared at her as she entered the room and, had it not brought forth so many emotions, she might have taken the time to admire her own talent. She took the canvas off of the easel and replaced it with a clean one, rolling it up and leaning it against the wall. She spent the afternoon painting a landscape, paying special attention to the flowers, and adding butterflies to spite Fiona. Again the sun was her timekeeper, and when it crept around the house to meet her, she cleaned up her messes and left.

She waited once again to return until almost a week later. She chose to continue working on the landscape from before, wanting to get the sky just right, and becoming frustrated when she couldn't. She thought back to the portrait she'd painted, again wondering at his effortless perfection when her actual effort was not at all what she wanted it to be. She eventually gave up and tidied the space, this time long before the sun came around the house.

She again stayed away, this time out of frustration, though she decided over time that during her next visit she would start something new. She hardly left the house for anything else, including church, though the following Sunday she wished she had after Edward and Lucy's return. Finally, after weeks of waiting, Edward had news about Rupert and Eleanor. And Katherine was surprised to hear the details regarding who was their saving grace.

At church, William had informed Edward that Arthur had reached out to some officials before leaving, and though he knew he would be out of town he directed them to reveal their findings to Mr. William Whyte, and his friends did not disappoint. According to his sources the couple boarded a boat for their homeland of Ireland, and William assured Edward he had been shown the documents proving what he'd heard.

Katherine thought while Edward spoke. They'd left weeks ago, so there was a chance they would have already arrived at their destination. She thought back to her childhood, how at times she would catch Eleanor looking wistfully into the distance, and when Katherine would ask what she was thinking about, Eleanor would talk about her family. She and Rupert never had children of their own, but both came from families they missed dearly. A smile came to Katherine's face and she sent a silent prayer up that they would live happily with their families for however long they had left on this earth. She considered writing, maybe using the connections Arthur had to track the couple down and send her final well wishes.

She also considered what Edward had just told her. She had found out about Eleanor and Rupert on Friday evening, and Arthur had left Sunday morning, meaning that he would have spent a part of Saturday talking with these associates of his, the day he'd said he was taking to prepare for his trip. It was one more kind thing he'd done for her, and she felt her heart swell.

She calculated in her head the time he had been away and how much longer he would be gone, as she wanted very much to extend her gratitude. Deep down she scolded herself for her earlier thoughts of disdain toward him, and the ones that still crept up from time to time. She considered writing to him but wondered if he would come back before it reached him, and chose to wait instead, returning to his home and the room to paint again and again.

She completed one of a bee on a daisy, and then another of a bird pulling a worm from the earth. She was much happier with these works, as she didn't have to paint the dreadful, unending sky again. She knew bees. She knew worms. She giggled to herself as she realized that all these years later they still had the ability to make her happy.

As she was tidying up the mess she'd made for the day she heard something of a commotion, and Mr. Burnley quickly entered the room to inform her that his master had returned home.

Katherine was sent into a flurry, wiping her hands, fixing her hair and smoothing her dress before leaving the room and descending the stairs.

"Miss Whyte!" Arthur exclaimed before she'd reached the floor. "What a pleasant surprise!" He took her hands. "Such a lovely sight to come home to. I truly look forward to doing it more often."

Katherine gave a small curtsy even though he held her hands. "My lord, I am happy to see your journey was a safe one."

"It was indeed, although every day was agony without you."

Katherine once again didn't know how to respond to such flowery words, so she smiled meekly and chose to change the subject. "I must thank you for your efforts in finding my parents' former employees before your departure. My brother Edward sends his gratitude as well. They were quite dear to us, as you well know."

He looked down at her and smiled. "Once again, no thanks are necessary, my lady, if it has brought some ease to your mind and heart."

"It has indeed," she assured him.

"Pray, to what do I owe the honour of your presence at this time?"

She smiled again. "I was making use of the painting room you so kindly offered me before your departure."

"Ah! I am glad to hear of it!" He let go of one hand but continued to hold the other to turn her back toward the stairs. "You must show me at once!"

"Oh, but sir! You have only just arrived home!" she

pleaded, feeling shy and uncertain about the work she had done. "Perhaps this can wait—."

"Nonsense!" he cried out with his usual, exhausting flamboyance, pulling her along as she continued to protest.

He practically dragged her up the stairs, babbling on about how much he missed her and how much he thought about her and how he'd had dreams about her, and every word spoken and every inch gained caused Katherine's thoughts to return to the negative ones she'd had about him. She was both nervous and modest and didn't feel at all mentally prepared for him to fawn all over her work. Deep down she wondered if he would even mean the words he was about to say. In the room the first piece he noticed was the bird and the worm that she'd been touching up only minutes before. He gasped and exaggerated, and while the things he said were meant to make her feel proud, the way he said them did quite the opposite, and she wondered again if he in fact liked it at all, or if this was all for show.

He moved on to the picture of the bee on the flower that she had spread out over the desk to dry days before. She listened as he used the word magnificent more than once as he moved around the room comparing them with some of her old works. Then as he unrolled one she had forgotten about, her heart ceased beating.

Chapter Fourteen

Arthur held it in his hands, turning his head slightly, furrowing his brow. He studied it for a long time. "I do not recognize this man," was all he said.

Katherine swallowed as her brain scrambled to remember words and how to use them. "I should think not, my lord. He was someone I knew in my childhood, and he has long since perished."

I have been on a few and have yet to perish… She heard Henry Bullock's voice clear as day speak the words in her memory and pushed it away.

"I was considering presenting my brother with that portrait, as they were the best of friends. My oldest nephew bears this man's name." She exhaled, satisfied with the words she had said though it didn't stop her heart racing or the dizziness that followed.

He looked up at her and smiled. "What a splendid idea, my dear. And so thoughtful." He set the canvas back down where he'd found it. "I should like to hear more about him someday."

Katherine gave a faint smile. "Perhaps someday," she replied softly, then took a deep breath to steady herself.

And in the weeks that followed, though she was terrified that perhaps "someday" would come to pass, instead talks turned to the planning of their wedding. Arthur had two more excursions in the future that he wanted to complete before they were wed, and with that information they planned for early July, seven months away. Fiona thought it was too long a wait, but Katherine was quite content to have the distractions that would come between the present and the future.

Again Arthur filled her time with teas and suppers and meetings and balls, and when Christmas came, he hosted a grand event in his own home, with Katherine at his side. Fiona was ecstatic throughout the evening, continuously reminding Katherine that soon this would all be hers. Katherine thought her mother was likely more excited for having been invited to an event for the first time in a very long time. Katherine had avoided inviting her mother to most things, which unfortunately meant William would not come either, but it was a small sacrifice if it meant Fiona came to learn her place. However this was Christmas, and Katherine dearly wanted to spend it with her father.

Arthur's gift to her for the holiday was the dress she wore that night, among several other heavy, expensive dresses in the latest fashion, and just like most of the things he bought her to wear she despised them. They were extraordinarily uncomfortable, and she would be exhausted after wrestling herself into them, let alone wearing them for hours on end. With so much time being taken up, and so much time already spent in Arthur's presence, she found no time or need to visit her painting room again since his return.

Late in January he was once again preparing to leave town for several weeks. By this time Katherine was once again fighting to remember the kind things he'd done for her that actually had some meaning, although she knew that in his mind that's precisely what he was doing every day. While he had showered her and her family with gifts and heightened their social standing among his friends, it was again becoming tiresome to Katherine. She knew any woman would be happy with sparkly jewelry or fancy dresses or party after party after party, but she was not. The more trinkets she was forced to wear and be seen in, the more she was beginning to feel like one herself. She was once more looking forward to his absence as it meant she could rest and be alone. This time, as well as the next, would have more meaning, she knew, as they would be the last before she became his wife, and the exhaustion became endless.

She was also aware of what little quality time she would have left with the only people in the world she truly cared about— Edward and Lucy and their two boys. And so she barely ventured out of the house. She attended every meal with them. They went for walks and played in the garden when the weather permitted. She even attended church in an effort to be near them.

It also meant having to see her parents. And while she still cared for her father as much as ever, being around Fiona was similar to being around Arthur. Perhaps even worse, as she'd only ever known Arthur to be as he was, but she knew an entirely different side of Fiona. The facade Katherine witnessed in society made her angry, and the incessant wedding talk gave her a headache. That was without mentioning the betrayal that had come with Eleanor and Rupert's departure.

Therefor Lucy made it her mission to turn the wedding planning into a positive experience, taking it upon herself to assist Katherine when needed, and helping Katherine avoid her mother in the process. Lucy accompanied Katherine to the dressmaker Arthur had acquired, and helped Katherine choose other odds and ends, including the foods that would be served at the ball.

And it was out on one such excursion, a morning in early March with Edward along to escort the two young ladies around town, that they overheard a conversation. They had since finished with the wedding business for the day and had made a stop at the market on their way home.

"...Mr. Bullock, and they have taken in the poor soul..."

Katherine had heard the last name Bullock from time to time, and it would usually cause her ears to perk up and her breath to stop so she could listen better. This time was no exception, and she pretended to look down at her skirt as the old man to her left continued to speak.

The woman he was speaking to responded. "A shame indeed. Young Henry was always such a kind lad. And his mother so lovely."

Katherine's heart jumped into her throat. *These poor people must have only just found out about his passing. And after all this time...* She felt as though she should offer them more details on the subject, until she remembered the first part she had heard. *Taken in... Henry's father George,* she thought, giving a small gasp. Now it was she who needed more details. She turned to the man and woman and spoke.

"I'm terribly sorry to interrupt, but were you speaking of Henry Bullock just now?"

The man nodded with wide eyes. "Yes, miss—."

"Has his father returned to England?" she spat out quickly, though politely.

Now he looked confused and cast a glance to the woman he was with. "Pardon me, miss, but George Bullock was hanged in America for treason."

This time it was Katherine who furrowed her brow. "I believe you are mistaken. George was imprisoned, sir. It was

Henry Bullock who was hanged."

The old man shook his head. "No, miss. George Bullock was hang—."

"I'm sorry," Katherine forcefully interrupted him again, her fingers up and palm toward the man for emphasis. Her heightened voice catching the attention of her brother, who made his way toward them. "I know very well that it was Henry Bullock that was killed, sir."

He shook his head again. "No, miss. *I'm* sorry but it was George who was hanged for treason. Young Henry Bullock is the one who was imprisoned all those years. And it is he who recently returned to England."

At this Katherine chose to remain silent and listen to the rest of the old man's tale.

"Poor fellow. He came back to England as any man would, for his lady, only to discover she has since married. And he took to his uncle's home in Bedford to, I suppose, decide what he should do now. It would be madness to return to America with all that's gone on."

After watching Katherine's face change, Edward stepped forward. "How can you be certain of this? I was among Henry Bullock's closest friends, and I was told he perished."

The old man smiled. "Then you should be happy to hear of his return!" he insisted.

"If Henry were alive, and had returned, I'm certain I would have been informed. How can *you* be so certain, sir?"

"My son is in the employ of Mr. and Mrs. Bullock of Bedford. He said Mr. Henry Bullock returned to England weeks ago."

Katherine was frozen and wide eyed, no longer looking at the old man but into the air beside him while she absorbed his words. This couldn't be right. She could feel her body shaking, starting in her core and radiating outward and causing her hands and knees to tremble.

She heard Edward thank the man and wish the couple well for the day, then he stood before her. He reached out both hands to touch her arms, and she instead clutched his abruptly.

“This man is not to be believed,” he told her, keeping his voice low and even in an effort to thwart the anxiety he could see rising in her with every breath.

“How can this be?” she whispered, her wild eyes blinking up at him.

Lucy stood by, blinking repeatedly, unable to form words, though her mouth hung open in stunned silence.

“It cannot. We do not know anything that man said is correct, Katherine—.“

“He would have written me! He would have, Edward!” she cried out, unable to contain the hysteria growing within her.

“Shhhh,” Edward hissed, trying to calm her. “He would have indeed, Katherine. If not you then he most certainly would have messaged me. It would—."

“We must go to Bedford and speak with his uncle,” she pleaded through trembling lips. “We must go. Now.”

“Katherine, I cannot simply—.“

“Then I will!” she shrieked. “I shall go alone. I must know what he said is untrue! It *is* untrue! He would have sent word were he still alive—.“

Edward put a hand over her mouth so to stop the screams. “Bloody hell woman!” he growled. Then he calmed himself and sighed. “I will take you to Bedford. We will see that what the old man said is false.”

Katherine didn't wait for them to finish their business in the market. She picked up her skirts and sprinted back to the carriage; Edward and Lucy struggled to keep up as she flew through the crowd, crazed and determined. She argued with Edward throughout the ride home regarding their mode of transportation. Edward said the carriage would be safer and warmer. Katherine refused, stating that horseback would be faster, and eventually they settled on borrowing the small phaeton Lucy's father owned.

He would have written...

She didn't wait for the footman to open the door, instead throwing it open and jumping out. She ran to her room, added extra layers to the clothes she was wearing, quickly packed a few things into a small satchel which she threw over her head and shoulders and ran back down the stairs.

If he were alive, I would know...

She sat vibrating and twitching while she waited for Edward to return with the phaeton, her thoughts racing and consuming her. He returned, but needed to gather a few of his own things, and she tried to calm herself but found she couldn't breathe as deeply as wanted to.

It could only be George. And I'm certain George will be happy to see us...

Lucy hugged her and wished her well before Katherine once again raced out the door.

Edward said nothing, not knowing what to say to this woman possessed. He kept the horse going at a fast-enough pace to keep Katherine quiet as she stared off into the abyss. He knew it would likely be nightfall before they arrived, and that should they actually speak with Henry's uncle, they would spend the night in Bedford. Edward was unsure of what accommodations the tiny town had, having only ever been there once when he was a boy.

They made a few stops to eat and rest the horse, and each time Katherine remained agitated until they were moving again. After one final stop within the town of Bedford to ask directions to the Bullock home, they arrived just as the sun was setting behind the layer of cloud that had plagued them all day.

And she felt it again as they approached the house—the warmth, the pulling sensation. She'd felt it a few times since Henry's death but had always thought perhaps it was his spirit still somehow being with her, watching over her, guiding her. And thus it made sense that she would feel it here, in this place where not only she and Edward were now, but also other people Henry held dear.

Edward rang the bell and the door was opened by a maid who, after Edward asked to speak with the master of the house, asked them to wait and then closed the door.

A few moments later it opened again and a middle-aged man stepped forward. He was tall, like George and Henry had been. His eyebrows were thick and some of the hairs were long and flowing upward, giving the appearance of wings above his eyes. He did not invite them in. He looked them over and the only word to come from his mouth was "Yes?"

Edward cleared his throat. "Mr. Bullock, my name is Edward Whyte, son of William Whyte of London, who was a friend of your brother George Bullock long ago."

The man said nothing, only giving a slight nod and turning his eyes to Katherine. "Is this your wife, Edward Whyte?"

"No, sir. This is my sister, Miss Katherine Whyte."

Katherine gave a small, quick curtsy. The movement almost caused her to pass out, and she realized she hadn't breathed in an eternity, not wanting to miss an ounce of what this man had to say.

"Miss Katherine Whyte?" Mr. Bullock repeated, his face remaining stern, though his eyebrows flicked together for a second.

"Yes," Edward continued. "She was engaged to your nephew Henry for a time. Henry was also my dearest friend, sir."

Mr. Bullock glared at Katherine, and then turned back to Edward. "My nephew is long dead, young man, and I cannot fathom your reason for coming all this way."

Edward inhaled and cleared his throat again. "Indeed, sir, and I ask that you excuse this intrusion. We were told some information earlier in the day, and, well, someone led us to believe that Henry perhaps had not died and was in fact staying here with you. They were quite insistent and, I suppose it brought us to hope that they were in fact speaking the truth. But as you've just said they were obviously mistaken. Our deepest apologies, sir, and condolences to your family once again. Good night Mr. Bullock."

Edward turned quickly and took Katherine's arm to lead her down the stairs. The door slammed shut behind them before they reached the bottom step. Katherine realized they hadn't had a chance to ask if George Bullock was present, but after witnessing his brother's demeanour, decided it was likely for the best.

"See now?" Edward said quietly as he took his place beside her on the phaeton. "The old man in the market was a loon, sister. We shall spend the night in town and return home tomorrow, and things will be as they were before this morning."

She gave a nod, though she stared forward, not willing to look him in the eye.

Edward gave the reigns a flick and the horse began to pull them. Again he allowed Katherine to be alone in her head as they continued out of the yard. Back on the road he sped the horse up slightly, hoping to get back into Bedford before they lost any more daylight.

"Are you hungry?" he asked, trying to be quiet but also having to speak over the noise of the buggy and the horse on the road. He himself was famished, having not had a proper meal since breakfast.

"I suppose," she said on a sigh.

The tone of her voice sounded oddly normal, even slightly pompous and irritated, lacking the urgency it had contained throughout the day, leaving Edward to believe he was right and things would soon be back to normal. He inhaled deeply, happily leaving the day's events in the dust behind them.

Katherine watched the horse, the road, the sky as it darkened, an owl as it landed and sat perched on the top of a tree. They had passed no one from Bedford to the Bullock house, and had passed no one since they left the house, but Katherine was sure she could hear hoof beats over the sounds of their horse, faster, at a run, and coming closer. She couldn't see anyone coming toward them, so she turned to look out the back, and could see someone racing toward them, coming up from behind.

Edward seemed to notice and looked back to follow her gaze.

"Seems to be in a hurry," he noted out loud.

"You should move off and allow him to pass," Katherine suggested.

Edward did pull to the side slightly, and then let out a small chuckle. "*Him*? What makes you so certain it is a man?"

"What woman would be out all alone at this time?" she replied with a cool wave of her hand.

"I suppose," he agreed, happy to see that she was, in fact, acting like herself again. He glanced back again and again to see how much ground the figure behind them had gained. The horse was definitely closing in now. Edward watched as the rider slowed the horse, but still had enough speed to pass them, which he did. Edward expected him to kick the horse back into a full gallop and leave them far behind.

Instead the rider stopped his horse abruptly, causing it to rear up slightly and turn to block their path, then quickly dismounted on the other side of his horse.

Edward yanked on the reigns and Katherine gasped as the wagon pulled abruptly to a stop, terrified at the thoughts that suddenly ran through her head: they were going to be robbed; Edward would try to fight this man; if he lost he could be killed; if Edward was killed Katherine could be taken, and who knows what would happen to her...

And as the man stepped around the horse, just as quickly as the breath entered her on a gasp, it was sucked from her body as she looked into the bluest eyes she'd ever seen.

Chapter Fifteen

"Good God," Edward whispered. "Henry?"

It sounded like a question, though they both knew it was him standing before them. His hair was cut close to his head and the hair on his face was just as long, giving the appearance he hadn't shaved for days, but there was no mistaking it was Henry Bullock.

Edward lowered himself off the phaeton and held his hand out to guide a stunned Katherine down as well, yet neither took their eyes off Henry, as though he were a phantom that would disappear if they blinked or looked away.

Edward let go of Katherine's hand and walked toward Henry. "We were told you were dead. Your uncle—."

"My uncle did as I asked should anyone come looking for me," he said firmly.

"Are you in some sort of danger? Are you hiding there?" Edward asked with genuine concern.

Henry shook his head.

They stood in silence for a moment, and then Edward broke it with a sigh that became a laugh.

"You're alive!" he cried out with joy, walking toward Henry.

Henry's face softened into a light smile, and the two men embraced one another, each patting the other's back firmly.

Edward pulled back. "How can this be?" he asked, shaking his head. "We were told you were hanged. The military men I spoke with, so many of them agreed—."

"I wrote to you. Both of you," Henry interrupted. "Upon my release I sent word to your parents' home and your home in London. I explained my absence as well as my impending return to England."

"We did not receive them. Perhaps because Lucy and I have moved to a different house. And Katherine has come to live there with us." He sighed again in disbelief. "How did you come to be imprisoned then?"

"My father," Henry said, suddenly becoming serious. "I was to be hanged, and without my knowledge my father switched our papers before we were discovered. He made them believe his name was mine, at which point he confessed to treason against the crown, if it meant my life would be spared. And then he..." He swallowed hard and looked away.

Edward patted him on the shoulder.

Henry's eyes came back up and landed squarely on Katherine, and as though she had no awareness of herself, she found herself drifting toward him, and set her right hand alongside his face. He laid his hand over hers and pressed it into his skin, closing his eyes and inhaling deeply the scent of her. Being this close she realized his body had changed as well, his shoulders and torso appearing more broad and muscular than she remembered. Then he pulled her hand down and his eyes landed on the sapphire ring she wore. The side of his mouth flicked up as she'd seen it do so many times before.

"I have yet to see you wearing this," he noted.

"I have yet to take it off," she whispered, desperately trying to hold back a sob. Him standing before her, holding her hand, suddenly became overwhelming and she closed her eyes against the emotion within her.

"I was told you are married now," she heard him say, causing her to open her eyes and look up at him. There was so much pain in his eyes, and she couldn't tell how much of it had been caused by her.

"No," she said, shaking her head lightly.

And with that one word the pain left his face on a small sigh that emerged from his lips, lips that then formed a smile, a smile that soon went away when it wasn't returned. "What is it?" he asked

"I *am* engaged... to someone else," she thought, adding the last part when it suddenly occurred to her that she was technically still engaged to him.

His eyes drifted away from hers and he took a step back.

"Henry, please..." she whispered, reaching out a hand and just missing his arm as he turned back to his horse and mounted it quickly.

"Henry!" Edward called out. "Be not angry with her! She believed you were dead. We all did! Years we grieved your death, Henry. Katherine most of all!"

That seemed to stop Henry's movements for a moment, and he dropped his head back to stare up at the sky.

Edward felt the need to take advantage of this moment. "We have all come to believe falsehoods about one another. The militia convinced us you were dead. Someone told you Katherine was married. We must be calm so we can determine what went wrong and how we shall move forward."

Henry shook his head and chuckled at Edward's words, then his eyes fell to Katherine. "Perhaps you should speak with your charming mother regarding her misinformation of your marriage and my sudden resurrection." With that he kicked his horse and galloped back in the direction he'd come from.

***

The next afternoon Katherine pushed through the front door to the Whyte estate quite forcefully. She hadn't rang the bell or knocked, and she walked past the new servants with an air of importance and went straight to the parlour, Edward following her closely.

William looked up from his newspaper. "My dear children!" he cried out. "What a pleasant surprise! To what do we owe the honour of seeing the both of you here?"

Katherine kept her chin held high. "We've come to tell you the news father!" She paused to remove her bonnet. "You are married to an absolute wretch of a woman."

Fiona's head shot up from the needlepoint she was doing. Katherine could see the whites of her eyes and was quite satisfied she had their full attention.

"Whatever do you mean?" William grumbled in a way that suggested it was not, in fact, news to him.

Edward spoke up. "What my sister is so... delicately trying to convey is that we've just come from Bedfordshire."

"Bedfordshire?" William repeated. "What business could you possibly have there?"

"None at all," Edward insisted with his usual sarcastic flare. "We did, however, track down an old and dear friend."

Katherine watched Fiona's lips purse and eyebrows flick upward as she realized what was about to come forth.

"Oh?" asked William. "Go on boy. Who did you meet?"

"Henry Bullock," Katherine answered, looking squarely at her mother. "He is alive and well and staying with his uncle."

"No!" William cried out, his face in absolute shock as he searched the faces of his children for any signs of jest. "We were told he died!"

"Indeed," Edward agreed. "It was, however, his poor father who was hanged, God rest his soul. And through some dreadful mess people were made to believe it was actually Henry, while Henry himself was the one put into prison and believed to be George."

Katherine continued on without missing a beat. "He spoke with us briefly about things he's done since his release, such as writing to tell us of his well-being— letters we never received. I can understand that Edward never received his, as we believe it was sent to his old home. However I cannot explain why we did not receive the one he sent here. Can you, mother?"

Fiona said nothing, but Katherine noticed Fiona's nostrils flare, something she'd witnessed before when Fiona was filled with rage but choosing to bite her tongue— a rare occasion indeed.

Edward started up again. "My sister and I were wondering aloud on our journey home if that was the real reason for Rupert and Eleanor's sudden departure. Perhaps they knew too much, and it threatened your designs for Katherine's future."

Again they paused briefly, giving Fiona the chance to explain herself, but when she didn't, Katherine picked up on their verbal assault.

"And what of his arrival here? He gave no details but mentioned he had been here and spoken with you. Do you deny it? That in your efforts to advance yourself you would lead *us* to continue to believe him dead and *him* to believe I am already married?" Again she paused, and again she received no response, so she shook her head. "Satan himself would fear your evil." She realized she was showing Fiona more emotion than she deserved, and that Fiona would not care one bit about the pain she had caused them all. Instead Katherine squared her shoulders, lifted her chin, and became what Fiona had worked so hard to create. Knowing the only thing that would cause Fiona any grief, she said in a loud, even tone, "You will not be welcome in my home, madame. I will see to it you will not be welcome in any home my fiancé and I might attend. Nor will your presence be required at my wedding." And with her head still held high in pompous defiance she swept out of the room.

The siblings returned to their home, both silently stewing in their anger, exhausted from their journey and the emotions that had beaten them throughout. Katherine wasn't sure how much sleep Edward had gotten, though she knew she had only slept a few hours, and the sleep she did get was fitful with dreams full of her deep despair. While Edward explained everything to Lucy, Katherine excused herself for the evening, having already grown sick of the whole situation and not wanting to hear it recounted. She'd spent twenty-four hours highly aware of the ring on her finger and lay in bed spinning it until she finally fell asleep.

When she woke up, she was happy to have slept well and dreamlessly, though she was still plagued by her conscious reflections and the guilt that came with them. She remembered her final thoughts as she had fallen asleep: should she return the ring to Henry?

All this time it had been a memento, a sacred keepsake to maintain the memory of him. But now he was alive, and it would appear odd to wear the ring given by her former fiancé when she married Arthur.

If I marry Arthur.

The thought suddenly struck her, though she pushed it away immediately. Of course she would marry Arthur! She had promised her father and dear Eleanor long ago. The union had already been blessed by the king himself. The wedding was mere months away, and many important people were set to attend. A dress was being made for her in a lovely pale shade of green. Arthur had set up her paint room, and Katherine had begun to collect things from here and her parents' house to move into her future home. There was so much that was already expected of her that she could not simply walk away now.

Not to mention poor Arthur. Though he could be tiresome and boring, he did seem to genuinely care for her. And he was so much older than she was, it could be his last chance to marry! She couldn't possibly do that to him after all the wonderful things he had done for her.

So with the decision having been set in her mind, she wondered what she should do with the ring. She wanted to keep it, deep down, still keeping with her a piece of Henry and the affection she had felt for him, since it had been the only time she had felt love and was certain she would never feel it again. But she also knew how inappropriate it would be.

And if she were to give it back, would he even understand and accept it, or would it be yet another crushing blow to him?

It was an argument she had with herself throughout the day, and she considered bringing it up with Edward, but decided to wait a few more days. This was still so fresh, though it remained unspoken the next day, Sunday, as no one could stand to revisit the topic just yet.

Katherine had always felt mixed emotions about Sundays. She didn't like large crowds, but she did like singing, and she absolutely loved the sounds of a large group of voices rising and falling as one. Though she would usually find herself bored by the sermon, it was something that Arthur insisted upon, therefor when he was home, she was expected attend with him. Edward and Lucy had attended regularly since the children were born, and so she knew that, should she ever feel the urge to attend in his absence, she could go with them. This day though she felt like staying home, not wanting to be near her mother just yet.

Until Lucy stopped her in the hallway. "Are you wearing that to church?" she asked, perplexed.

"I had no intention of attending church today," Katherine informed her, quickly glancing down to her simple house dress.

"You would have Arthur attend alone?" she asked, her face becoming concerned. Then she dropped her voice to a whisper. "Is it because of what's happened with..?" She nodded knowingly, though like everyone else, she still couldn't bring herself to say his name.

Arthur? Katherine thought. And then she gasped, realizing what day it was. Arthur was to have returned the previous day. She'd been so preoccupied she had forgotten entirely.

She dashed up the stairs to change, choosing a nice dress that she could pull on and arrange quickly. She already had her hair back in a loose braid, which she normally wouldn't have left the house in, but she was in a hurry, knowing Edward and Lucy were ready and waiting.

Although the young Whytes were understanding as usual, Katherine was frustrated with herself for having forgotten, but her frustration turned toward an absent Arthur. Her flurry, as it turned out, had been all for naught, as Arthur was nowhere to be seen. She did not listen to the sermon and the words of forgiveness, instead her thoughts were angry and spiteful, toward Arthur, toward her mother, sitting four people away from her, and toward herself. And as time passed, she dreaded the end of the service, knowing with it would come the awkward socializing she was no good at.

"And where is your darling fiancé dear?" Mrs. Margaret Turner asked once people had gathered outside of the church. "Will he be joining us at all today?"

Katherine was irritated by the question, mainly due to Margaret referring to Arthur as *her* fiancé. It was true, but it made Katherine instantly furious. She managed to smile at the older woman. "I haven't any idea, ma'am. I believe he's just returned to town from a business trip."

"Oh, pity. Such a polite man. Will he be settling in his duties once you are married? To spend time with his wife and children, perhaps?"

Nosy sow, Katherine thought, taking a moment to breathe in and out slowly, calming herself. "We have yet to discuss such things, Mrs. Turner."

Margaret Turner looked a mix of shocked and confused, as if to say, *Surely you should have discussed it already, before accepting his proposal.* But it was now obvious they hadn't. They hadn't discussed much, Katherine thought, beyond planning the day itself, and if Arthur had any visions of what he believed their lives should be once married, he had yet to share them with her.

Lucy, ever thoughtful, came to Katherine's rescue. "Perhaps we should pay His Lordship a visit to enquire on his well-being?"

Katherine smiled at her softly. "Yes, perhaps we should."

To save face Margaret turned her head, with an interested look, to join the conversation happening on her right.

An observing Fiona caught Katherine's eye, and pursed her lips in her usual obvious upset. Katherine's response was to lift her chin and look away.

And then the wave of warmth hit her, pulling her eyes to look to her left.

Henry was walking toward her, toward the group she was with, his eyes fixed on her.

William noticed him as well and turned to face him. He let a loud sigh. "Henry," he called out, holding out a hand for him to shake.

Henry took it, but was pulled in for a hug, William using his free hand to pat him on the back twice before pulling away and setting the same hand on Henry's shoulder.

William shook his head. "I cannot remember a time in my life when I was so happy to see someone, my boy. I cannot imagine the distress you've faced these many years. And I cannot apologize enough for the things that have transpired since your return."

Katherine had to look away from this, as the emotion in her father's eyes was something she had never seen outside of encounters with her and Edward.

Henry nodded, holding and reflecting William's sincerity. "Thank you, Mr. Whyte. You are long forgiven," he assured him. Then he let go of William's grasp and turned his body to face Edward and Lucy. "Mr. Whyte, Mrs. Whyte, how lovely to see you again."

Lucy, who could not hold back the tears, moved to embrace him quickly. The smile it brought to his face was genuine and continued even after she had backed away from him, though her hold of him lasted quite a long time.

Again his eyes fell to Katherine. "You look well, Miss Whyte," he said with a faint nod.

She had to fight against herself to stave off a shiver she felt emerge and travel through her body, and the motion caused her eyes to dart away from his. She closed them and cleared her throat. "Thank you," was all her mouth would allow. When she opened her eyes a moment later, he was inhaling to speak.

"Miss Whyte, Edward, might I have a word?"

While Edward nodded when he moved away from the crowd, Katherine could only follow them involuntarily, pulled in his direction as she always had been.

"I feel as though I should apologize for my conduct and my abrupt exit last week—."

Katherine shook her head. "Henry, no, you mustn't..." she whispered.

"Yes," Edward agreed, "it is not at all necessary—."

"It is though," Henry insisted. "I was a fool to believe everything would be the same as when I'd left. Much time has passed, and I've only just come to realize you believed me dead. Of course you have continued on with your lives, as well you should have. Forgive me."

Edward shook his head. "Henry, you have been through so much. Much more than we even know. I cannot fathom how you survived it."

At this Henry's eyes flickered to Katherine for a long enough moment, and she felt she understood what it meant. Then they looked back to Edward. "Perhaps we should spend some time recalling the past few years to one another," he suggested.

"Absolutely," Edward agreed. "Would you join us for supper today? I should love for you to meet my boys, see my home, stay for as long as you like. Lucy would agree."

Henry pressed his lips together in a nervous attempt at

a smile. "Perhaps another time, my friend. Another day. I have affairs of my own to tend to this day."

"Tomorrow then! I insist! Before you leave town again!" Edward declared before quickly giving the directions to their home, his presence as jovial and commanding as his father's.

Henry managed to grin. "Tomorrow then," he agreed quietly. He bowed his head to Edward. "Good day."

"Good day," Edward repeated, satisfied.

Then he bowed his head to Katherine. "Miss Whyte."

She felt as though she should have said something more. Edward had spoken. Henry had spoken. Katherine had watched silently, as she had always done, and immediately regretted it. She now wished she could, but she knew the moment had passed, so she gave a small curtsy and watched with a heavy heart as he walked away.

Chapter Sixteen

A female housekeeper opened the front door to Arthur's house, and upon seeing Katherine and her party, a brief look of panic crossed her face. She gave a curtsy. "Miss Whyte! I was not made aware that you would be arriving today."

Katherine blinked at the girl then squared her shoulders and spoke with an air of importance. "His Lordship is not expecting me. However he was absent from church this morning and I am curious as to why."

The girl did not open the door. "I was told to allow no one in, however if you would wait here, I shall see if he is willing to receive you."

"Why would he not receive me? We are to be married soon," Katherine narrowed her eyes at the girl, making a note of this situation, and thinking of firing the brat when she became lady of the house. "One day soon you'll be given no choice in the matter," she spat for emphasis.

The girl cleared her throat. "His Lordship has given instruction, miss."

Edward spoke quietly behind Katherine. "Perhaps we should return another time."

"No," Katherine said in a low even tone, holding the gaze

of the girl at the door. "We've come all this way out of concern for Lord Thacker's well-being and you will fetch him or so help me..."

The girl dropped her eyes and curtsied again, then closed the door, silently infuriating Katherine.

"What is going on?" she hissed to no one in particular.

Edward grinned at her ironically. "You seem particularly irritated by your fiancé today, dear sister. Any specific reason?"

She knew what he was hinting at and rolled her eyes, looking away.

The door opened again and Mr. Burnley stood in the way. "Miss Whyte, my sincere apologies. Please," he stepped back and gestured they enter. "My lord arrived later than expected last evening and continued to rest well into the morning. He has been informed of your presence and will be down shortly to greet you." Mr. Burnley led them into the parlour and instructed they sit to wait. It was a long wait, as made obvious by the large clock directly in front of the sofa they sat on. Lucy and Edward spoke quietly while Katherine sat breathing in and out angrily, her nostrils flaring.

"I'm sorry for the delay, my sweet," Arthur's voice rang through the room before he actually entered it. He approached them; his hands held out in front of him for Katherine to take.

She did not reach out to meet him. She stood, only to be at his eye level, and kept her hands folded while she curtsied accordingly. Her jaw remained set. "My lord, you appear well. We were concerned with your absence this morning."

He dropped his hands and rubbed the palms on his trousers. "Yes, well, I arrived later than I'd planned and was exhausted. So much so that I asked not to be disturbed for any reason today, at all." He was staring her down now, his words and tone making it seem as though this meeting was some inconvenience to him. "But as always I will make time for you." It was at this moment he looked her over. His eyes moved to Edward and Lucy and back to her. "Did you wear this dress to church this morning?"

Katherine swallowed the lump in her throat but kept her chin high. "Yes. I was hurried this morning believing I would be meeting you there, my lord."

He gave a pinched smile. "Then perhaps it is best I was not there after all." He did not give her proper time to be insulted, instead moving swiftly into the next sentence. "My darling I am still very tired and in no great mood for company. As you can see, I am well and I thank you for your concern, but I must ask you to leave so that I may rest. And I shall warn you now that tomorrow I will likely also be occupied all day with His Majesty to complete the business he sent me away on, so there is no need for you to expect me to join you anywhere." He grabbed her hand before she could pull away and abruptly, roughly, kissed her on the cheek. Then he said his parting words to Edward and Lucy—in a tone much more pleasant — and walked out of the room, leaving the responsibility of seeing them out to his staff.

Katherine blinked in shock at his abrupt exit, then stomped out of the house in a huff. She'd been right to be cross with him, it would seem, and he had made no real effort to change her sour disposition.

Lucy, never knowing what to say in times of tension remained quiet, but Edward was never at a loss for words. "Fear not sister. This day can still be salvaged," he proclaimed as he closed the carriage door behind himself.

Katherine rolled her eyes again at his chipper disposition. "Pray, tell brother," she growled with sarcasm, "I am entirely at your disposal."

"Well we can now spend the day inviting friends and loved ones to dinner tomorrow to welcome home your dear friend and mine, Henry Bullock."

"Oh yes Katherine!" Lucy piped up, happy to suddenly have something to distract her and look forward to.

Katherine sighed. "I'd rather not—."

"Nonsense!" Edward charged. "Your help is desperately required, and you know him better than anyone in this world."

She scoffed. "Must you? You must know how very difficult this has to be for him, and if you would like to know how it is for me, I would be happy to explain." She thought it would silence him, but her brother was never one to back away from a confrontation.

"Please do," he muttered, holding her eyes and challenging her.

She shrugged. "What would you have me say, Edward? You must know. You must!"

He stared at her, waiting for her to verbalize. "Go on, Katherine."

Unable to say the words he wanted to hear, or the ones she wanted to use to tell him off, she banged on the roof of the coach, signalling for it to come to a stop and she opened the door.

"Where are you going?" Edward asked, exasperated.

She didn't answer because she didn't know. She simply needed to be alone. She hadn't expected him to call her bluff, but she knew herself well enough to know that she wouldn't be able to make it through the first few words without falling apart. He'd been right— she was upset with Arthur for no other reason than existing right now. It wasn't Arthur's fault, any of it. He hadn't hung the elder Bullock or imprisoned the younger and sent back false information. He hadn't forced her to say yes to his proposal. He wasn't even the reason she was suddenly second guessing her shiny new engagement. Sure, she'd had uncertainties from the first time she'd met him, but now she had an entirely new burden to bear, and the weight of it was crushing her.

She jumped down and began walking, knowing this area of town well enough to feel confident she would make it home safely on her own. Though there was a part of her that hoped she would be attacked and murdered in some dank alley, ending her confusion and anguish and all the feelings she would rather not have anymore.

***

When Katherine awoke the next day she was quite relieved— she would have one more day's break from Arthur, and had she known yesterday would go the way it had ahead of time she would have enjoyed it far more thoroughly. But at least she would have today. It made the dreary day somehow brighter, and gave her a bounce in her step...

Until she got downstairs and remembered that Henry would be there within hours. She shouldn't have dreaded his presence, but she did. She dreaded it because she was yearning for it.

Every hour that passed made her twitch. Every ring of the bell made her breathe faster.

Edward informed everyone that Henry would be arriving with his aunt and uncle that lived in town. He had gone to their home to invite them the day before and found that Henry was in fact staying with them while he remained in town.

Several people arrived before the guest of honour, and Katherine's delight was increasing by the moment, until her parents walked in. Her father greeted her with a hug. Her mother acknowledged her by name, and Katherine responded by walking away, avoiding being in the same room as Fiona. Which made it difficult to interact with anyone else really, as most of the guests had converged in the parlour. Katherine chose to stay near the children in the foyer, playing on the floor with the boys, who were now four and two years old.

And as promised Henry arrived with his aunt Jeanette, while his uncle was unable to make it. Katherine knew Henry was there before she'd seen him come through the door. She did not stand to greet him or his aunt, feeling like she was hidden well enough around a corner to not be noticed. He disappeared and Katherine could hear him being greeted by Edward and Lucy, among others. While she wanted nothing more than to drown in his eyes, she felt the need to stay away, having made the choice, begrudgingly, to continue her engagement with Arthur.

Not that her efforts mattered. She felt a moment of light-headedness and knew he was looking for her. She felt the warmth within her growing, and though he entered the room without making a sound, she wasn't at all startled when he appeared in front of her.

He knelt down to be at her level. "And who, may I ask, are these strapping young men, Miss Whyte?"

"This," she said, digging her fingers in to tickle the toddler in her lap, making him squirm and laugh, "is my nephew Matthew. And this lad," she said, patting the other boy on the head, "is Henry."

Henry's eyes revealed genuine shock for a moment, and then changed when a smile crossed his face.

A smile that nearly made her come undone.

"Whose idea was that? If I may ask," he said quietly.

"I cannot be certain whether it was Lucy or Edward, or perhaps they both simply knew it was to be thus." She watched him watch his namesake as he played with a wooden horse on the floor. "They did, however, ask for my blessing," she added softly. She wasn't sure why she felt compelled to tell him that, but she did receive the response she'd intended—his eyes coming back to her, boring into her with purpose and meaning. And though she couldn't help herself in the moment, she regretted it when every emotion coursed through her all at once and she felt a familiar pulsating in her center—something she'd only ever felt with him.

She wasn't able to tear her eyes away from his, but was grateful that he had far more self-control, and turned to his namesake.

"Your name is Henry?" he asked the boy and received a nod. "My name is Henry as well. This is your brother then, is it?" Again the boy nodded. "And this, Henry," he asked, touching Katherine's hand gently, "who is this?"

"Aunty Kate," young Henry said with a grin, enjoying the attention he was receiving.

She watched him speak to the boys, so gentle and kind, and it made her long for the life he had promised her so long ago.

Henry Bullock grinned as well. "Aunty Kate?" he nodded, then he turned his head back to Katherine. "I like that. Well, young Henry, I'll ask that you take your brother to find your mum while I help your Aunty Kate to her feet please."

The boy did as he was told, taking his brother by the hand and leading him away.

Henry stood and offered his hand to Katherine, who took it with her right hand and allowed him to help her up. Again her ring caught his eye, and he smoothed his thumb over it.

She cleared her throat. "Do you want it back?"

He blinked at her. "Want what back?"

"The ring. You should have it back."

His face became very serious as he realized the meaning in her words. "No, Katherine. It is yours. It belongs to you."

She glanced away for a moment. "I believe it might be inappropriate of me to keep it, considering— "

"Not at all," he assured her.

She wanted to protest more, but she was afraid to offend him, and he'd already been through so much, so she tried to choose her words carefully. "I really must insist you consider it further."

He shook his head. "There is no need."

"Why not?" she whispered, feeling as though she were begging him now to take it back.

"Perhaps I am still holding on to some hope."

She froze, afraid to breathe.

"I know you feel it, Katherine," he whispered, taking a step closer until there were only inches between them. "For as long as I can remember it has been there, pulling me toward you, guiding me when I cannot find you. It kept me alive all those years I was locked away on that ship, and it lives within me still, as strong as ever. *It* will not allow me to take back that ring. It will not allow me to give up hope, as long as you are still Miss Katherine Whyte. I would speak to him if you would allow. I've heard he is a good man, kind and reasonable. He may simply let you go. We *are* still engaged, you and I, as long as we both have breath in us. Station be damned, I have just as much right as he. But only if you gave the word, Katherine. It is your choice to make. I cannot force your hand. I will not bring forth this conversation again, as it pains us both, I know. I shall leave it to you."

She was looking away now, absorbing every word, picturing the possibilities, and so he placed his finger under her chin to bring her eyes back to him.

"Promise me you will consider it," he concluded.

She gave a faint nod, and then he suddenly was gone, tearing himself away, walking back to the parlour, taking her senses with him. She sat on the stairs for a moment, regaining herself before she followed him, arriving in the parlour just in time for everyone to move to the dining room.

Fiona remained stone faced and silent through the meal, only speaking when asked a question, and only giving short answers. It was obvious she was upset with something as per usual.

Halfway through the meal, the doorman came in to announce that Arthur had arrived, and then Arthur himself entered the dining hall while Rosemary, Edward's housekeeper, scrambled to make a setting for him.

William seemed perplexed, yet remained jovial, commanding the surroundings and the circumstances as though he were in his own home. "We weren't expecting you!"

"No, and I must apologize for my sudden arrival," he said as he went to his seat. "I was quite stunned to have not received an invitation to this supper! I've only just heard about it perhaps an hour ago." He removed his hat and coat and tossed them at Rosemary, who wasn't ready to catch them, but did nonetheless.

Edward remained cool in his tone but challenging in his eyes. "Our arrival at your home yesterday was for precisely that, sir. However, if you will recall, you sent us away before any invitation could be given and insisted you needed the day for business."

Arthur took a moment, giving the appearance he was in thought. "Apologies. My coach was turned round and lost for a period of time. I arrived back early yesterday morning, and I required much time to rest and compose myself. I thought I would come visit my betrothed as last we left without parting pleasantries." He now took a quick look and noticed Katherine's glare. "Perhaps I should have waited another day, as it appears my beloved is upset at something," Arthur said, tearing his bread.

Katherine wished she were dead, as suddenly all eyes were on her, gauging her mood.

Arthur's statement confounded Henry. "What do you mean, sir?" he asked, not bothering with the propriety of introducing himself first.

Katherine's heart jumped into her throat, as she waited for Arthur to recognize Henry from the impromptu portrait she had painted of him.

Arthur turned his head to look at Henry, puzzled at the strange question from the strange man. "Perhaps she thinks my intrusion this evening rude. But I know for certain Miss Katherine will not want us to discuss private issues in front of so many people. We shall speak alone at a later time," he said, giving the appearance he was doting on his fiancé, when in fact it was *he* who had caused her such upset.

Fiona squared her shoulders. "How very noble of you, my lord."

Henry shrugged. "I wouldn't think it an intrusion to check on the well-being of your wife, sir. Especially after her abrupt departure, which was, as you said, without pleasantries."

Katherine could sense the irony within Henry's statement and shot a look to Edward, knowing he must have informed Henry somehow of their visit to Arthur the previous day, likely when he went to his aunt and uncle's home to invite them.

Arthur narrowed his eyes. "Well, she is not yet my wife, and again I would allow her the decency of *not* entertaining private matters in public."

"Perhaps you should have considered such privacy on the matter before you brought attention to her alleged mood in the presence of all these people."

Katherine had frozen in place, her eyes staring through the table before her, now terrified to lift them and make eye contact with anyone.

Arthur raised an eyebrow and looked Henry up and down. "I don't believe we have been introduced, sir. Lord Arthur Thacker," he said, giving his head a long nod, as though they were standing and it was a low bow.

William spoke up to introduce Henry. "Yes, Thacker. This is Edward's best mate from school, Henry Bullock. He has recently returned to England from—." William caught himself and cleared his throat, "— the colonies, where he spent most of his life." He looked toward Henry to see if he had caused any sort of offence and was relieved with the satisfied yet small smile and nod Henry gave him.

"Ah. I see," Arthur said, "well then. Welcome back to England, sir."

"Thank you," Henry said. He was polite but didn't look up from his plate this time.

"Tell me, Henry Bullock," Arthur said through a bite of food, "your thoughts on that silly war. I would so love to get perspective from someone who has seen both sides."

"I did not find it silly in any way, sir. I felt it was quite necessary," Henry stated, a bit of challenge in his tone. He was irritated by Arthur's nonchalance on the matter.

"Necessary?" Arthur scoffed. "You're not a patriot, are you Henry Bullock?"

"I'm an American," Henry replied, lifting his chin.

"You *sound* like an Englishman," Arthur pointed out.

Henry had to stop himself from saying what he thought Arthur sounded like. He was a guest in this house, and Arthur was almost family to these people. "I was an English-*boy.*"

Arthur continued, obviously looking for an argument. "Would you say you are no longer loyal to His Majesty then?"

Every eye was wide and moved from one man to the other, wordlessly. Katherine finally looked up and hoped one or both of them would look in her direction and read her eyes as she begged them to drop the subject.

Instead Henry stared him down, not willing to give Arthur a full explanation. While Arthur did not seem to notice, Henry was quite aware of the tension felt by all at the table who knew his story and chose to spare them anymore upset. "I would say I am loyal to my country, which is no longer at war with yours. There is peace there, and there shall be peace here." Henry was satisfied to watch Arthur give a nod, knowing it meant that while Arthur didn't agree, he also didn't know how to respond.

Fiona felt the need to break the silence. "Will you stay late for the celebration tonight, Arthur?"

"No, I have work to tend to in the morning at court involving my cousin, the king." There was a lilt in his voice when he referred to the king as his cousin, as if to make it known to the stranger that he was, in fact, a member of the royal family.

Henry was unfazed, thoughtfully inspecting a water glass to his right, happy to hear the pompous ass would be leaving soon after dinner.

Fiona continued. "I would think it better for you to wait out the rain, my lo—."

"Oh let the man make his own decisions woman!" William huffed at her.

"Forgive me!" she raised her voice to her husband again. "I am only concerned for the well-being of our future son-in-law!"

Henry's laugh was silent, but completely visible with a wide smile and shaking shoulders, made more evident by the dropping of his head. It brought all eyes to him again, at which he straightened up.

"Yes?" Fiona asked, obviously irritated at his lack of composure.

"Nothing, ma'am," he said, giving his head a shake.

"Oh, please!" Arthur chimed in, bringing his wine goblet to his mouth, "Obviously something is amusing to you."

"Yes, well. What I found amusing, I suppose, is the elder Mrs. Whyte referring to you as their son-in-law when you are nearly their own age. That is all." He moved his chair back and stood, ignoring the widening of Fiona and Arthur's eyes, and Edward's attempt to hide a smile of his own. "If you will excuse me a moment..." He stood and took quick, quiet steps out of the room.

Katherine chose to once again stare, unblinking, at the spot on the table just beyond her plate.

After a few minutes, the others in the room began to talk amongst themselves.

"Obviously a rebel," Arthur said, looking toward Fiona. "His manners are barbaric."

Fiona inhaled to speak but Edward was faster. "And what of your manners, sir? I would have expected better from a man of English nobility."

Arthur appeared taken aback once again. "My dear Mr. Whyte, have I caused you some offence?"

"Indeed you have, sir. Mr. Bullock is the guest of honour tonight. *You*, my lord, were not even invited, and yet you have the audacity and informality to speak to a guest in *my* house thus? Your behaviour with my sister yesterday and here just now has been nothing short of atrocious. Mr. Bullock has been to Hell and back in these past years. The things he has been through you could not fathom, nor survive I would wager, so I have happily welcomed him back into my life and my home and I will not stand for him being disrespected in such a manner."

"Please, then Mr. Whyte, enlighten me to his perils," Arthur said with much condescension.

Edward bit his lips at Arthur's smugness. "Not this night, Thacker," he said, giving back as much disrespect as he was receiving and being treated by a widening of Arthur's eyes. "This evening is not about you. No, this night is a celebration of my dearest friend's return. Perhaps another time, when you are more conditioned to listen rather than speak."

Katherine's jaw fell and she was once again afraid to breathe. She couldn't remember what had brought them to this point; she could only remember her brother's words as they bounced around her brain.

Like a candle being blown out, Arthur's demeanour suddenly went from challenging to hurt. "My dear friend," he said, shaking his head as he spoke with his regular flamboyance, "you have my most sincere apologies. You have mistaken my defence of myself and you sister as an offense and for that I am truly sorry. You are correct, sir, I was not invited tonight, and my presence seems to be something of a burden to your dear friend, Mr. Bullock. I shall retire then for the evening, and in my prayers tonight I shall ask God's forgiveness as I now ask for yours." He stood and came around the table to Katherine's seat and began to pull out her chair. "My darling, if you would please see me to the door?"

Katherine nodded and stood, and as she walked out, she noticed her brother also stand and follow them. Arthur took his things back from Rosemary and put them on, making sure to thank her most sincerely in front of anyone who could see or hear.

The door opened to allow them out and Katherine was glad to see the rain had stopped though it was still cool and breezy.

Arthur turned to her on the step. "I do hope you will forgive my behaviour these past days as your brother has stated it," he told her, taking her hand and kissing the back of it. Then he looked past her. "You as well, Mr. Bullock," he said.

Katherine looked over her left shoulder to see Henry closing in the space between them. She hadn't noticed the warmth that usually indicated he was close; though he was physically close enough now she could feel the warmth of his body against her back.

Arthur continued. "I do hope you will give me an opportunity to make a better impression, sir." He tipped his hat and left them at the top of the steps, and they watched him board his carriage and leave.

She was still watching the carriage rolling a block away when she felt Henry's hands rub her arms.

"Come inside before you catch your death," he murmured.

"I'm fine," she said, shaking off his grip. "What are you doing out here?"

He shook his head. "I needed a breath of air."

Edward was waiting inside the open door and whispered to his sister as she passed. “Fiona.”

Katherine looked around for her mother, confused. “What about her?”

“Have you not been wondering how Thacker got word of this occasion?”

She hadn’t truly given it much thought. Instead she’d been lost in a fog of fear and feeling and propriety. “You think she sent word to him?”

Edward nodded. “I believe she is worried that the presence of one fiancé has you doubting your commitment to the other.” They both turned to glance at Henry, who was several steps behind them and likely couldn’t hear.

The rest of the meal was pleasant among the friends still gathered, and they moved to the parlour when finished to play a few games. She watched from afar as Henry interacted with the other guests, noting he still had his charm when the moment called for it. But she also witnessed a sadness within him, so overwhelming to watch at times she felt as though it were overtaking *her*. She would get so lost in her mind, her brow would furrow, and she would stare at him until he would notice and she would be forced to quickly look away.

Since the events unfolded at the table, Fiona had been sitting with lips pursed glaring at anyone who dared to make eye contact. Katherine was still uneasy, knowing what her mother could be like, and knowing she would have to see Arthur again, perhaps as soon as tomorrow. The thought made her nervous. Arthur was a proud man, not one to be made a fool of. She wondered whether he had indeed seen the error of his ways and truly meant his apology, or if he was simply saving face in front of her and the rest of his audience.

She watched her father leave a card game, slightly intoxicated, and approach her and Edward and Lucy, who were standing near the door, discussing Lucy having just put the boys to bed. And before he could say a word his wife was at his side, mouth at the ready.

"How dare you speak such harsh words to a member of the royal family!" she hissed at Edward. "I did not raise you to be so disrespectful! What has gotten into you?!"

Edward inhaled deeply and sighed, calming himself, and though he spoke to her, he never moved so much as an eye muscle to look at her. "Fiona, I'll not bother responding to the fact that you did not raise me. I will say, however, that if you found yourself sharing Thacker's sentiments, you should have found yourself sharing his carriage. You are more than excused."

Katherine watched, with cool satisfaction, her mother's face contort and twitch, and knew that were they not surrounded by other people, Fiona would have lost control, screaming and perhaps even becoming violent with Edward for his insolence toward her and Arthur. While Katherine's dedication was becoming unclear, Fiona made no secret about where her devotions lay.

Chapter Seventeen

Days later Katherine awoke to find she was alone in the house, save for the servants. She knew Edward was working and that Lucy had planned on taking the boys to visit her parents that day. After several days full of people and conversation and awkwardness, she was quite happy not to make an effort. She knew there was a small possibility that Arthur could show up, however she hadn't heard from him since the party, and she didn't care how she looked if he did just appear out of the blue.

She brought her attention to sewing but grew bored after some time. She chose to find a book she had opened briefly the other day while packing some of her books into boxes for her move to Arthur's home, and once she'd found it, she made her way to the front steps. She didn't descend them, choosing instead to enjoy the shade given by the house on what was turning into a warm day. She sat on the top step and opened her book, lifting her head now and then to check her surroundings, or switching positions when her body grew tired or stiff. Eventually she heard footsteps approaching and glanced up in time to see Henry Bullock seat himself beside her.

"Good afternoon, Miss Whyte," he said as he made himself comfortable.

"Good day," she replied quietly, intentionally looking back down to her book, desperately hoping the coldness she'd been practising these few years would keep her voice from cracking and conveying the quivering her stomach had started at the sight of him.

Henry was quiet, waiting for more of a response from her. When none was given, he asked another question. "How long have you resided here with Edward and Lucy?"

She continued to look at her book though not to read, instead to focus on keeping her tone even and without emotion. "As long as they've lived in this house, so have I."

"You lived with them before then?"

She nodded and inhaled, choosing her words carefully. "I... did not... take the news of your... demise well at all. And while my father tried in his own way to... console me..." She licked her lips and cleared her throat, still not looking up. "My mother was far less supportive, as you can imagine, therefor William and Edward felt it would be best if I came to live with him and Lucy where I would have... people who understood, and things to occupy my mind, if you will." She could see him nod from the corner of her eye.

"You must visit the home of your parents often?"

She glanced in his direction and shook her head.

"Oh? Not even to visit our beloved Rupert and Eleanor?"

This time she turned her head, though she couldn't bring her eyes up, so she looked to the sidewalk below them. "They are no longer in my father's employ."

Henry was quiet for a moment. "How can that be?"

"Edward thinks, and I have no reason to believe otherwise, that perhaps one or both of them came to find the letter you told us you had sent. And the knowledge of your return would lay waste to Fiona's designs that I marry Arthur.

We believe there are other reasons, as well," she added quickly, hoping he would not think it his fault entirely, "though none so apparent."

"Such a pity," he whispered. "How I've missed that place."

"My father's home, you mean?" she asked, finally looking at him.

He nodded. "Yes. So many happy times were spent there when I was a boy. And then…" He didn't go on, remembering his promise to not revisit the topic of their betrothal, though he did not need to, she already knew.

She shook her head, pushing away the memories herself. "What brings you here today, Mr. Bullock?"

"Ah, yes," he said, coming out from his own reverie. He handed her a parcel, setting it atop the still open book in her lap.

"What is this?" she asked.

"I feel as though I need to apologize. For the way I acted the other night, toward your fiancé obviously, but also for the things I said in private earlier in the evening. I've thought about them for days now and feel as though I must have caused you some upset in both circumstances, and I am here now asking for your forgiveness."

It appeared to be a box wrapped in paper, like every piece of jewelry Arthur had ever gifted her. The thought of it being just another trinket gave her a pit in her stomach and caused her blood to boil. First he would not take back the ring, and now he would be so bold as to give her something else that would make her feel guilt and shame every time she wore it. Something that, like Arthur, would make her feel less of a person and more of a possession.

"Is something wrong?" he asked when she'd spent a

moment staring at it silently.

She picked it up and handed it back to him. “I cannot accept this, Hen—Mr. Bullock.” She regretted correcting herself then, as it made it seem forced, but she would have also hated how informal using his first name was as well.

He looked at her, perplexed. “How come?”

“In truth sir, no apology in necessary, but I believe it would not be appropriate for me to take it.” She felt like she was being too harsh and tried to soften her tone, though she found it difficult with the ice running through her veins at the moment. “Perhaps you should give it to your aunt.”

“Katherine, I found this in Philadelphia and it made me think of you. And truly, no one else in the world will appreciate it as you will.”

“Henry Bullock must you drive me so mad?!” she finally snapped at him.

He grinned at her and stood, taking the steps to the ground to be at eye level with her. “Until the day I die.” He dropped the package in her lap again and turned to walk quickly down the street.

She stared at the gift, wondering if she should open it, or wait and give it back. In truth she was worried she would love it, and she would feel bad for not hating it as she should. And if anyone in the world could know what she liked...

No, she decided, she would hate it. She hated jewelry, and she already had far too much of it. Chances are she would likely never find the occasion to wear it. The only piece of jewelry she’d consistently worn was the ring he had given her, and once she married Arthur, she’d convinced herself she would not wear it anymore.

She nodded in her conviction and opened the paper. First, she realized it wasn’t a box, but was in fact a painted wooden frame. And once more paper was removed her lips parted in astonishment.

Inside the narrow, framed box was a perfectly preserved blue butterfly, the size of her hand, the likes of which she'd never seen, not even in her books.

This cannot be real, she thought, examining the specimen closely. She'd never known of a butterfly this large and vibrant in colour. *If it is, it must be a newly discovered species.* Upon closer inspection she concluded that it had been alive at one time. And now she wanted to know everything she could about it. She realized she hadn't received a new book on butterflies or any insect in years, and the few she had were around a decade old, perhaps more. As she thought, she realized she hadn't touched any of them in a very long time, except perhaps to pack them with the rest of her books for her move into Arthur's home.

She needed a new book, she decided, one printed more recently, one that would identify this beautiful creature in her possession. She went into the house in a flurry, throwing on her shawl and a bonnet and setting off on her own with money in her pocket.

***

She returned home empty handed, unable to find what she was looking for. Another day passed without word from Arthur, and another, and Katherine found herself slightly disappointed, as her next plan of action was to ask him if somewhere in his vast collection of books he would have one like she was looking for, or perhaps he knew someone who could answer the questions she had about the butterfly.

She did find it odd though. Usually his time at home was spent with her, perhaps not during the days as he had to work, but the nights were usually at one home or another, making friends and business associates. *He's likely still licking the wounds to his pride inflicted by your brother...*

Only recently she had fully resigned herself to becoming his wife, and in that same stretch of time she'd seen less of him than ever before, so when Sunday came around she got up early to do her hair and don one of the difficult dresses he'd given her. She'd never worn this one, and was surprised at how low the front of it came down. She tried to adjust her breasts so they were not spilling over the top, but nothing seemed to work. She'd spent nearly an hour having Rosemary tie her into it, and just when she felt like she should change it for another one, Lucy called through the door to tell her they were ready to leave. She could already feel the judgement that would come her way and hung her head in dismay. There would be some satisfaction when Fiona remarked on it though, and Katherine could tell her mother where the frock had come from. She was thankful it was a cool morning and reached for a shawl in hopes it would cover her accordingly.

Edward gave no notice to the dress, which gave Katherine some confidence in the shawl she'd chosen, because if anyone would say something, it would be Edward. Lucy, however, did comment on how nice Katherine looked.

And as she thought more on the ride, she decided she would be more cordial to Arthur this day. Even though he'd been less than amiable, she continued to convince herself that it wasn't his fault. He had only been matching the tones and energy of those around him.

Henry is mad for him being your fiancé. It wasn't Arthur's fault.

Edward is just as conflicted on the matter as you are. It wasn't Arthur's fault.

Arthur was perhaps hurt at not being invited to supper, as he had alluded to. It wasn't his fault.

By the time they arrived, she felt pity for the man, and was even looking forward to seeing him after days apart.

Arthur was waiting for her at the door of the church with her parents. He took both of her hands and kissed her cheek as he had become accustomed to doing.

She allowed it, smiling at him as he pulled away. "So happy you could join us today, my lord."

He commented on how lovely she looked this morning, though that was something he always did upon seeing her. "Would you allow me a moment to speak with you in private?" he asked.

Katherine nodded, hoping she would now be getting an explanation and perhaps a sincere apology, and she was ready to do the same. Thus far he had given no reason for his absence from her of late and made no mention of anything being amiss that had caused him to stay away. He seemed his usual loud, flippant self in front of the crowd, and though Katherine was grateful that he appeared to be avoiding conflict, she was still nervous knowing nothing from the past week had in fact been resolved. As she followed him around a corner in the back of the room, she hoped his words now would calm her uneasiness.

He touched the shawl as it hung, the edges crossed over in front of her chest. "A shame you would hide such a lovely dress, an expensive dress, under such an unfit rag."

Katherine, though instantly angry, refused to give him the satisfaction of emotion or response to such a comment. She wanted to keep him on track. She wanted to keep *herself* on track, still making an effort to endear him to her. "Pray, my lord, what is it you wished to speak to me about?"

He blinked in confusion. "Simply what I just said. This

dress you are wearing, it is one that I had made for you, in the latest fashion and most expensive satin and lace, and it insults me that you would cover it at all, let alone with so unworthy a garment as this." Again he grabbed at the edge of the shawl, this time giving it a small tug.

"I beg your pardon, my lord, but it is a cold morning, having rained all night, and so very much of my skin is exposed to the wretched conditions in this dress." Somewhat irritated at the lack of acknowledgement of his errors, she now narrowed her eyes in a challenge. "Perhaps if, as you said, it cost such a penny, the dressmaker could have taken the time and used enough fabric to cover me appropriately."

Arthur inhaled deeply, causing his nostrils to flare. "I cannot imagine what you mean, my dear. It looks fine, just as it did when I saw it hanging in the window. You must show me what causes you such discomfort, so that I may know how to avoid it in the future."

Katherine's eyes narrowed slightly, not sure whether he was in fact asking out of concern, but as she opened her mouth to speak, he yanked at the bottom corner of the shawl and it was pulled off her shoulder. She quickly grabbed at it as it fell behind her and as she moved to readjust it, Arthur's hands were on her—one grasping her shoulder to straighten her and the other gripping her chin so she would look at him. Again she watched him inhale sharply, and again his nostrils flared as he did.

"The only problem I see, my lady, is that you chose *not* to cover such a vast area with any of the jewels I have given you." He moved his hand from her face, tracing a finger over her collarbone and down until he reached the crease in her skin where her breast began.

Katherine took a step back and then another and pulled her shawl back over her shoulders. "I am a lady!" she growled. "You are a gentleman and this is a house of God. You will not disrespect me thus—."

He closed the space between them, putting his hands around her and pulling her against him so that she could feel his hardness against her. "I am anxiously awaiting the day you become my wife, Katherine," he whispered against her ear. "Only then will you understand there is no disrespect between a man and his wife. No disrespect at all. Just your body and obedience—."

She shoved him away and wiped the moisture from the side of her face as she glared at him. He smelled very much of rum, she realized. "There is currently *much* disrespect between a drunken nobleman and a maid such as I. So help me sir if you so much as lay a finger on me before we are wed I have no apprehension that would stop me from speaking to the runners or the magistrate or the king himself, who I'm sure would be much appalled to hear of the conduct of his cousin and ambassador."

With that she rounded the corner back into view of everyone in the building and moved swiftly to sit with her brother and his family. The day was warmer now as the sun rose higher, and while a breeze still floated through the air outside, within the walls of this giant room, filled with so many people, it was stifling. Katherine was unable to tell if she was sweating from the heat or from the encounter she had just had. The air was heavy with moisture and smelled of dirt and sweat. She tried to convince herself she didn't need to breathe and kept each breath as shallow as possible.

Arthur chose to sit in a different pew with a jovial Scottish dignitary he was assigned to keep company, and Katherine wondered if this man was the reason Arthur had been drinking so heavily this early in the day. Katherine was thankful he was not sitting beside her today. She kept to herself like she usually did, hoping no one would notice her flushed cheeks. Several images of Christ stared down and judged her from all angles. She bowed her head to pray with the rest, the warmth from her cheeks radiating...

No, she realized, this wasn't the warmth from her cheeks. She felt a different warmth, on her right side. She opened her eyes and turned her head, and once again the breath was stolen from her body as she looked into intense blue eyes. The eyes she had seen only hours before in her dreams, dreams she only now remembered and made her feel even more shame, which she wouldn't have believed possible. She hadn't realized Henry was sitting in the pew in front of her, mostly due to the fact that she was avoiding eye contact with everyone in the building. She couldn't look away from his gaze. She felt her breathing quicken and her heart beat harder.

I went to church not seeking God, but seeking only you...

The prayer ended and Henry turned his attention back to the front of the room as everyone lifted their heads to do the same. There was standing, which she found difficult to do with weak knees. There was singing, which she mouthed silently. And another prayer, for which she squeezed her eyes shut. And finally, after what felt like days, the service ended. Everyone stood, including her family, waiting for the aisle to clear.

"Henry! Dear boy," William called when they stood, "I thought that was you." He extended his hand for Henry to shake. "Tell me, son, how are your new hosts treating you?"

"Like family," Henry joked with a wide smile.

Katherine tilted her head to the side. "New hosts?"

"Yes," Edward chimed in. "Henry has decided to stay longer with his aunt and uncle here in town, rather than returning to Bedford so soon."

"Indeed," Henry confirmed. "You look lovely today, Miss Whyte."

"Thank you, Mr. Bullock. I'm happy to hear you're

comfortable."

Fiona quickly filled a hole in the precession that was moving down the aisle and William took his place behind her. Katherine looked up to see Henry step out into the aisle, then hold his hand out in front of him, gesturing for her to go before him. She obeyed, following her father, and feeling Henry standing close to her side.

"Are you alright?" he whispered.

She swallowed hard and nodded.

He furrowed his brow as they stopped while the people ahead of them allowed others into the line. "I don't believe you."

She glanced behind her, and he took notice. "I'm fine. Really," she said quietly. "Your hosts did not join you today?"

He shook his head. "No. Those members of my family are Lutheran."

She took a step as the line moved. "Lutheran? Then why are you here?"

He was looking down toward the floor, but she saw the corner of his mouth flick up. "To check up on an old friend," he told her.

She couldn't tell whether he meant her. It was possible he knew other people here as well, although he had made no indication that he knew the people he was sitting next to. "Oh Henry!" she cried out, suddenly remembering and grateful to change the subject. "I must thank you for your gift. I have had days now to find the words but I still cannot. Is it real? I mean, was it alive once?"

He was smiling now as big as she'd ever seen. "Indeed it is real, miss. The man from whom I purchased it said the name, but I could not repeat it if I tried. He said it comes from a land far south of the colonies. I'm surprised you are not familiar with it."

"I'm afraid I am not. I believe it to be newly discovered, therefor the books I have from so long ago will not be of any service."

"I see," he said with a nod. "I am so very happy you like it, my dear," he said as they passed through the doors finally.

"Darling, there you are," Arthur called up from the bottom of the steps where he stood with her parents. He outstretched his hand as though nothing out of the ordinary had happened earlier.

With a sigh, Katherine parted from Henry with only a smile and dutifully came to meet Arthur but did not take his hand. Instead she kept both hands clutched firmly to hold the shawl closed. She forced a smile onto her face and greeted people alongside her fiancé as they left the church, something she had done a few times before. Arthur spoke to everyone who approached, answered their questions. Katherine tried to keep up, to answer questions asked of her and her thoughts and opinions, but she realized her life had not allowed for much information on current affairs.

She was asked a question on General Washington, someone she had never heard of, and Arthur laughed. "Women have no place in politics!" he told the man who had asked the question. Perhaps he thought he was doing her a favour, since she had stood there quiet, or perhaps he was still very much under the influence of what he'd had to drink before. Either way Katherine was again humiliated by him.

"I should go find my brother," she told the men as they spoke, realizing her family was no longer with them, and more than glad to have an excuse to be free of Arthur's company.

She searched but couldn't find Edward or Lucy. She rounded the corner of the street to search among the coaches for the one belonging to her family, or for their driver but was still unsuccessful. She weaved through the crowd of people, some she didn't know at all, others she did know, but just barely. She asked a few of them if they had seen her brother, or even her parents, and most had shrugged or shaken their head as they'd said "no, miss." She searched for a while. Finally she came across a man she knew had gone to school with Edward, and he told her they had gotten into their coach and left. She blinked at him, stunned, unsure of what to do or say next.

She thanked him and turned around to return to the spot she had left Arthur, but he too had disappeared. She followed her first instinct and went into the church to see if he had gone back in, but only a few people remained, and Arthur wasn't one of them. And as she descended the steps again, she saw what she knew to be his elaborate carriage rolling away in the distance.

They had left her, all of them. Neither party knew she was still here, and presumably neither party would think to come looking for her, assuming she was with the other. She thought about renting a carriage but realized she had no money with her.

She had never been in this part of the city alone before. It was a bright day, and she could see everything that was happening around her, but she still felt frightened, and she wondered how much of her unease was still from her earlier encounter with Arthur. It would be a long walk home. Arthur's home was closer, but how could she be sure he had even gone there? Besides, she was already angry with the bastard even before he had left her here, and had no desire to see him again today, let alone be with him in the confines of his house or carriage.

Henry. Or rather, Henry's Aunt Jeanette. Katherine had some idea of where she lived, though not specific, and it would be the shortest distance, that is if she could find it at all. She sighed; it wasn't the best option, and yet somehow it was.

Henry would get her home safely— she knew that much. She began her walk, a quicker pace than the "ladylike stroll" her mother would have insisted she use.

The sun was hot, and she had told herself she couldn't bring her parasol as she needed her hands free to control the shawl. And now the shawl was warming her more than she could have possibly guessed. She quickly crossed the street to seek some shade from the buildings as she passed them. Time went by. She stopped briefly to pet a cat that had emerged from between two buildings. She rarely saw cats, and her fiancé most certainly would not let her touch a stray. She felt her first tinge of joy this day here with the animal as it pressed itself against her fingers and rolled over onto its back to allow her to scratch its belly. Then it darted back where it had come from, to chase something Katherine couldn't see. She turned and crossed a street. Then another. She trudged on, feeling exhausted, and so thirsty. After a while of walking her lower back and her underarms began to burn as they were being rubbed raw by this horrible dress. Expensive or not, she hoped she was bleeding beneath it so she would have the satisfaction of throwing it away.

She wished it were any day other than Sunday, as the shops and buildings wouldn't be closed up like this, and she could stop and ask for help, or even just for a drink. In the distance she could see a few people walking in the same direction. People passed her going the other way, but she was too timid to ask these strangers for help or directions. Two women and one man turned off the street far ahead of her revealing the back of one, tall man walking all alone. He had a light brown jacket slung over his shoulder, and from where she stood, he appeared to have no hair.

And then she felt it.

"Henry?" she whispered. She wasn't entirely convinced it was him, but she wouldn't know unless she got closer. She quickened her pace, but when she felt like she was gaining no ground she lifted her skirts and broke into a run.

"Henry!" she called out when she felt she was close enough for him to hear her.

The man turned, and Katherine thanked God, on this holy day. Henry moved his coat to his arm in front of him and quickly came in her direction.

She was panting hard when she finally stopped running and set her fists onto her hips to catch her breath.

"Katherine! What on earth are you doing here?" he called as he continued to come toward her.

She stood but couldn't form words over her breathing, and her mouth was too dry to have tried otherwise. He finally reached her and gave her a moment to compose herself. "My family... left me... Arthur..."

"Arthur what?" he interrupted, his face concerned.

"He left me... as well... I have no way... to get home," she told him.

"Why did they all leave you?"

She inhaled deeply to steady her breathing a bit more. "Edward thought I was with Arthur. Arthur thought I had gone to find Edward."

He sighed. "I see. And you walked all this way alone?" he asked, though his tone seemed somehow accusatory. "Where are you going?"

She hesitated. She wasn't sure how to say it, and the tone in his voice made her doubt her choice. "I... I came to find you." She suddenly felt like she could cry. "I thought... perhaps... if I found the house you are in... you might help me..."

His face softened. The darkness in his eyes disappeared

and a smile formed on his lips. "Of course. I would be happy to see you safely home, my lady."

Katherine sighed, relieved.

"It isn't much farther. Are you sure you're alright?"

"Yes. I am quite thirsty, but I'm certain I shall survive," she smiled.

He looked at her with an expression of amusement. "Do you require that shawl? I would assume that dress is heavy and hot enough without it."

She dropped her eyes. "Yes... well..."

He waited for her response but one never came, which caused him to give a nervous laugh. "What is it?"

"This dress... does not fit me as it should," she muttered.

"Then why are you wearing it?"

She was becoming exasperated with this topic. "I did not know about it, and by the time I realized and was ready to change it for another, it was time to leave."

"Oh. You've not worn it before?" he asked, beginning to walk again at her side. He watched her shake her head. "The dressmaker did not fit you properly then."

She grimaced somewhat. "I did not meet with the dressmaker."

He stopped and looked at her with even more confusion.

"Arthur acquired it for me. This one and a few others," she told him.

He flicked his eyebrows up and continued walking. "Ah. Well if you were not measured for them it makes sense that they would not fit you proper."

"I suppose..." she muttered and then she stopped walking, wondering if the dress was some inappropriate scheme by Arthur. He'd bought her dresses before without incident, but of the five he'd most recently given her this was the first she'd worn. She made a note to check the others when she arrived home.

He led her into the house and took her straight to the kitchen where she consumed two cups of water. The house was empty, as everyone else still appeared to be at their respective place of worship.

"We will have to wait for someone to return with a carriage before we can leave," he told her.

She nodded, understanding.

"We should go sit in the parlour," he suggested. "You're likely exhausted after our journey."

Katherine followed him and seated herself on the sofa, though her breath caught and she slowed her descent as she was hit with a searing pain from the shifting of fabric over her sore skin.

"Are you alright?" he asked, turning at the noise she had made.

She sat breathing for a moment and staring forward. *It's only Henry. Henry is a gentleman, and he'd do anything for you,* she thought as an argument erupted between her body and her brain. "Would you... umm..." She swallowed nervously.

"What?"

She couldn't look him in the eye, but she felt like she would die otherwise. "Would you be so kind as to... if I stood up that is... to... perhaps... loosen the laces in the back of my dress? I'm in and incredible amount of pain—." She hadn't even finished her sentence when he nodded and took her by the hand to help her back up. She turned and felt him wordlessly begin, moving up and down her back until she inhaled a deep breath.

"Better?" he asked quietly.

"Yes. Thank you." She shifted her torso around under the garment until it was loose and no longer touching every inch of her skin. She felt him tie the ends loosely and move away from her again. She expected him to sit in one of the other chairs, but then was hit with both dread and excitement when he took his seat at the other end of the same sofa.

You're engaged to Arthur, she reminded herself. Arthur, who had humiliated her and then left her alone outside the church after accosting her inside it. She puffed out a breath and gave her head a subtle shake to release her fury.

"How do you suggest we pass the time, Miss Katherine?" Henry asked, choosing to ignore what he had just seen.

She pursed her lips together and looked around, then grinned at him. "Is that a chess board?"

The question made him laugh. "Yes. It shall be like our youth." They stood again and moved toward the table.

She gave a nod. "Yes. Like our youth," she grinned, "only without you trying to woo me." She glanced up and smiled, then looked back down at her hands. *You're engaged to Arthur.*

"Oh, I wouldn't say *that* ..." he said as he held her eyes, causing her to laugh loudly. He quickly moved ahead to hold out the chair for her and waited patiently while she sat and carefully adjusted until she was comfortable.

"If I remember correctly," Henry stated as he took his own seat, "I won many a game against you." He raised an eyebrow in an exaggerated and playful challenge.

Katherine forced her lips into a pout to hide a grin. "If *I* remember correctly, I *allowed* you win many a game to protect your pride."

Henry narrowed his eyes. "You're lying."

One of Katherine's eyebrows flicked up; the rest of her face remained still. "Am I?"

Henry shook his head, accepting the challenge with a wave of his hand to signal her. "You first, Aunty Kate."

They played in absolute, stone-faced silence. Their eyes would move from one another to the board and back again. There were long pauses leading to well thought-out moves. In the end, Katherine was victorious.

"Check mate," she said calmly after the final move of her bishop.

"Hmmm," Henry stared down at the board, making sure she had indeed bested him. "Well, you let me win so many times before, I was simply returning the favour."

Her smile was wide and her mouth fell open in amused disbelief. "Then we shall have one more game!"

"As you wish, my lady," Henry patronized as he moved pieces back to their original places. Again he allowed her to make the first move, and after another long silent game, Henry took her queen and won.

"It seems we are tied, my lady," he grinned.

She glared at him.

"One more game then?" Henry asked. "Winner takes all."

"All of what?" she chuckled.

"The glory!" Henry announced, triggering her to laugh again.

They began moving the pieces back to their original spots. She shifted in her seat for a moment, trying to find a comfortable position. Henry allowed her once again to move first, and it seemed as though it would be silent again until Henry spoke.

"How did you come to meet Arthur?"

She was staring at the board before them, her fist pressed against her lips in concentration. She moved it down against her collar bone to speak. "My mother placed me before him," she shrugged. "Or rather, she placed *him* before *me*. She introduced us. He began visiting the house..." she trailed off and gave a wave of her fingers and moved them back against her lips, bored by her own story.

The wave opened her shawl, though she didn't notice.

"I understand now," Henry said to her, setting his hand on his own chest.

"Understand what?" she asked, not taking the hint.

"Your shawl..." he said, trying to give her the dignity of not looking at her bare chest.

She finally realized what he meant and wrapped the ends of the shawl around her shoulders. "Thank you," she said quietly. She stared at him, realizing how different he truly was from Arthur. Not just physically, which was obvious, but in every other way. Arthur was spoiled and entitled, Henry was humble and patient. Arthur had taken advantage of opportunities to touch her, opportunities that were growing more aggressive. Henry had been alone with her more times than she could remember and had never once made her feel uncomfortable, including this instance, where she found she was enjoying herself. Arthur made her feel desired yes, as most men did, but Henry made her feel respected, which aside from her father and brother, was something only he could do.

Chapter Eighteen

"Ah, my boy, there you are," William called, appearing at the bottom of the stairs later that week.

Edward and Katherine had been upstairs searching for young Henry's favourite toy and were surprised to see their father as they descended the stairs.

"We have been sent an invitation to another wedding celebration in three days. This invitation arrived for you at my house," he said as he extended his right hand out to Edward.

"Whose wedding?" Edward asked as he took the folded paper from his father.

"I believe it is a cousin of Henry Bullock," William said.

Edward quickly read the invitation. "Indeed."

Katherine also looked at the paper over his shoulder. "I've never heard of either of these people," she said.

"You would know them to see them," Edward informed her. "The bride is Henry's cousin. She is much younger than any of us. Just eighteen I believe."

Katherine nodded in response.

"Of course we will go as well, father. Henry is like family. How gracious of them to include us," Edward said with a smile. They turned and began a slow pace toward the door.

"I trust Henry will meet several of his own relatives and feel most welcome," William noted out loud and then he stopped before the front door and glanced up from the floor. "Fiona insists upon coming into town in the morning with me, to purchase some clothing for the affair. Apparently the old windbag doesn't own enough dresses..."

"I am surprised she plans on going at all," Edward told him. "This will be a far less proper affair than the ones she has become accustomed to of late."

"Yes, well," William began, "since your sister has promised Fiona would be no longer be welcome at such occasions, people have thus begun to treat her as though she were a leper. She has been searching for any reason to leave the house and prove that she does, indeed, belong in society." He winked at his daughter and disappeared through the door.

Katherine smiled at this. She had not witnessed any mistreatment of Fiona by Arthur or his companions, however she had made herself scarce in Fiona's company, and hearing that her wishes on the matter had come to fruition made her feel powerful. She remembered how she enjoyed feeling powerful. It was rare but invigorating.

She'd only mentioned her wishes regarding Fiona once in passing to Arthur, and it seemed that he had again run with the idea. She couldn't be certain what he had said or to whom he had said it, but it was apparently enough for Fiona and William to notice, and that was good enough for Katherine. She would make mention of it to Arthur the next time they spoke, and if he were back to his sober, tolerable self, she would thank him for his assistance on the matter. She felt she might push it farther, still feeling as though the exclusion of her father were unfair, and even suggest Arthur invite William alone in future.

Nonetheless she looked forward to the ball. She sent word to her fiancé of the event along with where it would be, asking that he escort her, and she received word the next day that he would be happy to join her there. She had seen it as an olive branch, letting him know she would like to move on from his indiscretion the previous Sunday. With that she expected him to appear in the days before the dance was to take place, but he never did. Katherine wondered if he was busily wrapping up certain duties before their wedding, or if perhaps there were no events taking place of late, such as the teas and suppers he had fallen over himself to take her to before.

Or maybe he's ashamed of his actions...

And then the day of the ball a notice was sent to her home telling her that he would not be able to join her that evening. No excuse was given. Arthur himself hadn't even written it, she realized. The footman stood and waited to see if she would send back a response, and she did. She told him she was saddened to hear of his absence, and that she hoped he was in good health. She added that she would come to his home and visit him the next day, since it had been nearly a week since they had seen one another. She even went as far as to add that she missed him.

The coach ride was quiet. When they arrived Edward and Lucy left the coach first, then seemingly from nowhere Henry Bullock appeared and extended his hand to assist Katherine out.

"You look lovely tonight, Aunty Kate," he smiled down at her.

She wasn't certain how to respond to the compliment, but only grinned at what he had again called her.

He didn't let go of her hand, choosing instead to move it into the crook of his elbow and lead her into the assembly hall. Deep down, she was grateful for this— she knew this would be another event Arthur wouldn't be attending and felt awkward once again showing up alone with only her parents and brother to keep her company. But here, walking with Henry, she was grateful to be on the arm of a man.

And also, within her vanity, she was grateful to be on the arm of one so handsome. And tall. And polite. Who smelled wonderful...

She took a deep breath to steady herself and stop from going to the places she had just gone. She was engaged to Arthur. *Perverted, balding, absent Arthur...*

Again she took a breath. It was the life she had chosen. A life she had chosen only a few months before Henry had come back. A few months. What if Henry had come back a few months sooner? Would she have still said yes to Arthur's proposal?

The way Henry had made her feel, within only a few minutes of sitting with her at the creek when he first had returned. She had been confused then by the way his words and his face and his lips had made her feel, but over time that confusion had cleared and she realized it was desire. Arthur's face had never caused that kind of stir within her, ever. Really, no other man had.

They had stopped and were waiting in a line to enter through the doors. She turned her head to look at those lips that had captivated her to see what was so different from other lips she had seen in her life. And he noticed, turning his head to see what she was looking at. She lifted her eyes to meet his and gave a weak smile, quickly turning away again so he wouldn't see her blush. But she could see from the corner of her eye that he was still looking at her.

She hated herself quietly for a moment. She'd spent the years after his supposed death disciplining herself to appear indifferent and uncaring and purposeful, but since his return she found herself returning to her old, awkward habits, her eyes giving way to her emotions, tripping over her words, blood rushing to her face. She turned back to him and tried to cover it up. “Are you excited?” she asked quietly. “To see your family, I mean.”

“Yes. However I will have to be introduced to figure out who they are. Many of them I haven’t seen since I was a boy, and I hardly remember them. Or even what they look like.” He waited while she lifted her skirt to ascend the steps to the door.

“Perhaps I can help,” she told him. “I do know many of the people who are going to be here, even though they probably don’t know who *I* am.”

He looked at her, puzzled. “Why wouldn’t they?”

She shrugged. “I do not speak much. Mother always told me to only speak when spoken to at events such as this, and rarely does anyone speak to me. And, since my engagement, Lord Thacker has done most of the talking.”

He grinned at her. “Well, they will likely know *of* you, if they know you are engaged to Thacker. But since your—*he* is absent, you have *my* full permission to speak freely here.”

He had corrected himself mid-sentence, whether intentionally or not. He was choosing not to refer to Arthur as her fiancé, perhaps because he still felt that title belonged to him. She gave a smirk and shook her head but chose to ignore it. “Your permission is not required.”

“You *should* learn to speak more if you are going to become royalty, after all.”

She licked her lips and pressed them together, letting a sigh out through her nose. “I suppose,” she whispered. She stared into the empty space in front of her and was startled out of her thoughts when he put his mouth close to her ear.

“Katherine,” he murmured, “perhaps, just for now, we

can forget about that."

She turned to meet his eyes.

"Thacker is not here. Your father and mother have gone ahead of us, and your brother has once again left you in my care. Perhaps, just for a few hours, you can be you. You can speak to whomever you choose about whatever you choose."

Again she was mesmerized by his lips as they moved, causing her stomach to flip. His face was only inches away; his eyes bore into hers and she could feel his breath on her chin. And then his eyes found her mouth as well, and she felt her lips part. She wanted to feel his lips, to taste them, she realized. She'd felt that urge so long ago...

The doors opened before them, snapping her back into reality. They stepped forward and were asked their names by the doorman, who allowed them to continue on once he had checked the list in front of him. She let him lead her around the room, through the crowd, looking into every face except each other's. After a long few minutes of silence, they reached the other end of the room.

She saw her parents in a far corner, realizing she had passed right by them and hadn't noticed. Suddenly she felt like that young girl again, here with Henry, not sure of what to say. "Do you see anyone you recognize?" she stammered.

He looked around and shook his head. "Do you?"

She nodded at him then cocked her head to the right. "The woman in the gold dress. If I'm not mistaken, she is the mother of the bride. That would make her your aunt, correct?"

He nodded. "Yes. My mother's sister Francis. I haven't seen her since I was a boy." He craned his neck and squinted. "You may be right. Her face is similar..."

"Beside her, the man with the glasses is her husband. I cannot see anyone else clearly, but it's a start," she told him, smiling and hopeful she had perhaps done something right for a change. "Would you like to go over there?"

He brought his eyes to meet hers again. "If you wish. Or perhaps later. I am in no hurry to leave my present company."

Katherine smiled but rolled her eyes. Part of her longed to feel the way she had felt moments ago, standing in the doorway, close enough to touch. But the notion also terrified her, especially here with people— and her mother— all in view. She watched people begin to leave the grand room for another, where the feast was to be served. They turned to follow the crowd. Again Henry held out his arm, and again she took it. She gripped it slightly tighter; she felt dizzy, drunk from the thoughts swirling in her head. Being here pressed up against him did nothing to quench the thirst she felt— if anything it made it worse, made her want to know what other parts of his body felt like.

"Katherine?"

She spun in the direction of the voice she had heard say her name.

"Sam! How lovely to see you!" she cried out through a wide smile. She held out her free hand and Samuel Milton gallantly brought it to his lips. She felt the muscles in Henry's arm tighten briefly around the fingers on her other hand, though she paid it no particular mind.

"I'm surprised to see you," he told her. "I was told Lord Thacker wouldn't be here," he said, glancing at Henry.

She wasn't sure if it was jealousy she saw in Samuel Milton's eyes, but something was amiss. Sam hadn't formally courted her, but Katherine knew he had fancied her, and that she was locked up within the confines of her house before he was given the chance to do so. Not that it mattered now. It had been a lifetime ago. She was spoken for since then. *Twice over,* she thought. "He isn't," Katherine beamed at him. "I haven't a clue where he is tonight, in fact. This is Henry Bullock, a cousin of the bride and Edward's dearest friend." She turned her body slightly. "Henry Bullock, this is Samuel Milton. Another old friend my family," she laughed. She watched as the men shook hands and exchanged pleasantries, getting lost again briefly in Henry's smile and voice. She thought of the time she had spent with Sam; she had felt giddy and girly as any lady would when in the presence of a young man, but she had never noticed his lips in such a way, or longed to be close to him the way she was just now with Henry. Perhaps Sam had been lazy in his attempts. Or perhaps Katherine had been a silly fool who didn't know what to do with the advances he may or may not have made.

Or maybe it was that Sam wasn't Henry. Maybe what Henry had said to her the other night was true, about this mysterious connection being present since their youth, and they'd always known they were meant for one another. But what did that say about her present situation?

After the men got to know one another, Samuel politely let them be on their way. Katherine glanced around and realized that, as Sam caught up to his party, she and Henry were the last left in this room.

Henry looked down at her and smirked.

"What?" she asked.

"For someone who doesn't speak, you handled those introductions splendidly," he told her, flexing his arm to squeeze her fingers in reassurance.

"Well, I have been introduced to people, and witnessed many an introduction— "

"Or perhaps you are doing as I said, and letting you be you," he interrupted her. "You should do it more often, my dear. You are quite charming when you're being genuine."

His smile remained but hers faded away as they approached the room, and she knew that she would once again have to let go of his arm.

There were four large tables, one in every corner of this room, and a long table running directly down the length of it, with the bride and groom seated at the head. A few steps in, they heard William bellowing from the other end of the room.

"Henry, my boy! Come! Come here!" he called out, waving his arm. He began speaking again before they had stopped walking. "Henry! This is your mother's sister Francis. And her husband Nathaniel."

Henry gave a nod. "Yes, of course. Your daughter was already set to introduce us, but it seems as though you were faster, William," he said with his usual charm.

Katherine dropped her hand from his arm as Francis approached him for an embrace. When they pulled back Francis had tears in her eyes and Henry studied her face wistfully. They spoke of Henry's late mother, and Francis commented on how tall and handsome Henry had grown to be. Katherine suddenly felt out of place and though she wanted nothing more than to touch him again, she took a step back from the small crowd to observe like she usually did.

"William tells me you are currently staying with your father's sister Jeanette?" Francis asked him.

"Yes, they have been the most gracious of hosts," he replied.

Nathaniel spoke up. "I would expect nothing less. Did they come with you this evening?"

Henry shook his head. "They did not, as they had a prior engagement. However their governess did arrive with me, and they thank you kindly for the invitation."

Francis took his arm and turned him, leading him away

to where the bride and groom were seated. Henry glanced back to her, and Katherine took two steps to follow when she heard her mother's voice.

"Katherine!" She started in her usual snappy tone, but quickly corrected herself. "My dear daughter, Edward and Lucy are seated here with us," Fiona pointed. "Sit."

Katherine, doing all she could not to laugh smugly at Fiona's forced tolerance, instead took a breath and compelled her body to achieve her ice-queen posture as she sat and avoided her mother's eyes. Henry did join them eventually at their table, sitting beside Edward, three seats down from a now silent Katherine. It was now her own choice to not speak until she was spoken to, but she also had no words to say at the moment. She watched Henry, Edward, and Lucy converse with the people across from them, and they all seemed to be fascinated by a tiny, attractive French woman with a thick accent. Nicolette was her name, and the way she looked up at Henry from under her eyelashes made Katherine's blood boil.

Nicolette spoke quietly, but from what Katherine could gather by the responses the others gave, she was the governess Henry had mentioned earlier. Katherine slumped back in her chair, uneasy with the turn the night had taken. Henry was staying in the same house as this woman. It was no wonder she hadn't seen him in days.

Katherine's posture and expression caught Lucy's attention. "Are you alright?" she asked, which caused other heads to turn, including Nicolette and Henry.

"Yes, I'll be fine," Katherine muttered quietly.

"Are you certain?" Lucy inquired.

"Yes," Katherine lied. She sat up and kept to herself, picking at the food before her until the tables started to clear and everyone returned to the main hall for the dancing and celebrations. Nicolette came around to Henry and said something inaudible. Katherine looked away at that point, and together they left the table before she had turned back. Edward and Lucy left the table. William and Fiona left the table. Soon Katherine was the only one left in the room, other than the staff that were cleaning up after they had closed the grand doors between the two rooms.

It doesn't matter what he does, she told herself, *you are engaged. You are engaged to Arthur.* She repeated this affirmation to herself, Fiona's voice running the words through her head, as though it would help strengthen her will or take away her disappointment or at least force her to temporarily become the haughty woman she'd been striving to be for years. All it did was make her want to hang herself with the table linens. A maid came and asked if she was through with her plate and silverware. She nodded and took it as a signal that it was time to join the rest. She crossed the room and was about to round the corner when one of the doors opened again.

"There you are!" Henry said, his brow furrowed and his eyes concerned as he strode toward her. "What happened to you?"

Katherine was confused. "Nothing," she shook her head. "I just... wasn't feeling... well... and decided to sit for a moment longer."

He set his fingers under her chin and lifted it to look into her eyes. "Will you be alright?"

She pulled her face away from his touch and nodded. *I am engaged to Arthur.*

"Come," he said, again holding his elbow out for her to take.

She didn't. Instead she swept past him.

"Katherine," he said, catching up to her, "what's the

matter?"

"Nothing!" she said firmly.

He stepped quickly ahead of her to pull the door shut before she could leave through it. "Tell me what's wrong," he said, keeping his tone even.

"Nothing is wrong!" she cried out, loudly, irritated, unable to meet his eyes.

"Something is! Something is wrong! Did someone harm you? Or offend you in some w—."

"I am engaged!" she shouted directly into his face. It stopped him. It stopped her. It stopped the servants in their tracks. The only sound was the heaving of her breath. His face told her that he didn't understand what her engagement had to do with anything.

She swallowed hard. "Excuse me," she said quietly, and again she made a move to pass him.

This time, he had no choice but to let her.

***

Henry asked her for a dance. He'd seen Samuel Milton had asked her for a dance. Even Edward tried, but she had told them all no firmly. She sat alone. She stood near her father. Once in a while she would look around, meet Henry's eyes, and then avert them quickly.

Why had she screamed at him? Was she upset with him? He had barely seen her for days. When she emerged this evening, she looked lovely and well rested and her tone toward him had softened. He could have sworn they'd had a very intimate moment earlier in the evening; a moment that squeezed his insides and nearly made his head spin.

Or perhaps she was far more upset with her fiancé's absence than she had earlier let on.

She couldn't really have feelings for the pompous ass, could she?

He saw her standing close to a different group of people, but still near her parents, and approached them.

"On-ree!"

He had come to know the sound he had just heard as Nicolette's heavy accent saying his name, and he lifted his head to see her emerge from the crowd and put herself in front of him.

"Nicolette," he greeted her as he joined the others.

"Madame Francis says you are extending your stay and shall continue to live with us! Such happy news!"

He smiled. "Yes, I would like to spend more time with my family and close friends."

"Yes!" Nathaniel agreed loudly. "There are people to meet! Cousins! My wife will take you to see her brother as well. No time to waste boy!" He slapped Henry on the back, hard enough to sting through his jacket.

"Yes, Henry," William added, also intoxicated, "You should go, son! Be with your loved ones! And we will still see each other here and there before your return to Bedford, I have no doubt!"

"Very well, then," Henry said with a nod of agreement to a decision that had been made for him. Whether or not it came to pass in the sober light of day had yet to be seen. Still, he didn't like the feeling of having no control. It must be how Katherine felt all the time...

He turned his head, and once again found her eyes. They were sad, but also hard from whatever it was that had happened tonight. This time she met his for a longer duration, as though she were trying to tell him something, and then she blinked and they slowly moved away from him, lowering down to the ground in front of her.

He moved to her side. "May I speak with you? Alone?" he asked in a low voice.

She raised her eyes, but not enough to look at him. "No, sir. I am an engaged woman you and are a bachelor. It wouldn't be appropriate for us to be alone."

He sighed in frustration but would no longer press the issue. He left her alone for the rest of the night, until he was ready to leave and approached her party to say goodnight.

She was standing close; he could reach over and touch her if he dared. He could find no words to remedy the situation, and even if he could, his mouth and throat were dry with nerves.

Katherine nodded in response to his parting words to them all. "Enjoy the rest of your stay in London, Mr. Bullock," she said, her tone firm and flat, then she turned to fade away into the crowd to continue in her misery.

She had said her goodbye, he realized. She felt as though she wouldn't see him again. She didn't *want* to see him again. She was sad, perhaps, and definitely angry about something, but she held it all back to be the lady she was raised to be and still part on pleasant terms.

He reconsidered leaving the party, but he worried staying would only make things worse. And he had made promises to people who *weren't* angry with him. No, he would leave then as planned with Nicolette, but decided he would see Katherine again.

Very soon.

Chapter Nineteen

She'd planned to keep the promise as she'd written it, and ride to see Arthur; however he surprised her by arriving at the house late in the morning instead.

"Darling!" he said, coming toward her to embrace her lightly. "You look lovely today."

"Thank you," she said with a small nod of her head, happy to see he was acting more like himself and had kept his embrace of her brief and entirely appropriate.

It was another cool, overcast day, and he told her he'd been invited for tea with Their Majesties, and that she should dress and join him. She found the request a bit peculiar, as he had just told her she looked lovely. Nevertheless she did as she was instructed, though she avoided putting on any of the newer dresses he had bought for her, having not yet checked the fit and feel of them. She also had no desire to revisit the past, worried a conversation could start regarding the dress she'd worn the previous Sunday, and the fate of that dress, which she had indeed happily gotten rid of.

He told her on the ride that the queen would be giving a tour of her house to show her guests the works of art she and the king had recently acquired. Katherine smiled at this, happy he had thought of her, and beamed even more-so when he told her it would be the perfect opportunity to speak of Katherine's own talent to Her Majesty.

He helped her down from the carriage and held out his elbow for her. She took it, though her fingers felt odd and fuzzy somehow, and she had the urge to wash them immediately. Still, she held her composure and looked over to his face, inspecting it the way she had Henry's, looking to see if any part of Arthur stirred her in the same way.

He sat them on a bench in the courtyard and began a conversation with the people beside them while they waited.

Andrew and Jane, Katherine recited to herself, unable to remember their last name. They looked to be around Arthur's age. Katherine remembered that Jane had been a chambermaid to the queen before marrying her husband, a high-ranking officer in the king's navy. She couldn't recall his rank, however, and Arthur was no help, only referring to him by his first name.

"My lord," said Andrew, "I've been hearing of the good work you've done for His Majesty. There are whispers he may go so far as to make you duke."

Arthur laughed it off with a wave. "Well thank you, that's very kind. My work has indeed been steady of late, and I do so regret when I must take my leave and be away from my beloved for so long. I am, however, happy and humble in the knowledge that I can serve my cousin well and remain in his good graces."

This was a safe answer, Katherine thought, even perhaps humble, which was something Arthur never was. It pleased her.

"Better than good if he makes you a duke I should say!" Andrew agreed.

"Well you know I would never press His Majesty for

something like that for myself," Arthur said, gesturing toward the palace where the king was. "I will say, however, that young Katherine here would make a charming duchess. Wouldn't you agree?" He had set his hand on both of hers as they were folded in her lap.

Katherine smiled as the rest of them continued to cackle, but nearly all of her energy was going in to keeping away the shudder she felt building within her at his touch.

They were soon called in by a servant. Inside the drawing room it was warm and stifling, and Katherine found herself feeling even more claustrophobic sitting between Arthur and Jane as they spoke around her about a ship her husband had once been on that had recently been lost at sea. Katherine sat silent as Arthur all but ignored her, continuing to give his attention instead to other men and women of stature throughout teatime.

She hadn't realized it before, but she did come from a jovial family. Fiona excluded, Edward and Lucy, William and the boys were always smiling, laughing, joking at one another's expense. Even serious conversations had an air of humour about them. And while here there were several smiles and a few low chuckles, Katherine was hard pressed to find anything to actually laugh at. She inhaled and exhaled bitterly when an older gentleman— Duke Something of Somewhere— made the room wait for a punchline that got a few exaggerated guffaws and giggles, but Katherine didn't understand. Other jokes, it seemed, were at the expense of people the crowd seemed to think were below them, some American, some poor. She took a few long sips of tea so no one would see her lack of reaction.

Katherine didn't realize they were done until suddenly everyone stood and waited for the room to empty.

"Come, Miss Whyte," Arthur ordered, following the rest of the very important people.

She did as she was told, giving a pressed smile as she passed others along the way. They wandered through several rooms that displayed the queen's vast art collection. This was something Katherine was sure she would be interested in, as Arthur had raved about it, but she found that it brought her no joy. There was nothing in particular that caught her attention or that she truly admired. She couldn't follow along and paid more attention to the people around her and the room decor than she did to the works, trying to gauge how her own reactions should be by the rest of the people around her. She nodded when she saw them nod or followed suit if eyebrows were raised or a giggle rolled through the group. She'd never before paid attention to brush strokes or the use of this or the absence of that. She had always just painted what interested her for the sake of having it to fondly remember one day, or she had been drawn to a piece because of its subject or colours.

And though she waited and waited for Arthur to introduce her as a painter like he'd promised, he never did. And it wasn't for a lack of talking on his part. After the queen, it was Arthur who did the most speaking, regaling the crowd with his knowledge of her collection, and Katherine was quick to realize he was simply repeating, nearly word-for-word, the points he had already made to her in private. And though the rest of the guests, including Her Majesty, found his knowledge on the subject fascinating, Katherine was ready to jump from the nearest window with boredom. She was thoroughly disappointed with the entire afternoon, though she would never let him know.

They arrived back at her home just as her family was finishing supper, and she was stunned to see that not only were her parents at the table, but so was Henry Bullock. A flood of thoughts ran through her, but mostly she was hit with a wave of shock, having not been prepared to see him here, or ever again. She inhaled deeply and exhaled hoping no one would notice the colour running from her brain to her cheeks and making her dizzy.

Arthur greeted her parents, as well as Edward and Lucy all by name. “But I’ve forgotten your name, sir.”

“That’s quite alright,” Henry told him. “I’ve forgotten yours as well.”

Katherine pressed her lips together and bit down hard on them to keep from smiling. It didn’t help in the least that Edward met her eyes and was also doing a terrible job of hiding a smirk at Arthur’s expense. This, she thought, was the most interesting and entertaining thing to happen all day.

Arthur held out his hand. “Lord Arthur Thacker.”

“Oh yes, of course,” Henry said, waving his own hand dismissively instead of shaking Arthur’s. “The cousin of the king!”

She bit down harder on her lips and had to look away to the door, up to the ceiling, anything to take her mind off this spectacle while avoiding the eyes of one Edward Whyte.

“Katherine, dear,” Henry moved on, “you look well today.”

“Thank you,” she said through a pursed smile.

“She looks well every day,” Arthur corrected him.

“You know what Mister Thacker? On that I will have to agree with you,” Henry practically sang.

“*Lord* Thacker,” Arthur corrected him grimly. “Have you forgotten your manners as well as my name?”

“Yes,” Henry stared him down. “I believe I left them in America.” He paused there to inhale. “Now if you will excuse me,” he said, as he stood. “Thank you, my dear friends, for the lovely meal, but it would appear it is time for me to take my leave.” He gave a low, exaggerated bow, and left the room.

She'd been holding her breath, she realized, as the tension had grown. She looked at her family, who also displayed looks of shock and worry upon their faces. Edward and Lucy left to follow Henry to bid him a proper farewell. William and Fiona stayed to continue their conversation with Arthur, who had now taken a seat at the table.

Less than twenty-four hours prior she had hoped she would never have to see him again, even making a vow to herself, steadfast in her determination to marry Arthur, however the look she had just seen in Henry's eyes was suddenly embedded in her brain. She had been upset with him the night before and traces of that anger had continued to burn through her to this moment, but she hadn't thought until now to ask herself why. And she could come up with no answer except that she was perhaps jealous of the French girl — single and pretty and currently spending more time with Henry than she was. She also reflected on the fact that she hadn't been shouting at Henry to remind him that she was engaged, but to remind herself, as she had been doing all night. No, her frustration hadn't been with him, but with herself. The confusion and miscommunication between her head and her heart were driving her to madness.

She excused herself quietly— though she wasn't entirely certain they had heard or would care— and left the room for the front door. Edward was closing it as she approached, and she passed without a word to open it again and hurry down the steps to catch Henry just as he was stepping up into the carriage. Upon realizing she was there he stepped back down and turned to her.

"I should apologize for Arthur—. "

"No," he shook his head. "You must never apologize to me or anyone else for Arthur's words or actions, Katherine. It is him who is the buffoon, my dear, not you."

His words were soft and she felt them roll around her

like fine silk. "You looked so angry."

"I was. I am." He shook his head and cleared his throat. "Katherine, I could never be angry with you. Thacker is..." Again he shook away the thoughts in his mind, another flash of anger racing through his eyes.

Deep down Katherine was glad he was angry, hoping it was a shred of what she had experienced the night before, but still she felt the need to excuse Arthur's behaviour. "He has a lot of pride."

Henry snorted out a laugh of derision. "He has many, many things. None of which I envy." He paused and stared into her soul. "Except for one." He took a step back and gave another deep bow, then turned and glided into the coach again, closing the door before she had a chance to respond.

Katherine didn't understand what had just happened. The bow he'd made was again low and dramatic, and she felt as though he had meant to offend her by doing it. He hadn't even stayed long enough for her to apologize for her own actions the night before, which she'd had every intention of doing after bringing up Arthur. She returned to her family, dejected. The feeling of disappointment followed her into the night, into her dreams. The eyes that she had never seen be anything but kind and caring had been enraged and sad, and they haunted her every thought.

After that day, her routine with Arthur became its own version of normal again. She was convinced now that he had indeed been embarrassed by his drunken actions and had avoided her until it had blown over. Though to this day she still felt an apology would have been warranted, even expected, fiancé or not. Whatever the reason she was glad it was over and they could continue on as before, taking her mind off of Henry Bullock and his lovely, exotic new housemate.

She followed Arthur around on mundane business

excursions, allowing him to introduce her as his *beautiful* fiancé to whomever they would come across. Now and then they would plan or pay for something for their wedding. Church came again on Sunday and Katherine sat with him in the same pew as the king and queen, and as she left she caught a glimpse of her mother, whom she had never seen beaming with such pride until that very moment, watching Katherine walk with her soon to be husband and other members of the royal family.

And Katherine found it unsettling. She had spent her adolescence being scolded and mistreated by Fiona. She had spent her adult life hating Fiona and her opinions. She had spent the past few months avoiding Fiona and punishing her for what she had done to Rupert and Eleanor and Henry. Now to be exactly where Fiona wanted her, doing exactly what Fiona wanted her to do, seemed like the most grand betrayal—to herself and Rupert and Eleanor and Henry and William and Edward and everyone else Fiona had abused throughout her wretched life.

Chapter Twenty

Katherine had forgotten that Arthur had another long journey to make before their wedding, and she assumed he would warn her ahead of time; however he sent word one morning that he would be leaving town again that very day. She couldn't understand why he had not told her sooner, though maybe he had and she hadn't been paying attention. They had seen each other the day before, and though it was as boring a time as was to be expected, she hadn't sensed anything was amiss. He also sent her a necklace and asked that she wear it to church the Sunday he returned— the last Sunday before they were married. It was cold and thick and ornate; whether the weight of the necklace itself or perhaps the symbolism, Katherine felt as though it were choking her when she tried it on. She stared at herself in the mirror, blankly inspecting the heavy gold and ruby noose around her neck. She realized how low it hung, and it occurred to her she had never found the time to inspect the other dresses he had given her.

She found them and laid them on her bed. They all seemed to have a similarly low neckline to the one she'd worn when he'd attacked her at church. *Perhaps it was the dressmaker,* she thought. But then why would Arthur send her this necklace? *Unless he knew...* The anger she'd had from his abrupt departure flared into rage, and when she looked into the mirror to see the atrocious necklace again, she also saw darkness in her eyes, something she had witnessed in her mother. As she looked at the necklace, she set her hand on it, and noticed again the ring she'd yet to take off.

She missed him, she realized. She missed Henry's eyes, even though they still followed her in her mind. She missed his voice, the charming curl of his lip when he found something amusing. She had hardly seen him in the weeks since the ball. The despair crept through her suddenly and she felt as though she would die— that the ache within her belly would spread to her limbs and her head and her heart and she would simply implode.

She didn't lift her eyes, but she clawed at the necklace until it crashed onto the table in front of her. Her hands were shaking, her heart was pounding, her breath was short and shallow. She stood up and swept out the door, down the stairs and rushed out to the street. She paid a carriage to take her to her parents' home, though she had no desire to enter the house. She picked up her skirts and ran to the trees, remembering a time long ago when she had felt like this: suffocated, scrambling for freedom. She stumbled through the trees to the cool openness and stopped to catch her breath. Perhaps history would repeat itself, she hoped. Perhaps Henry would sense it and come to find her here again. He had to know she was sorry for all that had happened— she had said it right to him. Or rather, she'd tried to.

She lay in the grass, in their spot, closed her eyes and waited. She prayed to God. She prayed to Henry. She thought of his touch and the warmth of him against her and felt a tear roll from one eye down to her ear.

No one came. Insects buzzed past her. Something crawled onto her hand and then off. Time passed. The sun moved across the sky. The stream trickled slowly on its perpetual course. But no one came.

She had thoughts, she had dreams. Some of Henry, passionate and emotional. Some of her mother, angry and violent. Though she hadn't planned on falling asleep, the daydreams turned to actual dreams, the comfort of the past lulling her. She felt someone's warmth press against her back and somehow knew it was Henry but suddenly he wasn't there anymore. She knew she had to do anything and everything to prove herself to him.

She dreamed of throwing the necklace she had just received back at Arthur and slamming the door on him. She saw herself wrap her hands around Fiona's throat and squeeze until the woman stopped struggling. Fiona's eyes were closed and Katherine let her limp body fall. She ran through a house she didn't know to find Henry. *No, the palace* she realized in her dream, with its lavish looking décor and paintings for miles. Even though she was indoors, somehow it was raining. She wanted to tell him her feelings, that Fiona and Arthur were gone now, and if he wanted her, she would follow him anywhere. She found him in a grand ballroom, somewhere in a crowd of faceless people. She shouted but her words were lost in the noise of the people and the rain. She pushed through to get to him but gained no ground. Then she watched him take Nicolette by the hand, and she stopped. Suddenly she felt as though she would die, freeze to death. She began shivering, knowing within her, that he loved Nicolette and she had just murdered her own mother for nothing.

Katherine's eyes flew open, and then she slammed them shut again. The rain she had felt in her dream had been actual rain. The cold she had felt was real, the shivering in the dream was real. She struggled to sit up against the tremors and the numbness she felt in her limbs. She stood but fell down from the absence of feeling in her feet. She didn't know how long she had been asleep for, or how long it had been raining, but the ground seemed well saturated. She finally stumbled to her feet, managing after several attempts to find her way into the bit of shelter the trees provided. She leaned against one of them for a long time, panting from the effort, watching her breath disappear in the chilled air, until she felt steady enough to continue on to the house.

She found Peter and demanded through chattering teeth to be taken back to town.

Katherine could do nothing but sob throughout the ride home. She was weak and exhausted. A terrified Rosemary helped her to the stairs, up the stairs, into her room. Rosemary stripped her down and dried her off and dressed her. She started a fire in Katherine's hearth and moved her to sit in a chair in front of it. Katherine had cried herself dry by then. Rosemary excused herself and then returned with a tray of food a while later, before leaving again.

Katherine didn't eat the food she was brought. Once the shivering stopped and she could feel her toes again, she stumbled to her bed and was asleep almost instantly.

She awoke when Rosemary returned in the morning to check on her. Katherine couldn't breathe through her nose; her throat was dry and sore, and her head pounded with every beat of her heart.

"I knew you would catch your death!" the woman scolded her, shaking her head in dismay.

Katherine tried to speak, but found herself doubled over, coughing until she couldn't anymore. Rosemary made her drink water, which did help the dryness in her throat, but didn't do much else.

"Eat. I'll come back," Rosemary said setting a new tray on the bed beside Katherine.

Katherine did as she was told, forgetting about Henry and Arthur and Fiona and her own despair. The only thing she could feel was the pain that started at the top of her head, peaked in her throat, and resonated down into her chest. Every swallow of the dry bread was excruciating.

Edward and Lucy came to check on her, having been told of her condition by Rosemary, and passed the news on to William. He'd always been the more caring parent, doubly so when the children had been ill. He would always travel into town and come home with a trinket or toy or in Katherine's case, a book, his way of showing his love. And that seemed to continue into their adulthood as now he traveled into town simply to check on Katherine.

Fiona made no appearance at her bedside, which Katherine was grateful for. Her mother had never been sympathetic, even when they were ill, and Katherine currently wasn't in any mood for that. Though her mother had been joyful when she had last seen her, Katherine also felt guilty for the dream she'd had. She remembered the relief she'd felt wash over her in the dream when she realized Fiona was dead, and were Fiona to show up and be upset at Katherine for being sick in the first place, that guilt would disappear instantly, she knew.

Katherine woke up Thursday fevered, and Rosemary made her drink a rum concoction, several times throughout the day. She forced Katherine to drink water and stripped the shivering mess of a girl down to cool off, applying cold, wet cloths to her head and body and redressing her at some point. Some time in her fevered thrashing she vaguely recalled her brother coming in to see her but had no sense of time, or if it had even really happened, since she had also believed it had actually been Eleanor who had shown up to care for her at some point. Friday afternoon her fever finally broke, though she still ached and found it hard to breathe. In the evening she was able to eat again, and once she was finished, Rosemary held out a folded and sealed note to her.

"This arrived for you."

Katherine took it, and flipped it over a few times, not knowing what it was or why she should have it. She fumbled but managed to pull it open. She looked at the familiar writing and forgot she was ill.

Katherine,

My good friend Edward told me you have fallen ill. I will be praying for your full and quick recovery and I hope I shall see you at church again Sunday.

Your favourite person,

Henry.

She knew he meant it in jest, but she also knew deep down that he actually *was* her favourite person. And this meant he was no longer upset with her.

Sunday. She must improve by Sunday, if for no other reason than to be in his presence. She had no strength in her to be vigilant in her restraint. No, now she was guided by instinct. She wanted to feel better. He would make her feel better. She walked around her room and stretched her sore muscles. She brushed her hair and pinched her cheeks to bring the blood back up to her face. She drank water, and tea, and more water. She went down for breakfast Saturday, though she still ate very little. Rosemary told her that the sun would help, so Katherine sat in the garden and let it burn into her for as long as she could stand it. She could breathe through her nose again, though just barely. Headaches came and went. It began to rain again while she ate supper with the family Saturday night. She wore two nightgowns to bed and stoked the fire high to be sure she would be warm enough throughout the night and when Sunday morning came, she felt no different from the day before, but she readied herself for church anyway.

Edward's mouth gaped open when he saw her descend the stairs. "Good God girl! What are you wearing?"

Katherine stared at him. "A dress. It is Sunday."

"Absolutely not!" her brother cried out, concerned. "You've been ill for days and you still look a fright, Katherine. You will *not* pass your plague on to half of London," he said, more gently now, placing his hands on her shoulders. "Stay home again today and rest, sister."

"It is true, Katherine. You are still unwell," Lucy added meekly from behind him. "We'll give everyone your best and let them know you are nearly recovered." She smiled, trying to comfort her but knowing it was of little use. They picked up the boys and walked out the door without another word.

Katherine stood in the silence of the house, breathing through her mouth. She took a step back, and then another, feeling the stairs behind her. She sat, wrapping her shall tighter around her shoulders, holding it firmly against the base of her throat. The way Edward had looked at her, spoke to her on the way out, she didn't like it, not one bit. She stood and began her climb back to her room, to once again do as she was told.

It's only Edward, she reminded herself. It wasn't like it was Arthur or Fiona barking orders at her. *And Lucy agreed with him. It's only because they care.*

She often felt alone, but it was a rare occasion in her new life that she was *truly* alone these days, with no children or servants in the house, no teas and dinners and Arthur and conversation. She'd just spent days alone in her room, now she would spend hours alone in the house. She had spent most of her life cooped up in solitude, but in the years living with Edward and Lucy it occurred to her she may have forgotten how to enjoy her own company. She chose to again sit in the sunlight as Rosemary had instructed and read a novel her father had brought her that she had never touched, but she couldn't focus. Though her eyes followed along with the words before them, the thoughts in her mind were far more powerful.

Her brother this morning. Her mother and the dream she'd had. And Henry— always Henry. She'd been waiting for this day just to catch a glimpse of his lovely face. Now she would have to wait another week— if he even chose to attend a week from now. After restarting the same paragraph five times she shook her head and closed the book, deciding it was time to go back inside. In the study, she tossed the book onto the sofa and gathered up one of her needlepoint projects. She thought about how much she actually hated needle work, and how it had been months since she had picked up a paintbrush. Hunger brought her to the kitchen; boredom brought her back to the study. She picked up the book again, determined to pay attention this time.

Down the hall, she heard the door creak open and someone enter the house. She heard boots and the gait of a man, and since Edward gave the servants Sunday mornings off, she believed it to be Edward.

Her hoarse throat would not allow her to call out. She simply sat as she was, looking down at her book, waiting for whoever it was to find her, when she felt a flicker. Katherine's eyes widened and her head shot up at this— it wasn't Edward.

"There you are!"

"Mr. Bullock," she croaked, standing quickly, allowing the book to fall from her lap to the floor, then doing her best to stand still as the rush of blood dizzied her.

Henry laughed loudly. "Such formality!" he said as he approached. "You really must be ill." He stepped forward and took both her hands. "How are you feeling?" he asked softly.

She cleared her throat, then inhaled to do it again, and watched him smile with slight amusement at her helplessness. "Never better," she whispered.

He chuckled.

"What are you doing here?" she whispered.

"I did tell you I would see you Sunday, did I not?" he gave her a wink. "I thought it unfair that they left you alone even though you haven't fully recovered."

Katherine looked down and nodded, taking her seat again. She reached for her book and set it in her lap, but still wouldn't lift her eyes.

Henry sat on the chair across from the sofa. "Well you do seem much better than when last I saw you. Dreadfully pale, sopping wet, shaking like a leaf in the wind."

Katherine looked up at him stunned. "You were here?"

He nodded. "I brought the note myself. They let me see you briefly. They thought it... might help you, in some way."

She shook her head. "I do not remember you being there."

"I believe that. The things that found their way out of your mouth made no sense. What I could understand anyway. So much of it was whispered or hoarse."

She turned her eyes and her head away from him, praying for the blood to stay away from her cheeks. "I still don't recall any of it."

He glanced away. "When your brother told me, he was quite worried. Genuinely. I could see it in him. It terrified him, which terrified me. Then to see you. It was all I could do to..." His voice caught and he cleared his throat. "No matter," Henry concluded. "You survived. Praise God on this holiest of days!" He grinned at his own silly dramatic flair. It reminded her of why he and Edward were indeed such good friends, why he fell into their family so effortlessly.

Katherine smiled at him, truly appreciating his effort to make her feel better. She cleared her throat. "Henry, I want to apologize for my behaviour at your cousin's wedding. I haven't been… myself of late." She didn't know what else to say, but at least she had said this much.

"I'm aware," was his only response, his only acknowledgement, before moving on. "Now," Henry announced as he stood again and began walking to the door, "I shall make us some tea. You, shuffle the deck," he said, giving a nod to the table behind her.

They played a few rounds before he got up again and returned shortly after with their tea. The hours passed without a single care. The laughter was constant among them, and Katherine could not believe how lovely a time she was having. Nor could she believe how easy it was to do so. Somehow it was different than when they had recently played chess, which had been a quiet and serious time. She could speak freely here alone with him. She could laugh loudly and put her elbows on the table. It was quite possibly the best time she'd had… ever. She was happy here.

And the thought made her miserable. This could very well be the last time she felt such joy and comfort, she realized.

And of course, the moment the smile fell from her face, Henry Bullock's piercing eyes took note of it.

"Are you alright?"

Katherine nodded. "I am." She smiled, but as she did it, she realized it wasn't even a real smile. It was a flicker of the corner of her mouth, like she had seen him do so many times.

"He seems older than I would have anticipated." Henry said quietly, looking down to his hands and thinking this a good, safe way to open the conversation to see how defensive Katherine would actually get.

She turned her head from the window and raised her eyebrows slightly, acknowledging his comment as though she had almost forgotten he was there. "So you noted," she said, reminding him of his first meeting with Arthur. But then she nodded in agreement. "Yes. He is nearing forty years soon."

Henry nodded. "Well I suppose that is alright. He must be ready then to lessen his workload and raise a family."

She smiled meekly. "I do not believe there will be a family with him, Henry."

He raised his own eyebrows in surprise. "Do you no longer want children?"

She looked thoughtful for a moment. "I do not believe Arthur *does,* in fact, want to stay close to home. And I would rather not raise children on my own. Or have them raised by nannies and servants."

"He is a baron. A lord. He must create an heir, Katherine." He stared at her, and she stared back at him, her face not changing whatsoever. "So you would rather be in that, presumably large home, alone for the rest of your life?"

She smiled again, grateful for his concern. "Look around Henry," she chuckled. "I am quite accustomed to it."

He swallowed hard. This time it was Henry who looked into the air before him, unable to find the words, any words.

"Are *you* alright, Mr. Bullock?"

He shook his head slightly. "This is no way to live, Katherine. You've spent your life being abused and ignored and you're condemning yourself to it for the rest of your life."

Her face set as she'd practiced for years and she breathed in deeply to calm the blood rushing through her. She inhaled to speak, but abruptly shut her mouth when she heard the front door open down the hall and the children enter the house. And then the ambient sounds they made were pierced by a shrill sound Katherine had never experienced before.

"On-reeee!"

It was paired with the clicking of heels and the swishing of fabric that seemed to be coming closer. Katherine watched as Henry grinned and shook his head, then he pushed his chair back and stood.

"I was invited by your friend, Edward Whyte, as he thought you would be here," Nicolette said as she swept into the room, soon followed by Edward and Lucy with the boys. Immediately she began babbling about the house to them, going on about the room they were in and asking for a tour of the rest.

Katherine had chosen to remain seated. She noticed that Nicolette had placed herself beside Henry and had slithered both hands around his arm. She stared at them in awe of the ease of it all. This woman oozed sensuality; she needn't try, she just was. She also felt another surge of jealousy, and thus began another argument in her head, so when Nicolette and Henry turned to her for a response to whatever it was they had said to or about her, she had none. It felt like this was one of those moments when someone should speak for her, but no one was there to do so, and she felt like a fool.

"Is she mute?" Nicolette asked Henry.

"No. I think she may be exhausted from our day and the games. She is still recovering from a near deadly fever." He moved and knelt down in front of Katherine. "Are you alright?" he asked, looking up at her with concern.

She took a deep breath. "Yes. I think you may be right. I am exhausted."

"Indeed," he said with a nod before standing.

"Good then," Nicolette said, turning back to Edward and Lucy, and in the same movement slipping her arm into Henry's. "You should now show me the rest of your charming home!"

Katherine chose not to follow, knowing all there really was to know about the house, and not wanting to witness anymore of the spectacle that was Nicolette. Instead she quietly snuck away to her room to contemplate on her bed. Her mind shot quickly to the dream she'd had before she'd become ill, and were she not sitting she felt as though her knees would give way.

She had missed him so before this day. He had kept his promise to see her this day. He told her he had come to see her when she was at death's door. She'd had a wonderful day, and the thought of having to return to the world of Arthur after had seemed so grim that, had she been given a few more minutes alone with him, she may have reconsidered, and done it out loud so Henry would know she was willing to take him up on his earlier offer to speak to Arthur and end her existing engagement.

And then she remembered the grin he'd had before Nicolette had entered the room. Her mind became flooded with conversations from a lifetime ago, conversations of Henry's bachelorhood, and how he had never found someone who could make him happy. Perhaps, Katherine thought, after she had rejected him at the wedding once and for all, he finally had.

Chapter Twenty-One

Another week passed. She received a letter from Arthur, though she never got around to opening it. She passed the time walking around her block, making food she used to make with Eleanor—which Edward enjoyed with a nostalgic smile— and sewing. Henry's words haunted her: this was no way to live. But she would do it or die trying.

Saturday afternoon she was sitting in her room near her dressing table staring out the window when Lucy walked past the open door.

"What on earth?" she asked aloud, stepping back and then entering Katherine's room. "I thought you would be ready by now."

Katherine turned her head to look at her sister in law. "Ready for what?"

Lucy's eyebrows flicked together for a moment. "For the party—." She stopped talking when she saw Katherine's head fall back in an annoyance paired with a scoff.

"God, not another one!" Katherine moaned.

"Katherine!" Lucy said with slight amusement. "How could you forget? Henry invited us last week when he and Nicolette were here for supper."

"If you recall, dear sister, I was still quite ill and had retired to my room before supper had even been prepared."

Lucy nodded after a moment. "Ah, yes, well you've recovered now, so you must dress. Supper. Games. People! What fun it shall be, Katherine!" She didn't give Katherine the opportunity to argue, as she left the room swiftly at the sound of one of the children calling her.

"I've more than had my fill of people," Katherine muttered to herself. Still she stood and dressed, not entirely sure what the evening had in store or even where they would be going.

The ride was a quiet one, for which Katherine was grateful. She hadn't yet entirely regained her voice and having not said much of anything to anyone all week, her throat felt strong and moist. She felt hopeful she could speak easily this evening.

The house was lit in every visible window as they approached, and Katherine noticed it was the house where Henry had been staying with his aunt and uncle.

Jeanette and Fredrick, she reminded herself. Inside she was quite surprised when her mother entered the room, though they said nothing to one another. When Fiona finally spoke, she changed to the phony persona she portrayed to the rest of the world, speaking loudly, emphatically, smiling wide, and talking about Arthur.

Katherine stood back like she usually did while the others conversed. She glanced around the room. There weren't many people, which made sense since the house itself couldn't hold a party of people like her parents' home could. She counted eight others aside from her family standing or sitting in this common area. She saw Jeanette and Fredrick but didn't see Henry. She brought her attention back to her family and saw her brother's eyes staring at her own. She didn't understand why. And then she watched as he cocked his chin up so slightly anyone else would have missed it. He moved his eyes to his left and then back. She looked to her right and noticed an open door, and then looked back to her brother. This time, with a bit more motion, Edward nodded his head once to his left. Katherine glanced around the group to see if she would be missed, knowing deep down she wouldn't, and slowly crept away toward the door.

She felt the warmth already as she approached the door. She found herself in the dining room, also not as grand as her own, though she didn't really care.

"You came," he said from behind her.

She nearly fell to the floor after she smiled and turned. He was dressed in a pair of black trousers with a white shirt and a black waistcoat, as though he had prepared for an evening far greater than what had been described to Katherine. "I was invited, wasn't I?"

He approached her and took her hand. "You're the guest of honour." He bent his head and laid a soft kiss on the back of her fingers. Her knees nearly buckled then, and she found herself holding her breath.

"On-ree!"

Bugger. Katherine closed her eyes at the shrill sound that pierced the silence. In this moment she'd all but forgotten about the French woman. She took a step back and let out a loud sigh before opening her eyes again. But to her surprise, he seemed to have the same look of exasperation in his own.

"There you are!" Nicolette cried out, coming quickly toward them in a swish of skirts. "I was looking everywhere for you!" She placed herself at his side and set a hand on his chest. "Madame Jeanette says all the guests have arrived!"

"Good news," he said. He placed his hand on her back.

"Nicolette, you remember Katherine Whyte."

"Oui! I do this time, yes. And I think I remember why I had forgotten you the last time."

"Oh?" Katherine asked, raising her eyebrows inquisitively.

"Yes. All the time I am hearing about Miss Whyte and how beautiful she is. They say how all the men love her." She waved a hand around emphatically. "So when I met you the first time, I was surprised that you are not the great beauty I was told."

"Nicolette!" Henry cried out, his tone scolding. "That is quite rude of you—."

"No. You misunderstand!" she said, pinching Henry's nose with a giggle. "She is lovely, but I was expecting more, like a portrait of an angel. Different hair and skin and eyes. Even a halo!" she exclaimed on yet another giggle. "And that is perhaps why I forgot her the first time, because she is not what I was expecting."

Katherine simply stared in shock. She was used to people carrying on about how she looked. She had been told since adolescence that she was beautiful. She didn't feel as though she were superior to anyone because of it. In fact, the only solace she found in it was that it was the one thing her mother thought was good about her. So this was strange, and Katherine was unsure how to respond. She chose to excuse herself and return to her family.

Henry did the same, joining the rest of the party with his aunt and uncle, Nicolette on his arm. They worked the room, smiling and laughing. Katherine watched them make their way toward the Whyte family and took another step away, backing up against a wall.

Nicolette acknowledged and greeted everyone by name.

An air of confidence floated around her like nothing Katherine had ever seen before. Even Arthur's charming public persona couldn't compare to Nicolette. Her English vocabulary rivaled Katherine's, yet it wasn't even Nicolette's first language. The arrogant flip of a hand, the delicate toss of her hair, the way she set her fingers on her chest when speaking of herself, bringing attention to her visible bosom; all of these things combined told everyone in her presence that Nicolette was as feminine as they come, and it was a fact not be missed or mistaken.

Edward cleared his throat. "You seem very comfortable around my friend Henry, mademoiselle," he said loudly. His smile was innocent but his tone was accusing.

She flipped the ringlets that hung below her up-do over her shoulder, and once again set her hand on her chest. "Monsieur Bullock is very comfortable to be around," she told Edward wryly, and added a wink.

Katherine found herself swallowing hard and looking away, holding down the contents of her stomach in the same manner as she had after Arthur's attack on her in the church.

Arthur.

She suddenly had a new understanding of what it must be like for Henry to see her with Arthur. She closed her eyes and swallowed hard.

Edward nodded. "Yes, I can see that. What are *your* thoughts on the matter, Henry?"

Henry set his jaw and gave his friend a stony look. "What man wouldn't want to be on the arm of a lovely young lady?" he said, finally breaking into a smile to look down at the woman clinging to him.

"Lovely indeed!" Fiona chimed in. "And ladylike in every way."

Katherine couldn't help but feel her mother's comment

was somehow directed at her.

Fiona continued. "Have you given any consideration to a courtship?" she grinned, pandering to Nicolette as Nicolette had been doing to all of them.

Henry smiled sheepishly. "She may have mentioned it a time or two."

His comment made the group laugh.

"Henry!" Nicolette pouted. "It has not just been me," she told the group. "Many people have given us their blessing and told us what lovely children ours would be."

"Their blessing?" Edward asked wide-eyed. "Who would give their blessing on a union that does not concern them?"

"I believe what she means," Henry jumped in to defend her, "is that many people comment on our potential as a union. Not so much giving their blessing—."

"Your dear aunt and uncle have given their blessing," Nicolette interrupted. "They did at supper one evening."

Henry nodded. "Yes, after several subtle suggestions you made, if I remember."

"And isn't that really the only blessing you would need?" Fiona asked, seemingly enjoying being able to once again play matchmaker. "*Your* family! And *her* employer!"

"Who treat me as though I were also family!" Nicolette pointed out.

Fiona continued. "In that case, since Henry is like family to us, you have our blessing as well."

Katherine couldn't take it anymore. She slid along the wall, then pushed off and found her way back into the dining room, where, luckily, people were beginning to take their seats. She chose one at the far corner from where the host and his wife were sitting, hoping this evening would go as every other evening had throughout her entire life, and they would all forget she was even there. In her mind she flashed back to the vicious dreams she'd had, only this time the face attached to the throat her hands were clasped around belonged to Nicolette. The corner of her mouth flicked up at the thought. She squared her shoulders and steadied her breathing and sat on her hands to steady them. She had been preparing for times like this, and let the calm wash over her like water, ready to spend the rest of the evening being the cold, intimidating being she was rumoured to be.

She was pulled from her thoughts when Lucy sat across from her, and Edward took his place to the right of his wife. Katherine's parents chose to sit next to her, and Katherine was momentarily grateful that her father put himself between her and her mother. But then she realized that it was in fact Fiona who chose to sit where she had— next to Nicolette so they might continue their conversation.

Katherine once again stared into nothingness as another dark scene before her unfolded in her mind's eye. She wondered how long it would take to die if she stabbed herself with one of the knives here at the table. Or if one of the windows on the next level was high enough up to jump from. She thought about the tallest point of her childhood home, the turret above her father's private office, and how she had seen Rupert scale it to fix leaks. A fall from there would certainly kill a person. Even a fall from that window, which was on its own third level above the second one, past her room and up another narrow flight of steps. Landing on the stone path below would surely...

She shook the thoughts away and reached for the wine that had been placed before her.

Fiona laughed loudly.

Nicolette laughed loudly.

Katherine drank more wine.

Henry had chosen to sit beside Edward, across from Fiona and Nicolette, and conversed mostly with Edward and Lucy, though from time to time the shrill French woman would pull him into whatever they were babbling about.

And Katherine drank more wine.

The meal ended and the table was cleared, but someone suggested a game of dice begin at the far end of the table, and the idea moved down to their end as well, initiated by Nicolette, though Katherine was in no mood to participate. She moved to allow a very nice older gentleman to take her place instead.

She stood and smiled numbly at those who chose to play. She hadn't felt drunk until she stood up, but now as she noticed the room spinning, she also realized her lips and tongue no longer felt attached to her body. The gentlemen stood, Henry included, who had allowed sweet, small Nicolette to join him when she had asked to sit, and once Katherine had found her spot against the wall, they all sat again. Soon Nicolette was out of the game and stood close to Katherine to get a better vantage point.

"He is so handsome, is he not?" she asked quietly.

Katherine wasn't sure if she was the one being spoken to. She had to make eye contact before deciding that she was, in fact, the recipient of the comment. "Who?"

Nicolette giggled. "Henry, of course! Such a tall man. He is not fat."

Katherine forced her lips together, satisfied it was almost a smile. "I suppose."

"And so sweet. I haven't met a finer man here in England. And if I must go to America with him, then so be it."

Katherine felt her jaw fall and her lips part slightly

before catching herself. "I had no knowledge of him wanting to return. He... He's asked you to go with him?"

"Of course he wants to return! It is where he grew up, where his poor parents are buried. He is not going to stay here for much longer." She smiled matter-of-factly, as though his departure, which was news to Katherine, had long been confirmed. "I shall try to push for a wedding before the boat leaves, so you may all attend. That way, on the long journey we can..." She shook her head and spun her finger around near her chin. "What is the word? Con... Con... sum... Con... Consummate! Share a cabin," she almost shouted, excited to have come up with the word she was searching for. "Will you come, Katherine?"

Katherine was staring down at the table—through the table, wobbling as she leaned against the wall, barely listening anymore. "To America?" she muttered.

Nicolette laughed at that, believing it to be an intentional joke, when really Katherine had been confused. "To the wedding! If I can convince Henry to have it here, will you come?"

Katherine felt herself nod slightly, knowing it was the right thing to do, and then the game ended and another began, with Nicolette running her hand along Henry's back and taking her seat beside him once again. Nicolette seemed genuine in the lack of knowledge that Katherine and Henry were once betrothed. This meant that she wasn't speaking to Katherine out of spite or ill will, but rather that she saw Katherine as a friend perhaps, another young lady with whom she could share her feelings.

Katherine made sure to refill her glass before she left the dining area and moved back to the small sitting room near the foyer. She could have stayed and studied Nicolette, trying to figure out what she herself could do differently that would make her mother admire her, or at least approve of her. She caught herself and shook her head. Not only did Katherine no longer care for her mother's approval, but the more she stewed, the more she found Nicolette to be obnoxious and wanted nothing to do with her or her ways. Unless...

What if that was in fact what Henry wanted? He made no motion to remove the tiny human from his side or brush off her hand just now. He made no attempt to correct anyone who assumed he was courting her. And he had possibly asked Nicolette to return to Philadelphia with him.

She drowned the lonely thoughts with the contents of her glass. It was dark now, save for the orange glow escaping from the dining room around the ajar door. Then the light coming from it disappeared when a body blocked the doorway.

A body she would recognize anywhere.

"All alone again, I see," Henry said. Though she couldn't make out his features, she could hear the grin as the words had passed through.

"Yes I was just coming back," she told him and took a few steps toward him.

"No. Stay." He inhaled as though he was going to give her a reason but didn't follow up with anything.

"Shouldn't you get back to your game?" she asked.

He took a step in. "No. I lost to Nicolette." He turned then and closed the door until only a crack of light remained. "Or rather, I sacrificed myself to her."

She let out a small laugh. "Oh? That was generous of you."

He chuckled. "Yes, well I was taught a gentleman will always sacrifice themselves for love."

In a split second her drunken heart broke into a million pieces and those pieces fell into her feet. Then they were true, all the things Nicolette had hinted at. Marriage and Philadelphia and the blessings of Henry's loved ones. Katherine was suddenly glad for the darkness, as she could feel her head spinning and tears come to her eyes. She swallowed the lump in her throat. "I'm sure your lovely Nicolette is grateful for your sacrifice—."

"I wasn't talking about Nicolette."

She tried to remember how to breathe so she could speak, but the abundance of wine that coursed through her veins was making it difficult. She could barely comprehend her own thoughts, let alone the words he was speaking. "You've spent months here. With her, day after day. It would only make sense—."

"Nicolette is still a girl. A silly flirt. She might have knowledge of how to attract attention, but she does not understand what it actually means to be a woman and a wife and to run a house." He took another step closer.

They were interrupted by voices on the other side of the door, a man and a woman, and then the sliver of orange light disappeared as the door slammed shut.

Katherine sighed. "Perhaps we should go back…" She tried to turn but his hands on her shoulders held her in her place. She wasn't entirely upset by this as her knees felt weak and warm and unsteady.

"If you want to" he whispered.

"What I want…" She found herself laughing quietly at the thoughts that came into her head and put her hands over her face to hold them in before they fell from her lips. At this, he let her go and took a step back. She turned and her eyes adjusted to the room, now barely lit only by the moon outside. She took a step to her left, and then another, distancing herself from the temptation that was *him.*

"Why are you laughing?" he asked from behind her now.

She moved her hands from her face, pulling them down to either side of her neck, as though it needed help to hold her head up. She shook her head. "Henry I've wanted to end my engagement since the moment I became engaged. Months before you even returned." She turned and glared at him. "And you know that. You know me, my soul. Because you were right. It's there. I've always felt it. The day you came back to me and..." She dropped her hands to her sides. She had nothing to lose now, and the wine took away any other notion she may have had to hold back. "You were right about everything. This bond we have. And mostly how miserable I am," she whispered. She stopped talking, and he allowed for a pause.

"Good."

She furrowed her brow at his response, though she wasn't sure he could see it. "Good? You're happy I'm miserable?"

"I'm happy you finally realized you deserve nothing less than happiness. You would not have come to that conclusion on your own, as you were, before I returned."

The wine was suddenly taking her from laughter to anger and turning her limbs to wobbly mush. "Fine, you pompous ass," she turned back to him, with a few drunken waves of her hands, "I want happiness." She plopped down on the sofa that was behind her.

He laughed at both her words and her countenance.

The room became illuminated again as the door opened.

"Ah. Good. Edward," Henry said through a wry smile, "your sister has had entirely too much wine and thinks I'm a pompous ass."

Edward came to stand beside Katherine. "Well, she is not wrong," he laughed. He helped her to her feet and turned to lead her back to the dining room.

As she passed Henry his words echoed in her fuzzy head.

All of them.

"No!" She yanked her arm away from her brother and spun to face Henry again. "What did you mean? You said you weren't talking about Nicolette..."

He cleared his throat and lifted his eyes to look at Edward. "A few more minutes."

Edward sighed. "I don't know how much longer..." Then he nodded and disappeared through the door again.

Henry took a deep breath. "You said you want happiness —."

She shook her head and interrupted him. "*You* said you weren't talking about sacrificing yourself for Nicolette. You said she would not make a good wife. But if you are to be married," she slurred, "and she's going back to America with you—."

This time he interrupted her. "Who told you she was coming back to America with me?"

"She did. Just now. In there. She said she was trying to convince you to marry here in England so we could all attend your wedding and then she would return with you."

His eyes darted around the room as he absorbed her words. "Katherine, I understand you're not yourself right now, so I'm going to be very clear. As I said, Nicolette is a lovely girl. She's well educated and polite and quite popular with those she meets." He paused and sighed. "I suppose I've indulged her somewhat for the sake of peace within the house we both live in, because I don't like to be rude..."

I so hate to be rude… His words from years ago emerged from the back of her brain.

"…But she does not make me happy, Katherine. And she never will. And it seems," he took one step closer and dropped his voice to a whisper, "the only time I find myself genuinely happy is in your presence."

There was a rhythmic knock at the door, and Henry dropped his head in disappointment. "Stay close to me," he ordered. He snatched her hand and led her through the door, then dropped it and walked around to the far side of the table where his uncle was sitting. He held out a chair for her and took the one beside it.

"Your mother shouldn't see you like this," he said as he set a mug of water in front of her. "Drink this. All of it. Smile more, and perhaps we can fool her."

She closed her eyes and nodded, then lifted her face to look at him and smiled politely, though now she couldn't feel her teeth, and could only barely feel her cheeks.

He chuckled. "Close enough." He took a long draw from his own cup. "Nicolette!" Henry called out. "You should tell Katherine and I about France, dear. We have often discussed our mutual desire to travel there someday." He then adjusted himself in his seat, this time a bit closer, pressing his legs tighter against Katherine's, and resting his forearm on top of hers between them. She could feel his fingers curl loosely into the curve of the hand she'd rested on her lap, and imagined Nicolette could certainly see this, but when she glanced down quickly she was surprised at how casually his hand was draped beneath the table, as though he had no choice in this cramped space *but* to place his hand there.

Katherine could barely pay attention as Nicolette spoke. Instead she could only focus on the warmth at her side, his light touch and the churning she felt between her legs. She stared into the crowd, not looking at anything, but within her mind's eye. She shuffled her feet and crossed her ankles. Then without even realizing she was doing it, she lifted her thumb to brush it underneath his finger. She was pulled out of her reverie when he moved his head ever so subtly to glance in the direction of their hands. She realized what she had done and froze her body, only moving her head to look toward the opposite window so no one would see her blush. Once Nicolette moved on and Katherine felt the colour had left her cheeks, she returned to stare blankly at him for a moment. "You still want to marry me," she said, a look of whimsy in her eyes as the words he had spoken minutes ago had only just registered in her brain.

He laughed silently to himself, once again at her drunken manner, which he had never experienced. Once he had composed himself, he answered her with another nod of his head.

"I make you happy?" she asked, cocking her head to the side and looking at him, confused.

He gave one nod and set his cup down. "Yes. You do. You and only you."

Suddenly her eyes became clear and a sincere smile crossed her lips. "You make me happy, Henry," she insisted.

"I know I do," he said through a smirk. "And I truly think that, once this whole Arthur business has passed, we could make *each other* very happy."

She looked at him with fury in her eyes. "You laugh, as though this were the easiest choice imaginable!"

He returned her look. "The action, perhaps, may not be. But the choice, Katherine, is indeed the easiest in the world. You simply have to make it."

His words stunned her, and infuriated her further in

her intoxicated state. *It was not an easy choice!* she wanted to scream at him. Neither spoke for a while, giving her time to calm herself, both observing the goings on around them, Katherine catching her mother's glare now and then. And then a thought struck her.

"*Are* you planning on returning to America?"

He sighed and stared straight forward so not to meet her eyes. "I don't know yet."

"When will you know?" she asked, wishing he would look at her so she could gauge his feelings, though she had to admit her judgement was a bit askew right then.

"When your fate has been decided, so shall mine," he said, still refusing to look at her. "If you indeed choose this life you've resigned yourself to," he said with a wave to indicate the frivolity of it all, "I shall be as good as gone. I'll not wait forever, Katherine."

She gasped. She hadn't considered this as a possibility. She'd somehow brought herself to believe that even if she were to marry Arthur, Henry would be there, a part of her life, a friend, as he had made himself these last months.

No, she determined as the room spun around her. She could convince him to stay in her life. He had said so himself that he felt the pull toward her the way she did to him. It was the reason he was sitting here with her, this close, all but holding her hand. There was no way he could resist it, no way he could stay away. They could remain as close of friends as he and Edward has always been…

However, she wasn't convinced.

Chapter Twenty-Two

Before the evening was over her father had invited everyone to his home the next day after church for supper. Katherine remembered agreeing to it, however when she woke up, she felt extraordinarily worse for wear, and decided not to attend church in her condition. She didn't want to wake up. She remembered most of the evening and knew the reality that would come this day. With the amount of overthinking she already did daily, she anticipated only having to do more now. So instead she chose sleep.

Sleep that did not come easily. Her exhausted body pulled her into slumber, but her overactive mind would pull her back out.

I make him happy...

I have spent so much time and effort reforming myself, pushing people away, to become this new version of Katherine…

So many people would be disappointed…

A version of Katherine that's too much like Fiona. A version of Katherine I barely recognize…

I am happy with him, as much as he is with me…

The king has accepted our union, and is to be in attendance…

A version of Katherine meant to move on from Henry Bullock's death, who swore she would never marry…

The back and forth continued, in and out of consciousness until Lucy made a point of rousing her and practically dressing her before leading her down the stairs and into the carriage. Edward smirked at Katherine's condition, and laughed out loud when Katherine cursed him for marrying such a woman. It wasn't until the carriage was moving that Katherine noticed Lucy hadn't even entered it.

"W..?" she began to say, though she couldn't decide which sentence her lips should form.

"My darling wife will be joining us later for supper. Our parents are going to bring her and the boys in a few hours. You must be getting very excited for your wedding, sister. 'Tis mere weeks away."

She opened her mouth to speak, which she knew she should have, but no proper response came to her mind. Upon remembering this was only Edward with her, she raised her eyebrows and gave both a slight shrug and a small nod, then turned to look back out the window. "My head hurts."

He gave a small chuckle. "Just as I thought."

"They are not even home?" Katherine asked.

"No. Father had business to tend to first. Then, as I said, they'll be stopping by to bring my family with them."

"Then why are we…" she began.

"We also have business to tend to," he interrupted.

She didn't understand. She gave him a look that told him she didn't understand. She hated when he was evasive like this, but it reminded her that the only times he was ever this dodgy was when it had to do with Henry. Her stomach flipped at the thought that he might be waiting for her, though she dare not speak it out loud, or even whisper it to herself in secret. Not another word was spoken until they arrived at their destination and exited the carriage.

"Why don't we take a walk!" Edward suggested.

She recalled a time long ago when his behaviour had puzzled her so, and in that instance, he had also suggested they take a walk. Again she followed him toward the trees behind the house. *There is no way it could have the same outcome*, she thought. It was a thought that continued into the cool shade of the trees, and back out into the sun. And even when she felt it, and after she turned and saw him standing midway down the path, the thoughts of doubt somehow continued, that there was no way this would be the same as it was then.

"Miss Whyte," Henry said as she approached, inclining his head toward her.

She watched Edward hold Henry's gaze and flick his brow. It lasted but a moment and before she could think too much of it, Henry held out his elbow to her. She grinned and took it, wanting nothing more than to be near him in any way she could again, her inner arguments, her doubts, all falling away with each step. She had dreamed of him throughout the night and well into the morning, adding to the reasons she chose not to attend church. With one hand in the crook of his elbow, she set the other on his bicep as they walked the rest of the path. In the clearing, the sun was warm. Their stroll led them upstream several hundred yards from where they once took solace in one another. The ground rose up a few feet creating a short embankment. It was here Edward finally sat on the soft grass and began to remove his footwear. Henry joined him and they dangled their feet into the water. Katherine chose to sit beside Henry, though she thought it best to keep her feet out of the water and to sit with her ankles crossed in a ladylike fashion. She continued to listen to them talk, half listening, half daydreaming.

And then Edward stood. "I'll be back," he said as the

others looked up at him. He grabbed his boots and left the way they had come.

"Where are you going?" Katherine asked.

"I forgot something," he called over his shoulder before dashing toward the trees.

She glanced back at Henry and gave a small, nervous smile. Henry pushed himself up slightly with his hands and moved his bottom closer to her, which caused their arms to touch. And before she knew she was doing it, she had moved her head down, resting her temple on his shoulder. And they sat like that for what felt to Katherine like an eternity.

He inhaled. "Have you thought about what you're going to do with yourself once I go back?"

She sighed, but didn't move, waiting to see if she could call his bluff. "I suppose I shall continue doing everything I've always done."

"Ugh," he grunted. "That sounds dreadful."

It made her laugh out loud, her body shaking rhythmically and causing his to do the same. Then she became thoughtful. "How long of a journey is it again?"

"Well, coming here took just over two months. But the journey back may take more time if it's a heavier ship carrying supplies." This time he sighed, deeply, as though he weren't looking forward to it again.

She let that sink in for a moment. "Henry, do... do you ever... or have you ever, rather... considered...staying? What our relationship could..."

This time, it was Henry who laughed as loudly as she had. She lifted her head to look at him. "What? What did I say?"

"It wasn't what you said, darling, but how you said it. It's only you and me here. I've nothing on my feet, and you're lying against me, propriety be damned. And yet you still speak as though you're afraid I'm going to judge you or inform your parents of any unpleasant word or harmful tone in your voice." He put his arm around her, pulling her close, and she laid her head against him again. "We had a wonderful time last night, did we not? You were being yourself. And even though I wasn't sure you could possibly be more beautiful than you normally are, you are today. The light in your eyes and your smile..." He put his face into her hair and inhaled her scent, then kissed the top of her head.

She didn't move her head from his collar bone. He didn't move his face from her hair. She didn't feel beautiful. Her head ached. Her mouth was dry. Her stomach twisted inside out. She hadn't the energy to properly tend to herself this morning. Lucy had hastily done it all for her, from choosing the dress to pinning her hair.

She sighed. "I've considered all you said last night. And I've much more to consider, haven't I?" She felt him give a nod against her head. She was once again glad Arthur was gone. He would be here eating up her time, influencing her decisions. She could take her time and think clearly in his absence. She could spend time with Henry and Edward and Lucy, and maybe she could find herself again.

"They're back!"

It startled them both and their heads snapped in the direction of Edward's call out to them.

Katherine was still trying to understand who *they* were, when Henry began putting his boots back on. He stood and helped her up and continued to hold her hand as he led her toward the trees, and then through them to where Edward was waiting for them. Here, Henry let go of her hand, and Katherine suddenly felt empty. She moved to pick up her skirt and hurry up to the house with the men.

"Edward?" she heard her mother say when they came through the back door.

"Fiona," Edward acknowledged with a tone and a nod.

Henry was the last one in and closed the door behind them. They continued to stand where they were, Edward in front, Katherine behind him, and Henry pressed comfortingly against the left side of her back. She felt the urge to reach for his hand, but then felt it lay lightly against the small of her back.

"What are you doing here?" Fiona asked from where she stood down the hall, locking eyes with her daughter. "You were not at church this morning."

"Yes," Edward spoke for them all. "Katherine was not well this morning, and Lucy and I decided she should have been left alone to recover. By the grace of God on His holy day, she seems to be back on her feet and in great spirits, so I thought to keep her company on the ride out."

"Yes," Henry continued, in almost the same tone. "I arrived alone long before anyone else. I am also quite happy to see Katherine has recovered."

Fiona waved her hand and spoke quickly. "Ah yes there she stands, completely fine." She had rolled her eyes and walked away as she spoke, turning into the study as William came through the front door. He seemed delighted to see the three of them, a stark contrast to his wife, and was followed by Lucy and the boys.

"Husband, a moment of your time, in private," Lucy said firmly to Edward, leaning her head away from them.

They all finally moved forward from the door, though Henry stayed close to Katherine's side.

"How was your ride out, father?" Edward asked, giving his wife a concerned look and a nod as he picked Matthew up from the floor.

William chuckled as he removed his jacket. "Warm and loud," he said in reference to his grandsons. "Too warm for this blasted thing!" he grumbled as he tossed his jacket to the floor and gave it one dramatic stomp for effect, receiving a chuckle from the young people around him. "But uneventful thus far." He then took the tiny hand of the younger Henry in the room.

"Good. It is warm, indeed," he said, before shifting his focus to Lucy. "Shall we, my dear?" Edward said as he took a few steps to reach for the front door for him and Lucy to walk out, but before they reached it, it opened from the other side.

And through it walked Arthur.

Chapter Twenty-Three

Katherine let out a small gasp. Her eyes shot to Henry beside her, but he didn't see. Instead he took the smallest step forward and to the right, putting himself slightly between her and the baron. Katherine's instincts pulled her magnetically in his direction, just as slightly as he had done, until she could feel the pressure and warmth of him against her. And once he felt it, he leaned slightly back in her direction, closing any gap between them.

"Ah, there you are," William said loudly to Arthur. "I thought perhaps you'd gotten lost."

"Of course not," Arthur snorted, removing his gloves. "I had some things to tend to before I left. That is all."

"As did I," William said.

"Lord Thacker," Edward began, his voice doing little to hide his distaste for the man. "you have returned early from your business trip. What brings you all this way?"

"I came to see my beloved, of course. She has been ill, and I have been out of town." He shot Henry a glare and pushed past him to embrace her, for a far longer time than she was comfortable with. He pulled back. "Your sister Lucy told me you were bedridden and unable to attend church today."

"Yes, w-w-well I was... I've since recovered," she stammered.

Arthur stepped to the side and pulled her in again, increasing the distance between her and Henry. She watched the other men in the room as they all averted their eyes from the spectacle she was an unwillingly part of. Her father looked everywhere else. But Henry and Edward stared at one another with the same expression and furrowed brow, a shared rage behind their eyes.

Edward cleared his throat. "Well perhaps we should retire to the parlour."

Before anyone could respond Henry was out the back door, followed soon by Lucy and Edward, who still had Matthew in his arms. Young Henry was still holding the hand of his grandfather.

William paused and watched curiously as the door closed behind the young people. He blinked and glanced down to young Henry, then asked "Will you join us in the parlour, Arthur?"

"No, thank you. I would like to take my beautiful fiancé for some fresh air." He turned from William to look at Katherine. "Perhaps a walk to the stable?"

Katherine nodded, as she had always done, unable to look at anyone for fear her eyes would give her away. Arthur took her hand and led her out the front door. He told her of his trip, and as usual she nodded along. At one point she tried to add a comment of "That's interesting," but she was immediately hushed by him. "Don't interrupt, dear. It's rude," he told her with a shake of his head. He must have noticed the look on her face indicated she was upset because he stopped and turned and put himself in front of her. He took both her hands. "Katherine dear. I missed you so. And when I heard of your illness I rushed to the nearest church and prayed for your swift recovery." He had his usual dramatic breathlessness.

Katherine was unsure of how to respond. She settled on a thank you and began to stammer it out nervously. She couldn't pay attention to the words he was saying. Her mind was with Henry, stuck on her intimate moments with him earlier by the stream and the night before. Arthur continued to babble, about himself as he had always done, about the work he'd done and his correspondence with the king and the nobility he'd made friends with along the way, and the rumours and gossip he had heard throughout his journey.

But she was quite suddenly made *very* aware of what he was saying. She blinked at him, needing the time to replay the words through her head slowly to make certain she had heard them right.

"Were you engaged to Henry Bullock?"

Her breath was stuck in her throat.

"Your mother wrote to me to tell me that I should return to tend to you during your illness. When I informed her I could not, she wrote again to tell me I should return for... other reasons."

Edward had been right, she thought. It was Fiona who'd told Arthur to make his presence known in prior gatherings. She paid attention to the path before her now, worried she might stumble as her breathing had quickened and her legs felt funny. There was no point in lying, she realized. "I was, my lord. Long, long ago."

A darkness came into his eyes and changed his face, nearly distorting it into something she didn't recognize. "And his face graces the portrait you painted."

She nodded and swallowed.

"Pray, what ended this engagement?"

She once again found use for the stoicism she'd

practiced for so long, not allowing her face to betray how truly afraid she was in this moment. "My belief in his demise. I grieved for years, and then became engaged to you as my mother wished."

He barely allowed her to finish speaking before he began and had likely missed the last few words. "Had you not thought him dead would you be married now?"

This time she spoke quickly. "I believe we would, yes."

He inhaled deeply through his nose. "And do you also believe that he returned to England to follow through on his promise to wed you?"

This time she allowed herself a small pause to gather her thoughts and word them properly. She needed to protect herself, but more so, she needed to protect Henry. Her fear gave way to the notion that now she could bend the truth. "I cannot be certain, my lord, as I am not able to read the thoughts of men—."

"You are never to see him again."

She snapped her mouth shut and lifted her chin. "I beg your pardon?"

He too raised his chin, and again inhaled through his nose.

Katherine chose to continue. "My lord, I would think that impossible. Henry Bullock is one of my brothers' oldest and dearest friends. Nary a day goes by that they do not speak or see one anoth—."

"You are never to see him again or so help me I will have him hung!" he shouted, a sudden booming quality rattling her eardrums that could rival that of her father before dropping it slightly and speaking very quickly, stepping forward to growl them directly into her face. "Henry Bullock is a traitor to his country already. Therefor I'm more than certain His

Majesty will listen to reason, should another opportunity to prove Bullock's disloyalty present itself." As before, he caught himself and cleared his throat.

Her lips parted for a moment in disbelief and fear before she pressed them back together and swallowed hard. With that he knew she understood, and as quickly as the wave of darkness came over him, it faded away.

"Come darling!" he called back to her as he walked away. "I am famished. Our meal awaits."

She stood still, putting as much distance between them as she could. She walked slowly behind him, watching another carriage arrive for her father's planned dinner. She was repulsed; she felt herself shaking as she had during the worst of her recent fever. When she entered the house, she heard him loudly regaling the guests with yet another tale of his travels, the guests that included Henry Bullock, as though he were proclaiming directly to Henry all the reasons he himself were a better choice of husband for her. Upon hearing this she walked past the room to the study, examining the books on the shelves, wishing for something familiar and happy that would take her mind off her misery and prolong her absence.

And she found it, tucked away, dusty, long forgotten—the very first book on insects her father had ever brought her. She had forgotten to bring it with her when she'd moved to Edward's. She'd packed nearly all of her books from Edward's to take with her when she married Arthur and had never even wondered what had happened to this one, she realized. It brought the smallest smile to her face and her soul. She sat on the sofa and ran her fingers over the cover, then opened it to the first page. She wasn't intent on reading it, rather flipping through its contents for the sake of nostalgia. She wondered, as she turned the pages, when the last time was that this book had been out of this shelf, and then with another flip and a gasp she remembered quite quickly.

Pressed into the pages was a dried, flattened purple flower. Henry had put it there, she remembered, in the days before he went back for his parents. She fought to remember the experience, the words he'd said, but she couldn't. She could only hear Arthur's angry words as they echoed through her consciousness.

I will have him hung!

He wouldn't though, she realized, if Henry made good on his promise to return to America— if Katherine went through with her marriage— and he would be safe. The thought caused her eyes to glisten, and without realizing it, one loud sob escaped her, at which point she covered her mouth and breathed slowly to recover.

Looking down at the delicate flower frozen in time she knew she couldn't allow any of it to happen. It sounded as though a few other guests had arrived, and Fiona's phony laugh rang from down the hall. It was Fiona who had indeed informed her current fiancé about her former one. Fiona gave herself away every time she shot a look to Katherine in Henry's presence. Fiona would stop at nothing to advance Katherine and therefor herself, even if it caused harm to those closest to her.

Katherine shook her head, no longer willing to be the puppet. Henry had mentioned being told Arthur was a reasonable man, but Katherine knew now there would be no speaking with him as Henry had stated, wishing Arthur would simply back out of the engagement. She did not love Arthur. She did not desire Arthur. She no longer wanted any part of the life he had promised her. He did not respect her whatsoever. He had barked at her when she had interrupted him not even an hour earlier. Henry had never raised his voice to her. He'd never stifled her words or ideas. He'd never belittled her. He'd never disrespected her. A marriage to Arthur would ensure she experience all of those things and more. God forbid! She would run the risk of becoming her own mother!

No, not true, she thought. Her mother, like it or not, did possess some control of her house and marriage, something Katherine would never do as Lady or Baroness or Duchess Thacker. She had never been a strong woman, someone worth admiring. She'd always been meek and small, unless Henry Bullock was with her. He accepted her as she was, and it made her stand taller and sound smarter and appear stronger.

More than appear, she realized. She *was* stronger with him. She could be or say or do whatever she wanted in his presence, at his side, and he would not stop her. He would stand beside her, support her, propel her.

She stood then, her choice made, though deep down she knew no decision would have been made and final until *this* one was. In all reality, this was her only choice. Moving quickly, she scribbled onto a small piece of paper. She held the note in one hand and the fragile flower between the fingers of the other as she left the room.

Katherine didn't dare look at Henry as she entered the dining room where everyone was already seated, knowing Arthur and Fiona would be watching her closely. She did, however, lock eyes with her brother and hold his gaze across the table. His eyes had a question, and hers answered by jumping in Arthur's direction to her right and back again.

Henry witnessed the entire event. He noticed the seriousness in her gaze, the swift motion toward Arthur. And he very much acknowledged that she would not meet his eyes.

Edward stood as the others conversed amongst themselves and came to bend down beside her, putting himself between her and Arthur. "My dear sister, you look wretched," he said loud enough for Arthur to hear, and hopefully, be intimidated. "Are you alright?" She handed him the note.

We must stay until Arthur has long gone. You must keep

Henry here as well. We must all depart at the same time.

As discreetly as possible, she pressed the small flower into his palm with it.

"No, I am not," she said, meeting his volume and tone, hoping it would put some fear into the man on the other side of her brother, but also disguise the actions of their hands below the table. "I shall discuss it with you later."

He simply nodded and stood to return to his seat. He continued a conversation already in progress, not turning to relay the message to Henry lest it give them away. The rest of dinner moved along as usual, with Katherine keeping her chin up in defiance and barely responding when spoken to. The only eye contact Katherine chose to make was with her brother, though on more than one instance Arthur's eyes fell on her or he would try to engage her verbally. All of which she chose to ignore, bringing forth the attention of their host and hostess.

When the meal was over Edward announced he was taking his sons for a walk to the trees and the stream with Lucy, and invited Henry to join them. Katherine sat down in the parlour with the others and gave a small sigh of relief. This was Edward wasting time. This was Edward informing Henry and Lucy of the contents of her note. She smiled to herself and then settled in for what would hopefully be the last evening of pomp and pretense.

The time passed by more slowly than Katherine had ever remembered. Though she would have normally held her posture and pretended to care about what everyone was talking about, this time she didn't care at all. She leaned back slightly in the chair. She continuously checked the clock and sighed with boredom.

And again they noticed. William caught her eye, seeming confused, though Katherine was certain he was trying to hide amusement. Fiona glared at Katherine;

sometimes Katherine felt defiant enough to hold her gaze, other times she would pretend to pick lint off her skirt or check the cleanliness of her nails.

Still Arthur tried to engage her, asking questions regarding the topic at hand, and her response would be to give a nod or shake her head or even be so informal as to shrug. Arthur's eyes widened at the shrug, and Katherine was more than satisfied with the fire that raged behind them. Perhaps there was a chance he would find her behaviour unappealing and end the engagement on his own. It was a thought so enticing, it had Katherine eager to do all she could to make it so.

Arthur stood. "Well, my friends, it has been an absolute pleasure. Now I must take my leave. My love," he said, turning to Katherine, "would you be so kind as to join me for the long ride home?"

Katherine lifted her chin to look up at him, but did not stand, as she knew everyone in the room was expecting. "Oh absolutely not." She heard the small gasps arise, the loudest, she was sure, came from her mother.

Arthur's eyebrows gave a slight flicker toward one another, though he managed to maintain his composure surprisingly well. His eyes moved quickly to Fiona and the others in the room. "I beg your pardon?" he asked, smiling as though she were joking somehow.

"Absolutely not," she said again, no more or less firm, no more or less loudly.

Again the rage in his eyes was palpable. He cleared his throat. "Would you then, please do me the great honour of escorting me out to my carriage?"

"No," she said, and tried to emulate her brother's dramatic flare. "I'm suddenly overcome with the most dreadful headache and I choose to wait for the return of my brother and his family so that *they* may take me to the *safety* of their home."

"There is no need to wait," she heard from behind her, and turned her head slightly toward her brother's voice, "for I have returned. And just in time, it would appear." Edward walked around the sofa to stand near Arthur.

Henry continued to walk into a corner of the room within Katherine's eyesight. She noticed the smallest movement that brought her eyes to his fingers, where between them he twirled the flower. Her gaze drifted up to meet his eyes for a moment, and then her brother's voice brought her back to the situation at hand.

"Fear not, old chap," Edward said cheerfully to Arthur, giving his arm a nudge with his fist. "I shall deposit her directly to her chamber to recover from this horrible headache that has overcome her."

Arthur glanced down at his arm where Edward's knuckles had been, then looked back to Katherine. He gave a nod of his head and then thanked his hosts graciously, before exiting the room and then the building.

The room was quiet after Arthur left it; befuddled guests glancing awkwardly at one another, not sure what to say to ease the tension. Edward, never at a loss for words, was the first to speak once Arthur's carriage rolled past the window. "Wife!"

Everyone in the room started, some more than others, at his sharp cry.

Footsteps could be heard approaching the door and Lucy appeared. "Yes, husband?"

"Gather the children. We shall be leaving, as my dear sister is not well."

"Oh how dreadful! Of course, my love," Lucy replied, her

tone overly sweet and sympathetic, playing along and making it entirely evident why there was no woman in the world more perfect for Edward Whyte. "Gather the children, I shall," she repeated his words with a sly look. She then gave a small curtsy and disappeared again.

"I shall take my leave as well," Henry said quietly from his corner. He walked toward William and extended a hand to shake. "Mr. Whyte, once again your hospitality is much appreciated."

"You know you are always welcome to it, lad," William told him as the other guests in the room finally began to converse again. Henry spun on his heel and purposefully swept out of the room without thanking the lady of the house.

Katherine followed his example, kissing her father on the cheek but avoiding both her mother's gaze as well as her proximity. Edward's only acknowledgement was a curt "Mother," as he walked toward the door.

Henry's carriage was still in the yard when theirs was on its way out. Katherine stared out the window while the parents and children conversed. She waited until they were a safe distance— nearly halfway back to town— before suddenly rapping her knuckles on the roof, startling everyone else in the cab with them. As it pulled to a stop Edward reached for the door but Katherine was faster and threw it open. She was on the ground and trudging toward the carriage behind them before it had even come to a stop. The door opened and Henry stepped down, his long strides closing the distance between them quickly.

"What does this mean?" he asked, holding up the flattened flower between two fingers.

"Everything it always has," she said, her voice heightened and her breath heavy from the walk as well as her emotional state. "He told me I'm never to see you again. He forbids it," she told him. Her words fast and frantic, her voice deepening as she fought to hold back sobs. "I would die, Henry. I would die—." She was silenced by him then when he pulled her against him, holding her tight. She felt her fingers clinging to his back and was certain she must be causing him some pain.

"Shhh," his voice calming her, his hand smoothing her hair. "He is not wrong, Katherine," he said, laying his cheek against the top of her head. "Though it would not be his choice. It would be mine, and in truth, yours."

They were silent as thoughts ran amok within them, then she looked up into his face. "Marry me. Tonight. Tomorrow—."

"Katherine," he protested on a chuckle.

"I'll not live another day without you!" she hissed. "We should be married already! We should be well into our life together. We should have a small, cold house and horrible, loud children. Everything we wanted. All the things we promised one another."

He was laughing quietly and tucking a strand of hair behind her ear when she stopped talking. "Yes, my love, we should have all those things already. But before we can bring ourselves to such an insufferable fate, we have other things to take care of. I will return to speak with your father. You will end your engagement to Arthur. And immediately thereafter, the world shall be ours to do with it what we please." He pulled her in again until he felt her breathing calm. "Are you better now?" he asked against the top of her head.

She looked up at him and nodded, though confusion still furrowed her eyebrows noticeably in the dim light of dusk.

"What is it?" he asked, the look on her face causing him to grin.

"I don't know. I don't know what it is, but I always feel... stronger when I'm near you. Braver. Even now, I don't know what is going to happen, but I'm not afraid like I would be otherwise."

Henry only curled his lip up as he gazed at her. Katherine swallowed hard and nodded, then she let him press his lips to her cheek and leave her there on the road. She didn't want to have to face Arthur ever again. Truthfully, she had hoped Henry would say yes, and they would be weeks into their marriage before Arthur came to call again. But she remembered her appalling behaviour toward Arthur at the end of the evening and wondered if he might accept her resignation to their agreement after all.

***

A servant answered the door. "Mr. Bullock," she said with a small curtsy even though she'd just seen him less than an hour earlier.

"Miss," Henry said back with an incline of his head and scolded himself for not remembering her name. "I would like to speak privately with Mr. Whyte, if you would retrieve him, please."

The young lady nodded and opened the door wider so that he might enter the house again.

"No, thank you, miss, I would prefer to wait here. And if you would inform only Mr. Whyte of my request, I would be most grateful," he added with a charming smile and a wink. If he could play to her flattery, the better the chance would be that she would, indeed, keep his arrival from her mistress.

The girl looked immediately to the floor and Henry was satisfied with the rush of colour that came to her cheeks. She didn't reply, only giving another nod and closing the door.

Minutes later the door opened again and William's imposing figure emerged. "Is something wrong my boy?"

"No, sir," Henry said, taking a step back. Then he tilted his head to the side in consideration. "And yes. William, sir, you know I have the utmost affection and respect for you, and I am certain you feel as I do." William nodded and he continued. "Thus I hope that this conversation might be kept away from your wife, sir."

William's brows knit together briefly. "What is this about, Henry?"

"Your daughter."

William inhaled deeply and sighed, then gave a nod indicating Henry should continue.

Chapter Twenty-Four

On their ride home Katherine was finally able to tearfully tell Edward and Lucy what had happened with Arthur at the house, how he had come so close and shouted in her face. Before she knew it, she was also regaling them with her tale of a drunken Arthur putting his hands on her at the back of the church. Edward was furious, of course, and confirmed Katherine's fears from before, that had he, or Heaven forbid, Henry, found out about it, Thacker would have paid for it dearly, maybe even with his life.

At home she tried to sleep, but anticipation got the better of her. She wondered if Henry would come to the house with news of what had happened with her father, and she waited up until after midnight before finally retiring. Then, after tossing and turning and thoughts of both Henry and Arthur not allowing her brain to rest, she got up and moved to her table. She decided she'd write to Arthur, to tell him she no longer wanted to marry him. She didn't want to face him after how he'd acted— the darkness in his eyes and the violence in his voice. The only way she would see him again would be with a chaperone, though it wouldn't be fair to anyone involved to force them into that situation.

She wrote quickly, not of the whole truth, but of how his actions earlier in the day had frightened her. She also brought up his indiscretion at church weeks ago, insisting she had been having second thoughts about marrying him since. She wrote she could not marry someone whose emotions were so very unpredictable, someone who felt threatened by her dearest friends, and especially someone who would treat her as a prize — a thing he had won and now possessed. She sealed it and, feeling better, decided she was ready to sleep. Her first order of business in the morning was to have it sent over.

She let Lucy know, as well as the housekeepers, and was not at all surprised when she heard the bell ring in the afternoon. She waited around the corner and listened as Rosemary held her own at the door.

"I've come to speak with Miss Katherine," Arthur called out firmly.

"She is not here, my lord," Rosemary lied.

"Where is she then?" Arthur demanded.

"She did not tell me she was leaving, sir. I only came to know of her absence when I went to her room and she was gone."

"I shall come in and wait for her return then," Arthur told her.

"No, you may not. The master of the house is not here to receive you. Only the lady and her children remain, and they are entitled to their privacy, sir."

Katherine listened to the silence that followed with a smirk, wishing she could see his face.

"I will let Mr. Whyte and his sister know that you came to call, my lord," Rosemary told him, and then she closed the door and locked it before he could respond.

"Thank you," Katherine whispered from where she stood, not willing to move until she heard Arthur's carriage roll away.

Rosemary also did not move until she was certain Arthur was not coming back. She gave Katherine a nod and then went back to her duties.

Katherine debated sending for her brother, worried Arthur might return, worried that he might become angry, even violent. There were only women in the house, save for the two young boys, and though she was confident Arthur valued his reputation enough to respect their wishes, he was proving to be more unpredictable as time went on. Every noise caused her ears to perk up, at times holding her breath until it had safely passed. Again there was a ring of the bell. Katherine was upstairs and peeked out the window, and though from this angle she could not see who was at the door, she did not see Arthur's carriage or any of his servants. She tiptoed out of her room to the end of the hall and listened from the top of the stairs.

Rosemary answered the door again, and Katherine was immediately filled with both relief and elation when she heard the voice of Henry Bullock. She bounced down the steps and met him at the bottom, and through the still open door Katherine could see Edward emerging from the carriage as well.

Henry grinned. "Your brother invited me for supper this evening."

Katherine smiled back at him, all fears forgotten. "I'm glad to hear of it. You know you are always welcome."

"Indeed. I would have arrived sooner, but I spent the day gathering my things and taking a room at an inn."

"Oh? Have you worn out your welcome with your aunt?" Katherine asked, perplexed. She couldn't imagine him having done so, the charming gentleman that he was. And he was just as fond of his relatives.

He smirked. "Not exactly. Miss Nicolette received some

upsetting news and I felt it best I allow her and her hosts time to accept it."

"Oh?" Lucy asked having entered the room to stand near her husband. "From whom?"

Edward answered, closing the door behind him. "From Henry. He denied her advances once and for all, after speaking with our father."

Henry spoke up again. "And I know how terribly her presence vexed you," he teased Katherine. "So I thought I would make it simple for all involved and leave the situation. The *temptation,*" he said, giving her a wink.

Katherine didn't know whether she wanted to throw her arms around him for his actions or throw something at him for teasing her. She chose to glare and purse her lips to hide a smile. She immediately wanted to grill him to find out what had taken place between Henry and William when he'd returned to the house, but chose to wait until they were alone, hoping to steal him away after the meal.

Instead, much to both her amusement and dismay, Lucy did it for her, and of course Henry was happy to oblige, explaining he'd asked for William to meet him outside, away from prying eyes and ears and Fiona. They had walked around the garden, and Henry had explained everything. He said that Katherine no longer wished to marry Arthur, and he also said that William seemed relieved, saying that he himself had become weary of the man. Henry told William that he and Katherine still loved one another and wished to fulfill their original agreement. It did not take much consideration from William before giving his blessing along with his promise to keep it secret for as long as he needed to.

Katherine breathed a sigh of relief, and upon seeing the smiles and grins of the others at the table, one formed upon her own face and would not leave. Supper ended and the children were put to bed. While the adults retired to the parlour to continue their conversation about the future, the bell rang at the door. The sun had nearly disappeared, and a look of confusion and concern replaced the smiles that had been.

A servant came in to announce that Arthur had returned, and before she knew what was happening, Henry had Katherine's hand and was yanking her off her chair and around a corner. And none too soon because Arthur had pushed his way into the home this time.

"My lord," Edward acknowledged him dryly. "To what do I owe this intrusion?"

It seemed to catch Arthur off guard, as it took him a moment to respond. "I beg your pardon?"

Edward sighed. "You once again enter my house uninvited and unannounced, sir, and at so late an hour—."

"Your sister wrote to me this morning and I have come —."

"I care not for your reasons or excuses," Edward cut him off in return. "Nor do I care for your treatment of my sister."

Katherine's eyes widened as she looked at Henry, who only grinned back at her with one side of his mouth as he usually did.

"I wish to speak with her," Arthur demanded.

"I won't allow it," Edward replied. "She is my charge, sir. You may believe your requests for her hand or her company should be to our parents, but you would be wrong. I have cared for her these many years. The responsibility has fallen onto me, and while I have done it happily, I have also taken it most seriously. I will not enter her into an unhappy marriage, nor will I allow any mistreatment of her. And from what she has told me, a union with you would result in both. She insists it already has, in fact. And if you still believe you are entitled to speak with our father on the matter, I should tell you that he has been well informed of this decision and the events leading up to it, and I cannot imagine his opinion would differ from my own. I would also inform you that we have agreed to send her away with family for as many days as it takes your pride to calm itself."

There was a loud bang as Arthur stomped his foot onto floor as he spoke, nearly causing Katherine to let out a whimper of surprise. "How dare you! You damn fool! You have no idea who you are speaking to! My wedding to your sister is days away, and if she does not show there will be consequences to you and your entire family! You will become destitute, mark my words, Whyte. Your father, you, your wife— no one will associate with you, or have anything to do with your business. You will be run out of this town! If you are not banished from this land by the king himself! Believe me, I will see to it!"

"And I will see *you* to the door," Edward said loudly, moving toward him and directing him to the door.

"Your sister will marry me! She'd better be there! And I will be there waiting!" Arthur called.

"I'm certain you will be," Edward told him before slamming the door shut.

They waited for Edward to re-enter the parlour before they appeared around the corner and joined him.

"Can he do that?" Katherine asked. "Could he ruin you? Or father?"

Edward shook his head lightly, adding a chuckle as though the fact that she believed him was just as ridiculous as the words themselves. "He believes I am successful for knowing him. He forgets I was successful before him, and that without my stature and associates he would not have come to meet you, let alone marry you. No matter how breathtakingly beautiful you are," he added with a grin.

It did nothing to ease her mind or rid the crease that had formed between her eyebrows.

Edward paused and took in her demeanour. "If you are in fact worried, and still determined to marry Henry, then perhaps you should hurry things along."

Katherine thought that perhaps this was just another time when the words of men went over her head but was relieved when Henry spoke up.

"What do you mean?"

"Well," Edward elaborated, "Thacker cannot marry a married woman."

Katherine moved her eyes to the floor, unable to bring them to look at Henry to see his reaction.

"She's set to marry in less than three weeks. They've only just read the banns yesterday," Henry reminded his friend.

Edward nodded and gave a thoughtful look. "Then I suppose you have two." When everyone was quiet, he scoffed and spoke again. "With all that you've been through, with all the longing and the brooding, you cannot possibly be having second thoughts? Either of you."

"No. Of course not," Henry spoke quickly to dispel the thought. "I just thought, perhaps we would have more time to plan things. Even if we rush, pay for a license, would there not still be rumours? A scandal—." He was interrupted when Katherine let out a loud laugh.

She once again forced herself into the role she had created in the years since Henry's "death." "I care not for the opinions of mice. Let them scurry about under the floorboards," she said haughtily, crossing the room to lean her back against a bare spot on a wall. "I do not need a proper wedding, Henry, I've already planned two. As for the banns, of course we will avoid giving Arthur or even His Majesty any opportunity to object. I'm more than certain my father or my brother will accompany you, should you need someone to swear to our union. I'm sure my father would happily pay the fee." She smirked at him and lifted her chin. "You will marry me, Henry Bullock," she said firmly, finally.

The men exchanged glances, both confused and amused.

"The lady demands it," Edward said, his voice uneven as he held back laughter. "I suppose you have no choice now."

The next morning Lucy insisted on taking Katherine to shop for a dress for the occasion, against Katherine's protests. Lucy made girly demands to the first dressmaker, insisting they were in a rush and they must have something by midday. When it was clear their needs could not be met, they moved on to another shop that had a lovely dress of pale blue in the window. Lucy had to barter and promised to pay more to have it taken down, but she was quite satisfied with herself and practically forced Katherine into it to make certain it fit.

"Can you believe it is finally happening?" Lucy asked excitedly as she fluffed and straightened the skirt. Edward had left to meet Henry that morning. They had arranged to go to William, explain the plan, and indeed take him to fetch a marriage license.

Katherine smiled a faint smile but said nothing. Not that she needed to, as Lucy continued to chatter on while she helped Katherine out of the dress and then throughout the carriage ride home.

"Katherine aren't you the least bit sad that there will not be a party? I suppose it doesn't matter, after all. You're likely tired and bored with public affairs..."

Katherine let out a laugh. "No truer words have ever

been spoken, sister!"

"We can throw a ball to celebrate in the weeks that follow! Properly introduce you as Mrs. Henry Bullock..."

Katherine nodded along with every whim spoken aloud until she was finally able to stow away to the peace of her room. She looked over the dress again, thinking it wasn't even close to the fanciest dress she owned, and yet it was perfect for the union to Henry. If ever there was a symbol of their relationship, it was this dress: simple, comfortable, perfect, blue— like the flower, like the butterfly, like the stone in her ring. And with that she gathered up the dresses Arthur had bought her and gave them to Rosemary to keep or give away or sell or dispose of as she pleased.

Hours passed. Katherine went back down for supper with Lucy and her nephews, and the talk among the two women had turned from the excitement of the wedding to curiosity and slight worry over what was keeping the men for so long. Katherine was readying herself for bed before she heard Lucy's voice rise with excitement below and knew it meant the men must had returned. As Katherine slowly stepped down the stairs, she could hear her father's voice within the group. And then she saw their faces.

"What's going on?" she asked quietly.

Always in charge, William inhaled to speak, but Henry held up a hand. He motioned to the sitting area and sat beside Katherine, taking her hand before he spoke. "We traveled all over London to find a parish that would grant us a license. We explained ourselves to anyone who would listen. However no one could meet our time frame. It would appear most everyone is aware of your situation with Thacker. And those who do not respect him, at the very least fear him."

Katherine took a few moments to process but could only utter "What do we do, then? Look outside of London?"

"Therein lies the problem," William said, unable to hold back any longer. "The last man we spoke with seemed the most sympathetic, but he noted that, with Thacker being of royal blood, it was unlikely you would be granted a license anywhere within England, as anyone could step forward and object on the grounds of your betrothal to him."

Katherine brought her free hand to press her fingers to her lips. The other squeezed Henry's hand a bit tighter.

"It's not as though Arthur can drag her up to the altar," Lucy pointed out. "She still belongs to us, to her family. And she was already engaged to Henry, long before Arthur was ever introduced to her."

Edward sighed. "Aye, but it's nearly all been said and done. She'd never be free to marry anyone of her choosing unless Arthur were to find another to wed first."

With that Katherine stood abruptly. "Join me in the garden," she said over her shoulder to Henry as she moved from the room. He did as he was told, even moving quickly ahead to hold the door and close it behind them. She continued once the door was firmly closed. "If we cannot be married, then we simply will not be. There's no reason we cannot have a house and a family—."

"Katherine, you know what could happen in such an arrangement. We would lose our social standings. I would never find work—."

"I don't care!" Katherine raised her voice. She inhaled deeply, catching and correcting herself, knowing her frustration was not with Henry. She moved without realizing it, curling into him and lying her head against his cheek as her arms moved around his torso. They stood silent for a while, holding one another, breathing together, trying desperately not to let despair take over. "We'll go away."

"What?" Henry asked, pulling away, not certain he'd

heard her correctly.

She looked up into his face. “We’ll go away. Somewhere where no one can stop us. Ireland. France. Both are close enough. We always talked of Paris. We could be there within days.”

“The French are not on the friendliest terms with the English right now, darling. I cannot imagine it being easy to run off and marry there.”

“You’re an American, are you not?” she asked, cocking her head slightly sideways. “From what I understand, the Americans and French were allies—."

He shook his head, knowing what she was suggesting. “No, Katherine. Long ago I made your father a promise—.“

A loud breath in and out interrupted him. “I recall the promise you made, that he could know his grandchildren. And yet he might never have grandchildren if we do not.” She watched his eyes lose focus and knew he was considering it. “And I’m not saying we return to Philadelphia. I’m only saying we can use your status as an American or mine as English to help us get wherever we must. We can come back, Henry, as soon as we’re married if you wish. Or after we’ve become established. Borne children. Once things have settled and Arthur has long forgotten us.”

Henry pressed his lips together and swallowed, then nodded his head slightly. “I’ll find us a ship leaving immediately.”

Katherine pulled him close again, grateful that their fate was finally sealed.

Chapter Twenty-Five

Katherine had insisted they tell no one, but Henry could not. He felt as though the Whyte men were his family, and he could not just leave, taking their beloved Katherine away from them, without relaying his intentions. They spoke quietly in the house, and while they were indeed upset at the loss of both Henry and Katherine, they understood that there was likely no other way to escape Arthur before the wedding was set to take place. And Henry made certain to again swear to William that they would return, so he could meet his grandchildren as promised. A tearful Lucy was the first to retire, likely so she could weep in private, but not long after, William left the house. Katherine assumed it was also so he could grieve in private.

The next day Katherine spent packing. Lucy stayed close, but she also stayed quiet. While the conversation was light and chipper, several times she left the room abruptly. Katherine could only presume she was overtaken by emotion.

Early in the afternoon Henry and Edward returned to the house. The vessel they had found that would be leaving the earliest, and could accommodate two extra bodies, was two mornings away. They assured her it was that or they travel to Dover the next day, which would not guarantee them passage to the mainland. Katherine didn't mind either way. However the men were weary of the time spent in England, and after further discussion they talked themselves into leaving on the vessel from London.

The following day, Katherine felt uneasy, wondering if Arthur would come to call on her; if the palace guards or King George himself would arrive and threaten to drag her kicking and screaming to the alter as Lucy had suggested. Edward did not leave the house, feeling the anxiety of the women, and perhaps experiencing some of his own. Henry arrived mid-afternoon, having done his part throughout the day to secure their escape.

William came for supper that evening, again without Fiona. Katherine wondered, if a woman had known her daughter were about to leave on a long journey during which she was to marry, would she have come to bid her farewell? In most cases it was likely, but Fiona was not most women. And Katherine knew that William would not speak of her plans to Fiona lest it be immediately and urgently relayed to Arthur.

Before William left, Edward and Henry explained to him the plan they'd come up with throughout the day. Edward would accompany them to port, see them safely to the ship and return home.

"Then you shall need this," William said, producing a pouch from his jacket and handing it to Henry. "Consider it a dowry. And if you have no other use for it, use it to find your way back someday."

Katherine knew what that meant, and watched as her father's face turned a bright shade of red. She hadn't realized until that moment just how much she would miss the people in this room. She hugged her father, who held her so tightly in return she could hardly breathe. And when they finally pulled away, he had streams of tears beneath his eyes.

Then William turned to Henry and hugged him as well.

"I know you will do right by her. By all of us," William said with a nod when the hug broke.

"On my honour," Henry assured him with a nod of his own.

After one more long squeeze of his daughter's hand, William left the house.

Henry turned to face the rest of the company and take leave of his own. "I suppose I shall see you all in a few short hours." He bowed slightly to Edward and Lucy, and quickly kissed Katherine on the cheek. "My love," he acknowledged her with small incline of his head, and the look in his eyes took away the sadness that had overtaken her with the departure of her father.

She suddenly felt like this was a beginning, not an end, knowing the sooner he left her, the sooner she would see him again and being their journey. After so many years surrounded by people, she would finally be alone with him, and only him. "Goodnight," she said, and he turned to walk out the door.

***

Henry was dreading the journey, having spent so much time at sea in his lifetime, and felt awful having to keep Katherine confined as well. He was also sad to leave Edward and Lucy, as well as William and his relatives. But he was beyond ecstatic that they would finally be married and was excited to introduce them to Katherine as Mrs. Bullock upon their return. He only wished he knew when that would be. They would definitely stay away until after Arthur and Katherine's wedding date had passed. The group had discussed their plan, which included correspondence. The first place they could find that would wed them they would call home temporarily, and they would send a letter to both Edward and

William to inform them, but only after it was done. Edward would return a letter of his own to tell them any news he could find regarding Arthur. Edward and Lucy and William would spread the news that Henry and Katherine had finally married after all these years, and hope it would make it back to Arthur and even the palace, as the royals would likely tell Arthur to leave things be to avoid any scandal. But should he and Katherine be sent word otherwise, he was prepared to flee with her to another town, or more than one should it be necessary. He had been practically living out of his trunk since his return to England, and this would be no different. Even throughout his stay with his uncle and then his move to the inn, he hadn't truly collected anything new since he'd arrived, and it wouldn't take long to pack again.

Henry had fallen asleep knowing that Edward and Katherine would leave their home at approximately six o'clock in the carriage to retrieve him. He'd set everything up, and when Edward knocked on the door he could spring out of bed, quickly dress, and be ready for the ride. So when the knock on the door came, he did just that.

"One moment," he had called out, lighting a lamp and groggily dressing. He was done before he glanced at the clock in the corner and realized it was not even four in the morning. He paused, slightly confused, wondering if the clock had malfunctioned, but watched it continue to tick. After another knock on the door he finished pulling on his boots.

"Have you decided we should leave early? Well, earlier..." he asked as he took the last step and opened the door. He smiled— and was met by no one.

The sun hadn't risen yet, and Henry blinked several times, wondering if his eyes were playing tricks on him in the darkness, but still no one was there. He took a step out, and then another. In these early hours, the hallway was bare, no lamps were lit; the only light coming from the candle in his own room. Henry's eyes darted around again, but soon found himself wondering if perhaps in his groggy mind he had imagined the knocks had happened in a dreamy state of anticipation.

He turned and stepped back into his room, and that's when he felt a blow to the middle of his back with such force it took his breath from him. After that he felt nothing else—but saw what looked to be the blade of a broadsword had come through his chest and out. He wasn't sure what was holding him up until he heard a gruff whisper in his ear.

"You should have stayed dead the first time."

The blade disappeared, and Henry watched the room rise around him as his body crumpled to the floor. He felt the thud of his head as it hit but couldn't feel the pain. He couldn't feel himself breathe. And though darkness had overtaken his eyes, in the back of his mind he could see a face, the face that had haunted him and driven him and guided him through every moment of his adult life.

Katherine.

Chapter Twenty-Six

Katherine awoke with a start, pain pulling at every bone, every muscle, every nerve, only able to choke on what was left of the air that had been ripped from within her. And when it reached to point where she thought she might scream from it, it suddenly stopped.

She gasped and panted, drawing in a few deep breaths, and once her breathing steadied, she felt...

Nothing. No pain. No emotion. Nothing. The anxiety and anticipation she had felt before she had fallen asleep were gone. The fear she had always felt of her mother and more recently of Arthur was gone. The sadness she had felt for leaving her nephews and Lucy, her father and Edward, was gone. The excitement to marry Henry after the years of love and torture was gone. She felt only a numbness, an emptiness she couldn't describe.

She lay there, searching her brain for a reason: a reason for her waking, a reason for her pain, a reason for the emptiness, but nothing came to her. She wondered if something were wrong, if she should wake the house and make certain all was well, but what would she say? How would she describe her experience without possibly sounding as crazy as her mother? *What if you already are?* She chose to stay put and stare at the ceiling. She wasn't sure how much time passed, or whether any time had passed at all when she heard hooves outside and banging on the door downstairs.

She stood at the bottom of the stairs. She watched Edward open the door. She heard the words as they were said. She listened to her brother cry out for clarification and then verification. She watched his face as he struggled to understand. She looked at Lucy who was clawing at Edward's arm, her mouth open in a silent cry as tears spilled from her eyes. She watched them as they turned to look at her, to gauge her reaction, and it was then she realized what had been amiss earlier in her bed: all was not well.

She had known. Deep within her she had known he was gone, and with him had gone a large part of her. She had felt it exit her body. That part contained emotion and reasoning and reaction. All the feelings she'd felt when Henry was alive had died with him. That ever-present bind pulling at her, keeping them connected, had been severed.

She sat down on the step beneath her, aware of Edward and Lucy as their words and arms and cries swirled around her. She felt the tears, choking in her throat, swelling behind her eyes, but that was where they stayed.

The men had said he'd been murdered in his room, and his belongings taken. The innkeeper had wondered at the noise, found the door open and the body in the room. Likely a drifter who was long gone already. It didn't matter. It didn't change anything. But it stayed with her while she spent the next hours in her room. Daylight had come and nearly gone again when Edward came in, stood her up, fastened a cloak over her shoulders and led her down the stairs and into a carriage. She didn't know where they were going, lightly bouncing from side to side as the wheels moved beneath her. Edward didn't speak, for which she was grateful. They both knew there were no words that would bring either one any comfort. Lucy and the boys spoke softly to one another in the seat across.

The carriage stopped. The entire trip Katherine hadn't lifted her eyes from the spot on the floor in front of her. Only when the door opened did she move her head to see that they had arrived at her parents' house.

Edward sighed. "Father insisted."

Katherine gave one nod and followed him.

William met them at the door. His face was red and damp; Katherine couldn't tell if it was from perspiration or tears. Perhaps both. The men embraced before William grabbed Katherine and held her tight for a long while, his breathing quick and uneven. She could feel him shaking his head from time to time. She briefly recalled the first time they had thought Henry dead. Neither man had responded this way. Katherine's reaction had been different then too, she realized. Maybe deep down they had all somehow known he wasn't actually dead then.

William pulled away and held her shoulders. "My poor, poor girl. I just..." He shook his head again. "You'll stay the night. All of you," he announced as he let her go and turned to the rest of the room.

Katherine didn't bother excusing herself. She had been pulled from the solitude of her room in town, now she once again wished to be left alone with her thoughts. She climbed the steps to the second floor, not lifting her eyes but staring only at the steps in front of her. And when there were no more steps she was staring into the light-coloured fabric of her mother's skirt. She paused for only a moment and let out a small sigh before continuing her ascent and passing her mother wordlessly. She didn't realize anyone had followed her until she reached her door and heard Edward's voice speaking quietly to Fiona, and her mother's response...

"Do you think she might reconsider Arthur?"

Katherine's hand froze on the doorknob. She listened as her brother gave a stunned pause and asked, "Are you completely mad?!"

But in that moment something made sense to Katherine: Fiona had, somehow, brought about Henry's death. Just as she and Edward had known who had told Arthur about Henry before Arthur had confirmed it, Katherine knew it deep in her soul. Fiona must have hired someone to murder him. Or she had done it herself. Katherine had witnessed her mother's violence on more than one occasion and couldn't think of anything that Fiona had ever wanted more than for Katherine to follow through with her marriage to Arthur.

Somewhere deep within her, her breath escaped in a chuckle, and rolled into a maniacal laugh that caused her head to fall back. Then it fell forward as the laugh became a silent one that shook her shoulders. Her hand fell away from the door. She turned to look at the people by the stairs and held her mother's eyes as she closed the distance between them. She watched as her mother lifted her chin, ready and waiting for whatever she had to say. And the same strange place within Katherine that had brought forth her laughter also thrust forward her arms, making contact with Fiona's body.

Fiona missed the first steps as she was launched back through the air. Her foot caught as she scrambled for purchase and caused her to slide and then flip awkwardly down the staircase, her head hitting the banister hard before her limp body rolled the rest of the way.

Edward made a sound of surprise as he reached out in vain to grab any part of Fiona, then quickly ran down. He had made it only halfway before Fiona hit the floor below them, landing hard and heavy near her husband, who'd had his back turned.

The men were shouting in shock, calling to each other and to Fiona, who was not responding. Edward looked back up the stairs but Katherine had vanished. He took the steps in two's to quickly get to the top. He opened every door, searched every room, calling out for Katherine. The only place left to go was to the end of the hall and up to the turret William had built for himself to conduct his business in away from the rest of the family. A third floor, a place they were nary allowed as children, and never cared to enter as adults unless asked to retrieve something for William. They had made jokes of William being the king of this castle, and also of him locking Fiona in the tower like in so many fairy tales. Edward couldn't imagine any rational reason Katherine would go there, and that idea was more terrifying than what he had just witnessed.

***

Katherine stared out the open window, looking down at the land she had grown up wandering. This room was the only one on the estate that could see the entire grounds, with windows in every direction. She did a lap around the room, looking to the stables, looking to the driveway in the front of the house, and making her way to the back window. Her eyes followed the path she had walked thousands of times, past the paddock where she would play as a girl, past the garden where she would help Eleanor and Rupert harvest. She could see the treeline from here, and the river glistening in the moonlight beyond the trees. She thought of Henry, and their spot, and suddenly it was there again— the pull she'd always felt that told her he was near.

He was there. He was at their spot. And he was waiting for her. She pushed the window open further and pulled her body up, over the frame and out. Her feet dangled as she looked out toward the trees and gave one last push with her arms. The last thing she heard were her brother's frantic footsteps as he scrambled up the stairs.

Made in the USA
Columbia, SC
09 August 2022